Capturing Sin

Playing with Demons, Book 2

Sakura Black

Copyright © 2024 by Sakura Black

All rights reserved.

No part of this publication may be reproduced, distributed, or transmitted in any form or by any means, including photocopying, recording, or other electronic or mechanical methods, without the prior written permission of the publisher, except as permitted by U.S. copyright law.

The story, all names, characters, and incidents portrayed in this production are fictitious. No identification with actual persons (living or deceased), places, buildings, and products is intended or should be inferred.

Editor: Lyss Em

Book Cover: Artscandare

Interior Art: Etheric Designs

Contents

Foreword

Thank you for picking up this book!

Just a little word of warning, the book you are about to read contains swearing, violence and steamy scenes (monsters need love too). It is intended for mature readers.

Head to sakurablackbooks.com for the full list of trigger warnings.

Chapter 1

Fire arced down my back.

A scream burst from my lips as I staggered forward, twisting to get away from the source of pain.

Mocking laughter rumbled from the demon, orange eyes glowing bright within a skeletal face. He lifted his claws to his mouth, forked tongue laving over the bloodied tips. "Mmm, tastier than the last hunter."

I snarled, ignoring the wet heat running down my back and lunging forward with my knife. He dodged the first strike, straight into the second blade waiting. It slid between the bony plates that formed a natural armour across his chest, and I yanked sideways, cutting through the gap in his defences. He screamed as I sliced him open, black blood gushing down his middle. His claws dropped to his wound, and I sliced open his throat, finishing him.

The evil bastard probably deserved to bleed out slowly from the gut wound, but I couldn't risk that he'd survive it somehow. Who knew how many innocent people he'd devour if I let him escape.

I turned, looking for the next monster.

Gunshots ricocheted through the old factory, sparking off rusted machinery. Moonlight streamed through broken windows, barely illuminating the nightmare inside. Blood and bodies littered the ground. Most were demons, but a few familiar faces had my heart clenching.

My squad—alpha team—wasn't prepared for an attack on this scale. One crafty demon had led us into a slaughter.

Horned beasts closed in around Tia. Brain matter blew out the back of one, dropping it to the concrete. She swung her pistol to the next, but no bark of gunfire answered. Her hard features slackened in fear.

I was already sprinting towards them.

We'd all used up a fair amount of ammo on the patrol, catching too many demons slipping through the dark streets. I'd run out shortly after we'd been ambushed in the warehouse. Otherwise, I'd have picked off most of the demons currently distracted by Tia.

She yelled, drawing a short-sword from the sheathe at her back and swinging towards the two closest to her. She'd never beat four demons with just a sword.

Leo barrelled in, brandishing only a pair of short-swords. But my fiancé would be lethal with a pencil. He cut down one monster as they lunged for our teammate.

My blade sliced through the arm of another demon as it spun to greet me, getting lodged on a spike protruding from its elbow. I drew back, but his claws grazed my collarbone. Pain flared, but I shoved the sensation down, focusing on the monster and drawing him away from Tia.

Another beast growled beside me. I had a second to duck. Claws sailed overhead, and I swept my leg out, tripping the first demon.

But the second was faster than I expected. He slammed his fist into my ribs. Something cracked, and pain exploded, bursting through my side.

I wheezed at the sharp ache, limping backwards, blades raised.

The pair advanced on me with steady steps and vicious grins, sure in their easy victory.

To my horror, a third appeared from the darkness. The three of them herded me back, away from the other hunters. I swiped out with my knives to hold them off, but I could barely breathe with the agony threatening to pull me under.

"Leo!" I yelled, almost blacking out from the flash of pain.

My fiancé cut down his second demon, gaze finding mine. Familiar navy eyes widened, as if confirming how much trouble I was in. He took a step towards me, but a scream had him whipping around.

Tia cried out again, yanking my attention to her too.

A blood demon pinned her to the wall, fangs in her throat.

"Tia!" my fiancé yelled, panic lacing his tone as he raced towards her.

Leaving me with the three hulking monsters.

I didn't have time to feel the disbelief at his choice.

The monster in the middle lunged forward. I stepped into his strike instead of away, taking him off-guard. I sliced his throat open as his claws sank into the meat of my other shoulder. My knife fell from my spasming grip.

Pain screamed from the fresh wound, and I hissed as I dropped beneath the other demons' swiping claws, stumbling. I twisted with the momentum and sliced open the arteries in his thigh with a spray of hot liquid.

Gravity sucked me down as my strength drained out with the blood, leaving me too fast.

The third demon towered over me, grinning maliciously. Hunger burned in glowing purple eyes.

I tried to roll away, but he stomped on my middle.

A scream choked off in my throat as I felt something *give* in my side with a bright stab of pain. I coughed, agony searing my insides, and wetness spluttered up from my lips.

I urged my body to move, but I barely twitched on the ground.

This was it.

The demon tutted, leaning down until his face eclipsed the room. "Such a fragile thing. Don't die on me too easily. I'm going to gorge myself on your sweet blood for days."

I could hardly feel the dread past the torment holding my thoughts captive.

But I knew one thing. I'd never let a demon feed on me.

My strength was failing, but I had enough left for one last strike, and he'd forgotten about the second blade.

His lips peeled back, revealing sharp fangs. Fetid breath washed over me. He tipped my head aside, exposing my neck.

We lunged at the same time.

Fangs grazed my throat as I twisted and swung. My blade bit into his neck, and I yanked it free, causing maximum damage.

Demonic eyes widened in a moment of shock, and I collapsed beside him. The monster gripped his throat, scrambling to stop the bleeding even as his claws raked weakly at the base of my own throat, stopping short at my collarbone. Pain swelled beneath the sharp points, but it didn't feel much deeper than a scratch.

Glowing eyes faded, and his hand flopped to the concrete.

For a moment, all I could do was stare at the dull purple orbs locked onto me. Reality fuzzed at the edges as I fought for each shallow breath through the agony rebounding in my torso.

"Fall back!" A commanding shout boomed from the far end of the warehouse, underscored by pained groans and the sharp retort of gunfire echoing through the space.

"Liliana's down!" another voice shouted nearby.

"Leave her." My fiancé's smooth voice pierced the din. "She'll distract the beasts."

Betrayal sliced through my chest, adding to the misery already lighting me up.

"Leo...," I choked out, a wet sensation leaking down my lips.

Pain hazed the world around me, but with every laboured breath, it lessened.

Not ideal.

Footsteps thudded as the hunters fled. Growls trailed off as the demons gave chase.

Silence swallowed me.

My team, practically *family*, were leaving me to die. Led by my fiancé.

I was going to marry him in a few months' time.

We were going to start a family of our own. Buy a home together here in Riverside. I could semi-retire from hunting in favour of domestic bliss. Even my uncle had given the nod of approval when I'd brought up dropping to part-time.

My hands shook as I tried to press them to the deep gashes in my side beneath the edge of my vest. I couldn't be sure, but I thought something vital had been pierced. Like a lung.

Which would explain the wheezing, damp sound I couldn't stop making.

It sounded like a death rattle.

My thoughts drifted for a moment as I stared up at the steel ceiling beams through the gloom, wondering what would happen when I died.

How fast would Leo move on? Would my uncle even bother to hold a funeral for me? Would anyone miss me after I was gone?

I blinked as someone touched my wounds. A biting pain seared my chest, setting my lungs on fire and yanking me from the fluffy cloud of nothingness I'd been suffocating on.

"S-Sstop!" I hissed, my slurring barely audible.

A monster blinked into focus above me.

Sunshine eyes bored into me, glowing blindly bright. "Hold on."

I tried to bat him away, my hands slapping uselessly at his arms. By some miracle, I narrowly avoided impaling my palms on the bony spikes protruding from his shoulders.

The demon arched a silvery brow at me. "Why don't you conserve your strength for something useful? Like living," he drawled, voice warm and smooth.

I tried to bare my teeth but couldn't summon more than a glare with the dizziness washing over me.

He lifted my hand, my pale skin looking peachy next to his dark-grey shade. The beast ran a forked tongue along a large gash on my forearm, ending just below the oversize watch clinging to my wrist.

Revulsion had me twitching in his grip, but I couldn't even feel the pain his feeding should have caused.

"C-Can't you let…m-me die in peace?" I coughed, and my blood speckled his sharp cheekbone.

The love of my life had sacrificed me on the battlefield. Wasn't I suffering enough?

A small smile twitched the monster's lips. "This isn't your end, huntress. Not if I can help it."

His meaning tried to sink in through the haze, but I couldn't understand what he was saying.

"This will hurt, but you'll thank me for it when we both wake up after a little nap together. If I can be brave enough to save my enemy, you can be brave enough to accept what it means."

Ragged wounds bled freely from gunshots high in his chest. He raised his forearm, claws widening an already deep gash bisecting his grey skin.

Bright blood dripped from the cut, splattering my lips. I coughed, distress seizing my chest at the damage I'd already taken. I tried to spit out the liquid, but it trickled over my nose, making it impossible to breathe.

The golden sunbursts around his eyes seemed to glow even brighter, a fiery corona amid a sea of black pupil and sclera. He gripped my jaw, claws pricking my cheeks as he forced my mouth open.

Blood filled my mouth. It burned like cheap gin as it slid down my throat, oddly heavy. Heat raced through my body, scorching me from the inside.

The hold on my face slipped, and the demon's eyes rolled back. He crashed down beside me, but I barely felt the impact against my arm.

Fire filled my wounds, and I screamed.

White-hot agony cut the final threads holding me conscious.

"I don't fucking believe it." A harsh male grunt yanked me from the darkness. Something cool pressed to the pulse in my throat.

I peeled open bleary eyes. Everything ached. Even my eyeballs seemed to throb as I tried to take in the sight before me.

A familiar face hovered over me, steel beams cutting behind him. He removed his fingers from my throat. It took me a moment to place the man through the haze—Jayce. The cocky beta squad hunter who'd been gunning for my position in alpha for years.

Jayce's eyes narrowed. "She's asleep. Not fuckin' dead. There's barely a scratch on her. You sure she was even injured?"

Everything came rushing back.

I wasn't dead. But my fiancé and the rest of my team had left me behind to die here.

A different kind of pain lanced through me before I remembered *why* I could wake up.

The demon.

Clearly, if I was alive, and apparently in one piece, then it was because of whatever his blood did to me.

But why would a monster help me?

Maybe I'd hallucinated the whole thing.

I pushed weakly at Jayce, and he obliged with a snort. "Classic pampered princess, taking a royal doze on the job. Don't take your irritation out on the poor peasant to wake you too." He stood, allowing me a better view of my surroundings.

My whole body shook as I half rolled to face the unmoving demon lying right beside me. His blood-smeared chest rose and fell in a deep, even rhythm.

One thought screamed through my head.

He shouldn't be here.

I reached for him, shaking his shoulder at the base of the spikes protruding from his grey skin. Even that much movement had spots blooming through my vision. Nausea slithered inside my stomach, but I didn't stop, pushing weakly at the demon.

He'd saved me. But he was about to die.

Panic set in, reducing my attempts to wake him to a frantic pawing.

"The fuck is she doing?" Jayce muttered. "Trying to attack it?"

My fiancé stepped up beside Jayce, a gun in one hand and a bloodied sword in the other. He raised the blade above me, almost in slow motion.

"No!" A hoarse scream burst from my lips, and I fought the weakness in my body to push at the demon harder, trying to shove his bulk out of the way.

I knew what was coming, but I couldn't stop it.

Sunshine eyes fluttered open, locking onto mine.

A wet crunch sounded.

He jerked, lips slackening to show the tips of fangs.

"No...," I groaned, the sound breaking to a whisper.

"She must have hit her head on something," Jayce muttered, toeing me in the ribs with his boot, sending another wave of nausea through me.

From my peripherals, Leo peered down, leaning on the sword embedded in my saviour, face unreadable before he pasted on a fake smile. "How wonderful, my sleeping beauty lives."

No thanks to him.

"Come on, beta squad's almost done with the last of the bodies." Arsen, another alpha hunter, stepped up beside Leo. "Huh, never seen such a spiky grey-and-white one before. Must be a rare beast."

"All right, we should probably get *Dozer* here back to medical in case she broke a nail," Jayce snorted.

I caught the edge of a shrug from Leo but couldn't look away from the twin dying suns staring back at me.

A *demon* had saved me. And it had cost him everything.

Jayce leaned down and hauled me roughly into his arms. Dizziness rolled me under, sucking me back into the abyss.

Chapter 2

Three weeks later...

"Oh, you'll love court. Honestly, you'll have such a great time if you get to go. It's so interesting." My boss smiled wide, leaning his forearms on the desk between us, caramel eyes crinkling at the corners with the edges of his excitement.

I blinked.

Letting his words sink in as I straightened in my chair.

"So, just to be clear, I told you I was almost *assaulted* by two men, and you think I'll have fun if I go to court to convict my attackers?" I tried to keep my voice within human hearing range, but the decibels were rising awfully high.

The hellhounds caged in the room next door were probably howling.

He frowned, as if considering my words, and shook his head in clear dismissal. "I didn't mean it that way. Why do you have to be like that?"

I couldn't cope.

I was about 3.2 seconds away from a throat-punching spree. But I was no longer the violent maniac I used to be just three weeks ago, before I'd swapped from operational demon hunter to scientist.

So, instead, I took a deep breath. In and out. Nice and slow. Calm. Controlled.

To top off what had been another spectacularly horrifying day in the hunter's research division, last night, I'd been cornered by two thugs in the car park outside my run-down apartment.

Instead of breaking their bones—like the old psycho hunter me would have done—I'd fled and called the police like a sane, upstanding citizen of Riverside.

Though, if I was being honest with myself, old me would have stabbed the bastards too, somewhere particularly painful, to *really* put them off ever trying to harass vulnerable-looking women late at night.

It was probably a good thing I no longer carried a weapon. The thought of harming more people that violently turned my stomach, even if they might have deserved it, just a teensy bit.

Now I was being punished by this conversation, though, because I needed a few hours off to give a statement to the police.

Even though it was a waste of time. Riverside wasn't one of the biggest cities in England, but the chances they'd catch these guys based on my description alone was slim to none.

It wasn't like I could just ask my uncle for the camera footage either.

I knew he'd seen me getting attacked last night, unarmed and still recovering from my injuries.

He hadn't sent help.

My uncle claimed he'd mounted cameras outside my apartment building for my safety. Yet he'd only installed them after I'd woken up in the medical room and tried to flee the city.

Leo had run me off the road and hauled me back in secret, on my uncle's orders, no doubt. I regretted ever giving my ex-fiancé a key. Not that he needed one, given the hunter chapter, and therefore my uncle, owned the damned building.

The incident in the warehouse had turned my world upside down, and I wasn't sure how to process everything that had happened.

And what it meant.

All I knew was that I didn't want to be a part of the hunters anymore. But I'd have to bide my time while I came up with a way to escape. Lull my uncle into loosening the leash a little first.

"Anyway, enough chit-chat. We're here to discuss your performance." Martin cleared his throat, trying to regain the upper hand in this abysmal conversation.

I waited as patiently as I could. The closest thing to professional I could do right now was a blank poker face. This was not what I wanted first thing in the morning, but being a scientist within a hunter chapter apparently meant seven-a.m. meetings and long, blood-filled days.

My boss reclined in his chair. "I am concerned about your future here, given your apparent issues with being able to handle the workload."

It was all I could do not to launch myself over the table and throttle the idiot. That, or cry.

To my horror, moisture swam across my vision.

I quickly lifted my glasses, rubbing at my eyes as if I were tired, not on the verge of a breakdown.

I was fine.

Everything was fine.

Just a totally normal person with her shit together.

Definitely not crying at work.

See? Fine.

"I can handle it," I said, keeping my tone even despite the near waterworks.

It wasn't that I wanted this job, exactly; it was that I couldn't stomach the alternative.

He shot me a condescending look, one of his all-time favourite expressions. "If that were the case, then we wouldn't be almost three weeks into you taking this position, and still without a single valid test result. Dr Smythe has seen those same compounds react to the blood and tissue samples she has taken. Might I remind you, *Liliana*, that you were the one who requested a transfer into the research division."

He loved to say my name. It was one of those stupid little things that made him feel powerful. Or maybe he'd once read in a self-help book that it made people respect you more.

I nodded repeatedly, trying to project confidence. "Not just a result or two. I'm right around the corner from a breakthrough."

There was zero chance of that.

Because I'd stopped running most of the tests they wanted after my first day playing scientist.

His flat look called me out for the liar I was. "The hunter prime will be kept appraised of your progress. Or, rather, lack thereof."

Only years of practise stopped the fear showing on my face. Somehow, I managed a tight smile. "I understand. I'll try harder."

Martin smiled back. And it was as vicious as any demon I'd come across. "See that you do."

Sensing we were done, I stood, leaving Martin to his silent gloating.

I strode from the room with my shoulders thrown back like I had nothing to fear. Closing the door firmly behind me, I let out a small breath, closer to a choked sob than anything, and checked my father's watch. It was the only thing I had left of him, since my uncle, the hunter prime, had taken the rest of my inheritance for "safekeeping."

The small crack in the glass aligned with the big hand like it was trying to hide the fact that I was officially late for my next scheduled appointment of the day.

"Shit," I muttered, hurrying down the narrow corridor and swiping my pass to enter the last room on the right.

This place was a maze of secured rooms, most I didn't even have access to, even now that I'd changed to the research division.

A thin woman hunched over a microscope, her loose-fitting lab coat splattered with vivid red marks. Greying hair was piled up into a high bun, similar in style to my dark locks. Where hers was neatly slicked into place, mine were a mess of loose wisps, a distraction of strands still falling into my face.

With my half-Thai heritage to thank for my five-foot-three skinny frame and baby face, most people thought I looked younger than my twenty-four years. My freckles and the recent switch from contact lenses to oversize wire-rimmed glasses only seemed to add to that, but I had nothing on Cara. She'd already hit retirement age and looked as unbending and unmarred as steel.

Cara didn't bother to look up as I entered. The door clicked shut at my back, sealing me into a fresh hell.

"What took you so long?" she asked, not bothering to look up from the microscope she peered down. "Humanity isn't going to save itself, *Dozer*."

"Sorry," I muttered, ignoring her use of the dumb nickname Jayce had started the whole hunter chapter using, and hurrying over to grab the samples from the fridge that I'd prepared with her yesterday. "My meeting overran."

I furiously ignored the horror show twitching near the back of the lab.

Cara switched off the microscope and finally faced me, severe features pinching. She held her narrowed stare for another long second, where I fought not to fidget under her scrutiny, clutching the tray of samples.

With a huff, she slid down the cat-eye glasses from her head to glare at me through them instead. "If you don't want to be here, go back to the other meatheads upstairs."

A part of me had always wanted to be a scientist but not like this. I wanted to help make the world a better place: cure an incurable disease, uncover a breakthrough that reduced our impact on the planet, help us understand a rare animal species to boost conservation efforts. This bastardised version of long-ago crushed dreams was a cruel joke.

Yet I couldn't face being an actual hunter anymore.

Not that this was much less horrifying. At least as a hunter, I'd given the demons a quick, clean death if I could. You didn't blame the wolf for killing the sheep. It was their nature, instinct driving them. Or so I'd thought.

It seemed I'd underestimated their capacity for premeditated evil as much as their ability for good. They were like us in that way. Just people.

I stretched my lips into a brittle approximation of a smile, waving her off. "I'm happy right here."

"Aren't we all?" a hissing voice sneered behind me, but I ignored the poor demon currently strapped down to the operating table, slowly bleeding out.

The sharp stench of bleach covered most of the metallic blood, but I'd grown so used to both that neither fazed me as much as I wished it would. Touching the red stuff was a different matter altogether.

"Good." Her nose lifted with her own self-importance. "You're meant to be learning from my work and making yourself useful to our team."

I already knew this, but Cara loved to remind me I was beneath her. She was one of those people that had to tread on others to feel tall.

I nodded, fixing my fake smile in place. "Yep, Cara, I'm super excited to help."

Her thin brows creased.

I was laying it on too thick, but the quiet whimpers of the wounded demon behind me were burrowing through the thick walls I'd erected around my emotions.

How could anyone stand this? Even three weeks ago, I wouldn't have been able to stomach this kind of cruelty. I'd stayed out of the research side of things, putting all my focus into making the streets of Riverside safe for humans, while trying to find a way to retire from the violence as much as my uncle would allow.

I'd always thought the research was a necessary evil, but I hoped like hell I would have been deeply unsettled if I'd known what it truly involved.

"Yes, well, let's go over how to administer the test compound again. This can be the trickiest part, I've found." She waved a hand towards the demon strapped to the table, as if their struggling for escape were such an inconvenience to her.

"No, please! Not again!" he wailed, thrashing on the metal.

I swallowed hard, bracing for another day of pretending everything was okay while dreaming of escape. If I was lucky, the screams in my head would drown everything else out.

Chapter 3

Locking down every emotion deep into the pit inside me, I twisted the lever and eased into the office.

The gentle tapping of fingertips on a keyboard reached out. My uncle continued to stare at his laptop screen, ignoring my entrance.

Somehow, it was cooler inside the office than in the climate-controlled lab where I'd watched Cara poke at demons all afternoon. When Martin had slithered in and snidely informed me I could no longer leave early because my uncle wanted a word, I'd panicked. Clearly, my boss had tattled about my lack of results.

I closed the door silently behind me and lingered in front of the solid wood.

Rich mahogany dominated the room, almost as much as the man who owned it.

A plastic chair sat opposite a grand desk of expensive wood, swallowing the middle of the space.

Weapons lined the back wall—half display, half armoury—accented by wooden panelling. It held his favourite guns, from simple pistols to customised Italian double-under shotguns and high-powered assault rifles.

Last week, one of the demons had got loose, and I'd seen my uncle grab a shotgun off the wall and blow their head off.

The bloodstains had been a bitch to clean off the walls, especially while trying my best not to add vomit to the mix of fluids and brain matter. I had a fairly hardened stomach after all the gore I'd seen, and caused, over the years, but I'd come out of that warehouse three weeks ago a different person. Now the sticky feeling of blood drying on my hands was unbearable.

The typing continued, and I turned my attention to the man who ruled my life.

He was in his late forties, the only evidence of ageing the salt-and-pepper shades of his buzz cut and the fine lines between his brows. Probably from all the scowling. He was still in peak physical condition despite the countless injuries he'd picked up over the three decades he'd served as a hunter.

There wasn't an ounce of fat on him, just stringy muscle and bitterness.

My uncle reminded me of gristle. Unpalatable and tough. He'd always had the look of someone who'd been chewed up by life and spat back out.

I used to wonder whether he'd always been this way, or whether the death of my aunt had played a role. Now I didn't care. I just wanted to spit him out too.

He closed his laptop and leaned back in his creaking leather chair, steepling his fingers in the ultimate power move of zero fucks to give.

Making me wait was a psychological tactic he employed often.

I bit down on my tongue, forcing myself to wait him out.

I counted the scars on his hands, from the thin slice of blades to the ragged stretch of claws. He had them in abundance. Thick ropes of the white tissue crossed his knuckles from where he'd split them open too many times.

It made sense. Bones were much stronger than skin. Not that a little blood ever made him stop hitting his unlucky target.

I should know.

For a moment, the fantasy of escaping him, and all the violence he represented, made it hard to breathe. The longing burrowed so deep that I knew it had always been there.

He jerked his chin towards the basic seat, purposefully uncomfortable, and I obeyed in an instant, bringing myself below his level, throned in the plush office chair.

"You're healed now?" he asked, running a critical eye over me like he could see my wounds through the lab coat and clothing beneath.

Fear gripped me, but I had to say the words. "Yes, Uncle."

It was closer to the truth than it should be. I'd broken my ribs, punctured a lung, been cut and bruised all over, practically bled out, and yet because of a *demon*, just three weeks later, only dull aches and extra scars remained. Even crashing my car the same night had only reopened the deepest wounds.

He nodded.

Rearing over the desk, he struck.

His palm collided with my face, whipping my head aside. Disorientation swam for a moment, and I blinked hard, staring at the weapons wall. Straightening in my chair, I ignored my throbbing cheek, clinging to my neutral expression.

Of course, his solution to me getting injured was to hit me. At least this time was an open-palm slap.

From him, that was practically a hug.

"You know we must maintain an image of strength to run this chapter. Your theatrics compromised that," he said.

I wasn't sure I'd call being almost murdered by demons "theatrics," but I understood what he was getting at. Me going down in battle made him look bad, especially given how minor my injuries seemed when the team had returned for clean-up with reinforcements.

Now that I was healed, he was expressing his frustrations.

He'd been mercifully ignoring me since my failed escape attempt. Retribution was coming, but it seemed he was letting me stew in the horror of anticipation. For now.

I locked down my instinctive reaction to bite back. Revealing my anger would only incite more pain.

"Apologies, Uncle." I inclined my head.

His eyes narrowed. It was the neutral acceptance he wanted, yet he hunted for any excuse to unleash more violence. He craved it like a junkie.

"Don't think I'm not aware that you also broke up with Leo."

More anger piled onto the bonfire raging inside me, hot enough to eclipse the stinging warmth across my cheek.

"You want to discuss my love life?" I asked, fighting to keep the acid out of my tone.

His expression darkened, telling me I wasn't quite as neutral as I'd hoped. "He's a strong match for you."

"He also left me to die," I murmured, voice lacking inflection. "Loyalty is important, is it not?"

He fell silent, watching me with a cold calculation I'd been taught to fear.

"What will I do with you, Liliana?" he asked, like he genuinely cared what my response might be.

I sealed my lips shut. If he wanted me to speak, a deep furrow would appear between his brows after a brief stretch of silence.

Expression smooth, he continued on, "Martin tells me you're being difficult."

One day, my boss would get what was coming to him. It might not be by my hand, but I had to believe karma would hunt him down and tear him into tiny, insignificant pieces.

Then I hoped one of the hellhounds got loose and pissed all over his remains.

I fought the twitch of my lips at the violent fantasy. One look at my uncle's flinty grey eyes killed any joy.

"Results take time." I kept my tone even, firm but respectful. "But they will be worth it. The benefits to our cause will be significant."

He quirked a brow. "So you claim, but I'm growing impatient. We need to try something more...radical."

My throat dried up, and I swallowed painfully. "Radical how?"

A cruel smile split his lips. Terror sliced through my middle. Like any predator, it was never a good thing when they showed teeth.

"No more of this sample bullshit." He waved a hand. "You will switch to live testing."

"No," I breathed. The denial fell from my lips without my permission.

The predator stilled, and I tensed on instinct.

"No?" he asked, voice deceptively soft.

"I mean... I'll have to figure out the best tests to run..." I trailed off, panic scrambling my thoughts.

"Martin says blood demons would be easiest to start on. And your aunt's notes confirm it was her next theory. You will dose yourself with trial compounds and feed them to your subject."

I felt like I'd been punched in the chest, my lungs seizing. The thought of letting a demon sink their fangs into me was terrifying, and my uncle knew it.

It was a horror to most hunters, but it held a special place in my nightmares.

It was the retaliation I'd been waiting for. I'd tried to escape him, and now he was dragging me deeper into the darkness, trying to drown any spirit I had left.

"I know this might be...uncomfortable, given your father's death." His eyes were unyielding.

It might have been over a decade ago, but even the day after it had happened, he'd been able to talk about his brother's murder like it meant nothing. I was sure taking over from my father as hunter prime, leader of the Riverside hunter chapter, helped ease the sting.

I'd watched a blood demon drain my father dry when I was eleven years old, and now my uncle wanted me to offer up my veins to the same kind of monster who'd killed him.

I shouldn't have been surprised, but some naive part of me still clung to the idea that maybe, deep down, there was something redeemable about my uncle. He'd loved his brother in his own way.

They were cut from a similar cloth, after all.

He sighed, like acknowledging that I might have emotions was exhausting. "If you can't do this, Liliana, I can find you a volunteer."

He didn't mean a willing one.

The threat was one he'd held over me before. Some random person would be taken off the street and held "for the greater good." Other scientists and the operational hunters were too valuable to become lab rats. The work could save thousands of human lives, so as much as my uncle wanted to protect humans, he'd do what he thought needed to be done.

As much as I didn't want some random person kidnapped to become a guinea pig, I also wasn't sure I could face the idea of a demon's fangs sinking into my skin.

There wasn't enough oxygen in the room. I held my stinging face in a composed mask, through years of discipline alone.

I had to get out of here.

"Let me plan the experiments, and we can go from there," I said, trying to keep the desperation from leaking into my tone.

My uncle stared me down, trying to assess my façade for any cracks. Any weaknesses that he could exploit. He'd burrow his claws into any hint of vulnerability and keep digging until I shattered.

After an agonising few minutes, where I begged my lungs to operate in a normal rhythm, he finally released me with a sharp jerk of his chin.

I stood, wincing at the scrape of the chair legs against the timber flooring. It took every ounce of my control to walk at a sedate pace to the door, open it gently, and close it softly behind me.

My hand shook as I smoothed a stray hair back that had fallen from my messy bun.

I'd made it out, but I was more trapped than ever.

Chapter 4

"Ah, my sad little feast is back," a smooth voice said. "Come to feed me more of your delicious pain?"

Stepping into the lab, I slammed the door behind me, reeling from my uncle's demand.

No part of me was ready to face this demonic bastard, but I had a schedule to keep. A lie to portray.

The monster caged in the corner smacked his lips together, obnoxiously loud. "Mmmm, so much agony today, feast. What happened?"

I gritted my teeth, refusing to look at the creep as I went about half-arsing my tests as quick as I could.

"Aww, don't you want to talk about it? Let me guess, one of the other meatbags said a mean word to you, huh?" His grating voice held a false sympathy laden with mocking in his faint American accent. "Why don't you come over here and open my cell? I promise to end all your pain," he purred.

I glared at the skeletal demon, taking in the way his spindly fingers clutched the metal bars. Eager desperation lit eerie red eyes.

He licked his lips, pointed tongue swiping down to his chin to catch the drool. "Come on, feast. Let me have a sip. I'll bet you taste even sweeter than my last treat."

"Fuck off," I snapped. "I'm not in the mood for your fear-munching crap today."

His last *treat* was a teenage girl he'd been found torturing. Alpha team had tracked the demon to an abandoned barn on the outskirts of the city, finding a horror show inside. The rest of the girl's family lay in pieces around her as he broke her bones, one by one.

I was a mess of conflict these days. Maybe not all demons were evil, but that didn't mean they were all good either.

A part of me longed for the simpler days when I'd believed in the hunter cause. No questions asked. I'd seen the horrible things demons did to humans. They were the monsters we needed to eradicate from our world.

Three weeks ago, things had been black and white. Then I'd been saved by the enemy, and my world had been thrown into shades of grey. More so with every demon captive I'd spoken to since.

Last week, I'd tried to convince a few of the less psychotic hunters that demons might not all be the mindless, evil beasts we thought. I'd even brought it up with Martin and Cara.

Unsurprisingly, I'd got nowhere.

Most hunters were recruited after a demon had murdered a loved one in front of them or they'd been a victim of an attack themselves. It didn't help that we had vicious demons like this one in captivity.

I sucked back the urge to sigh, instead pipetting a small vial of the demon's blood and combining it with one substance Cara had synthesised. The set-up here was an odd mix between a pharmaceutical lab and torture chamber.

All the lab work made me feel like a fraud, but it was play with chemicals or kill demons. At least the work I was doing now could help humanity. I'd been given a project designed to limit demon powers and even stop them feeding on us.

Surely stopping monsters devouring the fear of innocent humans was a good thing, right?

"Fear munching is how I survive." The demon sniffed.

"No. You suck down fear to gain power," I pointed out, watching the vial for any noticeable changes. "You eat and drink just like we do to actually sustain yourself. Why don't you become a fucking tandem skydiver or something? Feed on voluntary fear instead of being a homicidal maniac?"

He tutted. "Only the strong survive. Even an idiot like you must know that."

"Wow, a demon is getting philosophical with me. Are we bonding?" I tossed back.

"Such inner turmoil, huh?" The demon mocked me as I worked, but I was getting used to it by now. "You humans are so emotional all the time. It's delicious, but it must be exhausting. Come here, and I'll take it all away."

"Do you ever shut up? I thought you snacked on fear, not irritation." I concentrated on my work, trying to tune him out while I dripped the formula onto the glass slide, placed on a cover, and slid it under the microscope. Lifting my glasses, I peered down it.

As expected, the demon blood remained unchanged. The cells drifted amid the substate like unimpressed blobs, silently telling me to go fuck myself.

I sat back from the microscope, switching it off. Rubbing at my eyes, I shoved down the frustration and readjusted my glasses, brushing back a few strands of my chestnut hair that had fallen into my face.

Another day, another failure.

I checked my watch, stifling a groan.

Most of the science staff were given their own lab and freedom, but since I wasn't even a scientist, just a nerd that no longer fancied butchering people from another realm, I was given all the menial tasks and far too little time to do them.

My uncle's demand swirled around my mind. If I accepted this project he was forcing onto me, would I even still have to experiment on the fear demon? Or would I spend my days letting blood demons sink their fangs into my skin and steal my life through my veins?

"Until next time, fear muncher." I gave the demon a sarcastic wave and stalked towards the door.

He snarled, trying to lunge through the bars, slamming his forehead in his haste. His claws swiped through empty air, and I quirked a brow. There was no way for him to reach me. I was over three metres away, and he was trapped behind reinforced steel bars. He was acting like a rabid animal.

Or a demon.

With a huff, I left him to his captivity.

I sped through my evening tasks, restocking the labs for the other scientists while discreetly checking the demon captives were still alive. Some I tried to feed the cereal bars I'd stuffed into my pockets this morning, but most wanted nothing to do with me. And who could blame them?

I ignored the grumble of my stomach. Since I'd been trying to sneak the less violent captives what little food I had, it didn't leave much for me.

I'd also caved this morning, spending my whole daily budget on a drive-through breakfast muffin and cheap coffee on my way in. I didn't regret my morning splurge though. A little comfort food was overdue at this point.

My demon saviour's dulled sunshine eyes knifed through my mind.

Walking into the lab, holding my final test subject of the day, I flashed a fake smile at the caged demon. "Hey, Mags, how's it going?"

She hissed in response, tail lashing like a whip behind her back.

"That good, huh?" I asked.

She'd refused to speak to me even once, so I'd named her to make myself feel better. I hoped she was one of the good demons, but how could you tell who was innocent and who was an evil serial killer determined to turn my hometown into a human all-you-can-eat buffet?

Stifling the guilt at keeping her captive, I went through the motions, grabbing samples and equipment from the fridge and cupboards, pretending to get to work.

I leaned over the workbench, pipetting some unknown cocktail of chemicals into a tube and adding different samples of Mags's blood. They were old and dead, probably taken by one of the other few scientists I rarely saw. I would get no useful data, thankfully, but if anyone walked in on me, it would look real enough.

This was why Martin was breathing down my neck, but a part of me didn't want to discover anything at all about the demons and their weaknesses.

How would I be able to fake getting bitten by a blood demon? My mind swam with the implications of what I'd been told to do, and whether I could escape the plans my uncle had for me.

I couldn't just run off. I'd been dragged back so easily last time, and that was before my uncle had installed more security measures to tighten the noose. I was saving hard for enough funds to disappear into the vastness of continental Europe, planning to live off-grid until my uncle gave up the search, but I needed more time and the right opportunity to take off when he least expected it.

Wiping down the workbench, I cleaned off any traces of poison and blood before peeling off my gloves and throwing them in the hazards bin.

I checked the time, the oversize watch mocking me as the large hand hit twelve.

For most people, seven p.m. was a good time. Normally, you'd have finished work already. Probably eating dinner at home with your family, or going for drinks with your co-workers, possibly even on a romantic date to a fancy restaurant.

For me, it signalled the end of my twelve-hour workday.

I released a slow breath, wiping damp palms down my lab coat. "Time to run the gauntlet."

Chapter 5

Grabbing my bag from the staff lockers, I slung my coat on and hurried up the stairs.

The basement of Riverside's hunter HQ was a ghost town, not a single soul around to witness my act of bravery.

Except for all the captives trapped down here, hidden in various cages and cells.

I shoved thoughts of the poor demons aside. If I let myself dwell on their situation, or the weight of my guilt, I'd stop functioning.

With a swipe of my unmarked pass, the reinforced door topping the staircase buzzed me out. I spilled into the cavernous warehouse with a sharp inhale at the assault of noise. The sour stench that accompanied violence thickened in my throat, and I immediately regretted the action.

Two young guards sat at a table by the door, playing a card game. They barely glanced up, doing a quick visual sweep to check I wasn't smuggling a hellhound under my jacket, before returning to their game without so much as a hello.

I'd take being ignored by a hunter any day.

A cheer rang through the room. The usual evening crowd surrounded the spotlit fight cage in the centre of the vast space. Armed hunters sprawled in cheap foldable chairs around it, getting their blood pumping before their nightly missions.

Sometimes the fights were training—testing the mettle of new recruits or getting in some extra practise with a new weapon—but mostly it was for sport.

I moved, swift and silent, hurrying past them and praying to whatever deity might listen that they let me go unnoticed tonight.

My stomach dropped as I recognised a demon in the ring. A weary female Cara had made me take samples from yesterday. Like Mags, this demon had refused to speak to me, but after Cara had left, she'd listened to me ramble about inane things like the pollen count or how much I loved Italian food while I'd tried to clean her wounds and slip her a protein bar without getting clawed.

"Ah, well look who it is!" Jayce waved at me, leanly muscled frame sprawled across a chair at the edge of the crowd. "What's the matter, *Dozer*, too scared to watch demons in action now? Or are you off for more beauty sleep?"

A few chuckles answered as the hunters around him glanced my way. I ignored the back of a certain scarred sandy-blond head as my ex continued to watch the fight.

I'd never got along with Jayce. He'd always envied my position in alpha squad, claiming nepotism was the reason I was there and he'd been stuck in beta for so long. He wasn't the only hunter to think that either.

In a way, they were right—everything I'd had, I'd earned through blood—just not in the way they thought.

But Jayce had dragged me back to base after the incident that nearly killed me. Not my teammates. Not my fiancé. Not my uncle.

When they'd called in beta team to help what remained of alpha go back and erase the evidence of demonkind, Leo had told everyone I was dead. Jayce had checked me for a pulse anyway and found me miraculously alive.

Of course, given I'd looked relatively unharmed, he'd joked that I was being a typical princess and taking a leisurely doze. Hence the new nickname. I knew from the whispers that most hunters thought I'd been faking my injuries for attention like a spoiled brat, which made zero sense.

If they knew the truth, though, they'd call me a traitor and lock me up right beside the demons.

I stretched my lips into an imitation of a smile, pretending nothing Jayce said could affect me. "Night, Jayce. Good luck out there today."

I gave him a small two-fingered salute without stopping, hoping that for once he'd just let it go.

He kicked out an empty chair, and it slid into my path with a screech.

More eyes turned on me, burning with judgement.

"Stay and watch. It's only right you see off your former teammates before we head out and do the real work." Jayce's forest-green eyes met mine, filled with challenge.

"Sorry, can't tonight. I've got plans." I shot him an apologetic smile as fake as his gold Rolex.

He stood, taking a menacing step closer, trying to intimidate me even though he didn't have much more than a handful of inches on my short height. "You're going to sit and watch these satanic pricks fight to the death with us, and then you're going to watch us leave for our missions. Missions that *you* should be on too. If you weren't such a coward." He raised his voice towards the end, accusation ringing out through the warehouse.

A hush descended, the small crowd turning their attention wholly to me. Even the forced fight slowed inside the ring, until the meaty thwack of flesh hitting flesh stopped altogether.

At least my humiliation bought them a reprieve.

My cheeks heated under the scrutiny, but I squared my shoulders. "My work could help neutralise demon abilities, putting them on a level playing field with us. I'm sure you'd like for the demons to slow down enough for you to actually hit one."

Another few chuckles went up as people lapped up the show.

Jayce scoffed, "Putting on glasses doesn't make you a scientist."

"Picking up a gun doesn't make you a hunter," I snarked back, pushing my granny-style wire-rimmed glasses up the bridge of my nose. As an operational hunter, I'd worn contact lenses to fight in.

Leo finally twisted around in his ringside chair, a few rows in front of Jayce. His features sharpened until they almost glinted like a knife under the low lighting.

The rest of alpha squad and his usual groupies lounged around him.

Tia, the only other female besides myself to make it up the ranks into alpha squad, sat closest. Her manicured hand fell away from his knee as he stood slowly, interrupting whatever Jayce had been about to say with a harsh scrape of his chair.

She shot me a venomous glare that I chose to ignore. I'd wanted to be her friend, thinking we could look out for each other in this male-dominated organisation, but she'd always seen me as competition.

My dumb heart ached at the sight of my ex-fiancé, the hidden wounds he'd left stubbornly outlasting the physical ones I'd gained from the incident that had destroyed us.

We'd only been broken up for a few weeks, and he'd shown zero signs that it affected him.

Sometimes I could barely look him in the eye.

He sauntered over with the lethal grace of a trained fighter, effortlessly intimidating with his steroid-pumped bulk and the three slashes from ear to temple where a demon had scarred him.

Jayce jerked forward as the bigger man patted him on the shoulder a fraction too hard.

"She's got you there, bud. Let poor Dozer here get back to her evening." He shot me a condescending smirk. "Maybe she's got a date to get to."

A harsh titter fell from Tia's glossy lips, underlined by sniggers from the rest of alpha squad, as if the idea that I could be seeing someone was that ridiculous.

I ground my molars so hard that I worried I'd need to see a dentist.

Leo had made it clear when we'd broken up that he didn't care about me. In all honesty, I wasn't sure he ever had.

Still, the bastard had made sure none of the other hunters would look twice at me. Spreading some bullshit about how I was still madly in love with him and he wouldn't take too kindly to anyone taking advantage of me when I would obviously only be hooking up with them to make him jealous.

As usual, it was all about his ego. I was just an accessory to it.

It made me want to go out and fuck the nearest stranger, just to prove I could, but it was bad enough when my uncle threatened me with the lives of people I didn't know.

"Yup, met this cute guy on one of the dating apps." I flashed Leo a shit-eating grin. "We're meeting at his place."

His square jaw ticked, as if the thought of me with someone else irritated him.

A kernel of hope unfurled in my chest before I stomped it out.

He'd left me for dead. I would have taken on a horde of demons to save him. It had literally been our job, and he hadn't fought for me.

But he had for Tia.

A self-assured smirk curved her plump lips, as if she could hear my thoughts.

My ex might hunt down monsters infiltrating our world, but something just as evil lurked behind those dark-blue eyes.

"Well, try not to die tonight." I gave Leo and Jayce a mocking salute, and before either could spout more venom, I sidestepped the pair and strode for the exit.

Leo's voice boomed behind me, "Did I say you could stop!? Fight, beasts, or I'll execute you both."

My heart stuttered at the cold cruelty, but I couldn't free them.

I was just as trapped.

Chapter 6

Spilling out into the night, I sucked down air, letting the chill calm my frantic pulse.

Boots crunched broken glass as a pair of hunters patrolled the rear of hunter HQ, dark coats hiding the weapons I knew were strapped beneath.

The men halted a few feet away, content to watch me from the shadows. One dug a phone from their pocket, shooting off a quick message.

No doubt updating my uncle on my whereabouts.

Smothering the urge to flip them off, I reached my car at the edge of the parking lot without incident, unlocking the old hatchback with the manual key and sliding behind the wheel. Stale cigarette smoke tried to choke me with the joys of used cars. At twenty-four, it was the same age as I was, and had already had countless owners.

I just had the one.

"Come on, old girl, you can do this," I muttered, twisting the key in the ignition.

She spluttered a few times.

Then silence.

"Today? Really?" I let my head thunk back against the headrest.

I twisted the key again.

The engine fought to tick over with an ominous rattle, but no spark breathed life into it.

My hand tightened on the steering wheel, worn smooth by time.

The last car had been written off when I'd tried to flee Riverside. I didn't want to leave the town my family had lived in for generations. I just wanted to leave the cult of killers and mad scientists.

Since a speed camera had caught me right before the crash, the insurance company wouldn't pay out either. So the paltry savings I'd had left, after paying for my cancelled wedding, had gone into buying this pile of rust.

Now I saved every spare penny to fund the escape I'd been plotting ever since.

Taking a fortifying breath, I left the glaring money pit behind and headed for the only bus stop on the quiet industrial estate.

My uncle's demand rattled around my skull. It had haunted me all afternoon since he'd issued his ultimatum—either I suffered or a random stranger would.

I'd hoped leaving work meant I could leave my problems behind too, but of course, there was no escape. Not for me.

I glanced over my shoulder. A dark silhouette cast a menacing shadow under the street lamp, further back along the road, watching me walk to the bus stop.

Nobody else waited at the small shelter, and I quickly ducked beneath it as the first specks of rain hit my glasses.

The drizzle became a downpour, and I smirked at my tail, getting drenched on my uncle's orders.

A bus groaned in the distance, turning along the access road, and my uncle's guard dog slunk closer.

I boarded, paid, and took a seat, fighting not to snarl at the hunter who'd followed me on board. Instead, I watched water stream down the window as the vehicle trundled along.

Riverside blurred behind the glass, the small city passing me by in a sea of lit buildings and darkened parks. My thoughts whirred, circling over and over as I tried to come up with a way to defy my uncle, but no solution jumped out of the darkness.

Eventually, the bus pulled onto the main street, and I shook myself from my depressive thoughts in time to hop off into the rain. Despite the gloomy weather, people strolled along beneath dark umbrellas, darting to and from pubs and restaurants.

To my surprise, my tail remained seated, but I knew better than to think I'd be left unsupervised.

Right on cue, a familiar woman in running gear and a suspiciously large coat stepped under a lamp-post across the street from me, giving me a two-fingered salute.

A small smile tugged at my lips as I returned the gesture. Rhia was one of the few hunters who didn't seem to believe the rumours—whether it was me being handed my position in alpha because of my family name, or the latest ones about me faking my injuries in the warehouse ambush.

I wouldn't say we were friends, exactly, but we shared a mutual respect. It wasn't easy being a female hunter in a male-dominated organisation, and I'd helped her with extra training sessions over the last year since she'd joined.

She kept her distance as I headed along the busy street, confirming my thoughts. She must have been out hunting with delta team before getting diverted to watch me. My uncle having hunters monitor my every move "for my protection" wasn't helping my image as the pampered hunter princess.

The glowing lights of my favourite Italian restaurant called to me, but I was already going to struggle to afford car repairs, let alone an actual meal.

A vicious memory surfaced, taking me back to another rainy night, behind another restaurant.

Of my father's voice telling me to run. Of my legs failing to move.

The hungry growl of a demon.

I shoved the memory back before it could suck me under. It had taken me a long time to pull free from the nightmares of my past. Some nights, they still won.

I continued the long walk home, winding through the quieter streets until I was alone with the rain and my thoughts, save for the occasional scuff of a shoe against the pavement from Rhia, trailing behind me.

The ghost of my father's death haunted me.

If he'd have had the defensive serum that my uncle was pressuring the scientists to develop, maybe he'd still be alive, running the Riverside hunters. He'd pushed me to my limits with training, even though I was still a child, but my uncle shoved me past them.

My father might have been a cold bastard, but didn't I owe it to his memory to stop more people from being killed by parasitic demons?

I couldn't face letting a demon bite me, day after day. But what kind of monster would that make me if I let some innocent person suffer in my place? My job already made me sick, witnessing all those demons captured and hurt while I just stood by and did nothing.

Or worse, helped keep them there.

Sometimes the weight of my guilt was too much to bear. I'd wake with the lingering sound of screams in my ears. The image of demons begging me for help.

The echo of their torment seemed to follow me into the present.

I paused, frowning as another muffled scream pierced the haze of memories again.

My heart pounded as I spun, assessing the street for threats. Rhia was nowhere in sight.

A thud sounded from deep within an unlit path, just a few paces back.

Another pained cry rang out, and I plunged into the darkness.

Halfway down the alley, a horned beast pressed Rhia against the bricks, drawing me up short.

Fear held me in its vice as I absorbed the familiar scene.

This was how my father had died. Just a few streets over.

The monster buried his face against Rhia's neck, and she screamed against the hand clamped over her mouth.

"Not again." The plea slipped into the night, and I sprinted towards them.

The demon reared back, tearing bits of Rhia's throat out. Blood dripped from his fangs as he hissed at me. It stained his mouth like smeared lipstick.

He dropped his prey, smirking as I closed in. Horror churned my gut as Rhia collapsed at his feet.

I cursed myself for coming unarmed, but there wasn't time for regret as I swung for his smug face. He dodged in a blur of speed. Demons were naturally fast, but the fresh blood meant he'd easily outpace me.

He cocked his head, branched horns catching the moonlight. "You know what I am, don't you?" Thin lips split wide, showcasing a nest of fangs. "Surely such a weak little girl can't be a hunter too?"

His hand darted out before I could flinch, gripping my throat and shoving me into the bricks hard enough to see stars. Claws dug into my neck, and I shoved down the fear that my next breath would be my last. With a snarl, I slammed my knee into his balls, but he swept back, narrowly avoiding the blow.

I slid into a fighting stance, the wall at my back. Adrenaline narrowed my focus to the monster before me, licking a drop of my blood from his pearly claw tip with a look of ecstasy.

"It's almost too easy." The demon sniggered, eyeing my raised fists. "Not much sport in devouring a skinny runt, is there? You're barely a mouthful." Glowing red eyes ran the length of me, leaving a sticky feeling in their wake.

"If it's so easy, why are you backing away, leech?" I hissed back. "Come take a bite, see what happens."

He took another step back with a smirk. "I'm a touch full for another snack actually, but don't worry, I'll come find you when I'm hungry."

He turned and walked off, sauntering down the alley.

And I just let him go.

"Fuck!" I snarled, darting to check on Rhia instead.

It was against hunter code to let a demon escape, but I'd always choose protecting lives over taking them.

Moonlight cast a chalky complexion to her skin, dotted with raindrops like the night already mourned her loss. In vain hope, I pressed a hand to the wound in her throat.

Blood and ragged flesh met my fingers.

I heaved, stomach cramping at the slick sensation. Bile stung my throat, burning as I retched beside the downed hunter.

I spat thickly, clenched my jaw, and pushed my fingertips to the other side of her throat, even as the logical side of me knew she should have bled more from a neck wound that size.

No flutter answered my touch.

I let my hands fall away, wiping the blood off onto my trousers before the wet sensation could make me vomit again.

Rhia's eyes were frozen wide with the terror of her final moments.

My head bowed with the weight of another death on my conscience.

Another person I couldn't save.

If I'd been faster, or stronger, maybe things could have been different this time.

Drawing a shallow breath, I ignored the metallic tang and sour bile tainting the air and grabbed my phone from my pocket. I dialled the number for clean-up, quickly rattling off the location and details.

My uncle was many things, but he wasn't stupid. If the authorities found too many suspicious bodies, they'd start digging into what caused such strange wounds.

Now another person would be listed as missing; another family would go without closure. We could hardly tell Rhia's parents that a *demon* had murdered their child, or how the same monsters had killed their son too.

It was why she'd joined the hunters in the first place: witnessing a soul demon suck the life from her brother. A familiar story amongst the organisation that ruled my life.

Biting the inside of my cheek, I scrounged up the courage to really look at her.

She wasn't much older than twenty, but laugh lines rimmed her bloodless lips. A cut diamond glinted on her dainty ring finger, even though protocol demanded we hunt bare of any accessories or identifiers.

Guilt carved deeper into my chest. Somebody out there loved her. Waited for her to come home.

Would they have fought the demon to save her?

Car brakes squeaked, and I stood, shoving back the depressing thoughts.

The hunters were nothing if not efficient. A van blocked the end of the alley, parking straight over the pavement to lower the risk of being seen. I lifted Rhia's cooling body into my arms, thankful I'd kept up with most of my training, and carried her away from the violent scene.

The vehicle's side door slid open, and I wordlessly handed Rhia over to the stout man in coveralls lurking inside.

"That's the second of ours tonight." His upper lip curled. "No monster to dispose of too?"

My throat closed off, leaving me with a blank stare to offer in response. He sighed and, with a harsh slam, closed the door, and the vehicle peeled away.

I lingered in the alley, stewing in my guilt. In the what-ifs.

Not all demons were good. In fact, most I'd encountered were attacking people.

How many more would die with fangs in their throat?

If feeding on Rhia had hurt that demon, she'd still be alive. The compound my uncle was pushing to develop incapacitated demons. If it was in human blood, death by fang would be a thing of the past.

We could forge a weaponised cure to stop blood demons draining us.

If I embraced my uncle's latest demands and planned my escape for afterwards, when he'd be most distracted, then I could save countless people from the same fate as Rhia. As my father.

My uncle was as evil as some of the worst demons I'd come across, but ultimately, he wanted to save human lives. Regardless of the terrible cost.

What price was I willing to pay?

I straightened, coming to a harrowing decision. I tipped my face back, letting the rain wash away my failure, along with the stray tears that had escaped.

Nobody else would die. Not if I could help it.

Chapter 7

"I'm glad you've seen reason," Martin said, walking slightly ahead of me down the corridor the following morning.

The "for once" was left unspoken, dangling awkwardly, quite like I imagined his saggy balls did.

I pasted on a fake smile, drawing level with him. "I know, it's highly surprising given my condition."

He frowned, unsure of what I meant or whether to question me further.

Confusing him on social norms was the one joy I had in this pit of misery. The only condition I had was a bad case of reality.

What did one do when they realised they'd been raised in a cult?

And then chose to semi-willingly go along with the madness. For now.

After Rhia's death last night, I'd resolved to carry out the tests my uncle demanded, while biding my time until I had enough resources to escape him for good. If my last attempt had taught me anything, it was that I'd need a solid plan, money, and to start hoarding four-leaf clovers.

A door opened along the corridor, letting an agonised scream out behind Cara. The blood-spattered scientist exited her lab with the confident step of someone wholly unfazed by the pain she caused others.

It took everything in me not to flinch.

"Ah, Dr Smythe," Martin said. "Good day." He tipped an imaginary hat to her as we passed.

She blushed, looking coyly up at him from under her lashes. "Dr Burke," she murmured. "A pleasure, as always."

I wanted to vomit all over them both. Who flirted in a mad scientist's torture den?

Apparently I was the only person to hear the screaming. Maybe it was in my head.

Martin cleared his throat, walking a little taller as we made it to the last lab on this floor. "Expecting your answer, the hunter prime arranged for a fresh subject to be prepared last night."

Of course he had.

Because he'd snapped his fingers, so I'd come to heel like an obedient pet.

I subtly wiped my damp palms on my lab coat, shoving down the urge to bark like a crazy person, and gave him another fake smile. "Excellent."

Martin nodded his approval. "It's already caged inside. Since you need this one healthy, to better simulate real-world conditions, our usual methods for obedience are unsuitable." He held up a small remote, barely the size of his palm. "This controls a reinforced collar around its neck. It will tighten, asphyxiating the subject."

I eyed the device, letting the reality of what was happening sink in.

Of course I'd need a way to stop the demon from ravaging my veins, killing me in seconds. Choking the life out of it would probably do the trick, but I'd had no idea we had such weapons here.

I swallowed, pocketing the offered remote, ignoring the nausea that came with it.

"I know you're fairly new to the practical side of experimentation, so I can supervise the first few feeds, or ask Dr Smythe to." His gaze darted behind me, towards where his paramour had disappeared along the corridor.

"No!" I softened my sudden denial with a weak smile. "I mean... I wouldn't want to take up any more of your precious time. You both have your own important tests to run, and the quicker we can discover compounds to deter the demons, the more lives we can save."

The words tasted like ash on my tongue, but the worst part was the element of truth to them. The lines of what I was willing to do were so blurred I couldn't tell which side of them I fell on.

His stare cooled. "Yes, well, I've left you some guidance on proper methodology on the bench."

I shifted my weight.

I was determined to conduct the tests on myself, and whatever poor soul was trapped in my lab, but the reality would be a blood-drenched nightmare.

A voice in my head yelled at me to run away, to turn back and leave with my veins intact. There was enough darkness weighing me down already.

After a long pause, Martin huffed. "No time like the present, Liliana."

Biting my lip, I brushed past my passive-aggressive boss, scanning my pass and unlocking the door.

My nerves were a jumbled mess, but I pushed inside, letting determination harden me as I locked away every soft and squishy emotion I had.

I stepped into the room—and froze.

The door clicked shut behind me, trapping me in with a ghost.

His broad form had grown since I'd seen him last, somehow packed with more muscle across his bare chest and powerful arms. He radiated violence, dripping with a vicious energy I'd not felt before.

Charcoal skin seemed to draw in the light, reflecting off the bony spikes topping each shoulder and the violent horns rising from his short hair. The pale strands were only a shade darker than his bleached horns. A tail swayed side to side, flashing over each shoulder and revealing the heart-shaped spade on the end, more spines protruding from it, begging to sink into flesh.

Even his face was designed for battle: short spikes edging his brows, cheekbones sharp enough to cut, square jaw hard enough to take a hit.

Thin tribal tattoos covered every visible inch of his flesh. The intricate white linework almost glowed against the dark backdrop of his skin.

A thick metal collar banded his neck, littered with scratch marks.

The blood demon trapped behind the wall of glass had been the one to set me free.

He'd haunted my nightmares for weeks, a replay of his lifeless eyes staring up at me. Sometimes I dreamed he woke up, and I killed him over and over, even though it was Leo who'd wielded the sword.

Other times, he tore through my arteries like tissue paper.

"How... I thought..." I couldn't form a full sentence as I struggled under the battering of emotions. Relief. Guilt. Fear. Sorrow. Disbelief. "What are you doing here?"

His upper lip hooked into a sneer. "Waiting for a manicure. What the fuck does it look like I'm doing?"

I blinked at his acidic tone. It was low and raspy, like he sucked down poison to survive rather than blood.

The polar opposite of the demon who'd saved my life all those weeks ago.

I started noticing other things, little details I'd glossed over in my shock.

He was taller, close to seven feet, and thick cut muscle stacked his frame. Every point seemed sharper and every spike longer. Even his curved horns rose higher.

His face was more brutal than I remembered too, the angles harsher, jaw squarer, eyes deep-set. Their colour glowed an eerie silver within their black abyss, rather than the warm yellow I remembered. Starlight, not sunshine.

I stepped closer, getting a better look as my eyes tried to convince my brain that it wasn't him.

My saviour was dead.

And he'd not miraculously risen from the grave I'd helped put him in.

Chapter 8

I cleared my throat. I had to get my shit together and do my damned job. Another freak-out would only derail my new-found purpose.

Apparently I thought all demons looked the same, and I'd become a demon racist on top of all my other crimes against them.

I flipped the lights on, bathing the room in their harsh glare.

The demon hissed, squinting at me, but stayed in the middle of his cell, weaponised tail swaying like a viper ready to strike.

They'd assigned me the smallest of the seven labs, a storage room in its past life. A scuffed workbench took up half the usable space, and the glass cell at the back claimed the other. Flimsy cabinets lined the walls, and a yellowed mini fridge hummed in the corner.

It was basic, but it would do.

I didn't exactly need much to inject dubious substances and feed myself to a monster.

Martin's instructions lurked in neat cursive on a crisp sheet of paper resting on the stainless steel worktop. Why he couldn't just email me the notes was beyond me, but the secret nature of our work made him almost as paranoid as my uncle.

As I'd expected, his first instruction was to take a baseline.

"Of course," I muttered.

Dread coiled in my gut.

I was really doing this.

I replaced the sheet and turned to face my fears.

The demon watched me, unblinking.

Instinct screamed at me not to do this. It went against every ounce of logic to get closer to a starved predator.

What did one even say to the demon you were about to feed?

Open wide, here comes the aeroplane? I hope you're hungry? Try not to choke?

An inappropriate chuckle spilled out as I stepped up to the barrier separating us.

The demon quirked an arctic brow, looking down at me like I was the dirt under his claws. "Something funny, hunter?"

Well, my whole life was a joke, but I didn't think I'd get much sympathy from my captive.

I clamped my lips closed, shaking my head. "So...um, I'm going to feed you now."

His tail stilled, eyes searching my empty hands. "I don't want your dead blood."

He didn't just mean from a corpse. Bagged blood was considered "dead" to them too, which was part of the reason these tests were so important. For a demon like him, feeding off a live person was the sole source of boosted nourishment.

"I'm aware." I unlocked the hatch in the thick plexiglass screen. Sliding the window open to the first notch, around the width of my forearm, I secured it into place using the mechanism at the side.

Most of the labs and cells used traditional steel bars to hold demons, but my uncle had given me the only one with bullet-proof glass. The bars were cheaper and easier to find, but you had to watch out for a demon's jabbing tail or getting clawed if you strayed too close.

I was getting as close as one could. I'd already be at this parasite's mercy with his fangs in my flesh, but at least I wouldn't have to worry about his spiked tail shredding my face too.

I clenched my fist and held my forearm up to the open hatch, careful not to poke my hand through in case he ripped my arm off. As it was, my arm blocked him from reaching through and grabbing me, but he could still decide to slit my wrist with his claws. Or tear through my flesh with his fangs like the bastard blood demon had done to Rhia last night.

If my subject had been caught recently, he'd probably still be at full strength. Feeding him regularly wouldn't help the physical power imbalance between us, but there wasn't much I could do about it.

I fished out the small remote from my pocket and held it up so the demon could see. "This is connected to your collar. Try to hurt me, and you'll receive a little...punishment."

The thought of using it on anyone, even a parasitic blood demon, turned my stomach. But there was already a fair chance this experiment would get me killed.

I might be done with violence, but would it ever be done with me?

He eyed me, suspicion swirling in his stark gaze. Dark pupils expanded, feeding on the spikes of silver haloing them amid the blackness. He glared at my pale skin, pressed into the palm-sized gap.

A forked tongue swiped out, moistening his lower lip. "Why would a hunter offer themselves up as a snack?" he mused, tone slathered in mocking.

I arched a brow. "Does it matter?" I wasn't going to explain myself to a parasite. If he was smart, he'd figure it out before long. "If you want, I can throw you back in with the others and find a more peckish volunteer."

Unfazed, he pinned me with his sharp gaze. It scraped over me, inspecting every part and finding it lacking.

"If a hunter wants to get bitten for kinks, who am I to judge?" he drawled, finally moving up to the glass separating us. He swaggered the two steps with the arrogance of a predator, somehow oozing confidence and derision in such a small space.

Yep. Even a demon thought I was beneath him.

Loved that for me. Thanks, universe.

I shoved down the urge to sigh, instead fortifying my nerve as he towered over me, at least half my height taller and twice my width. I almost wished for the steel bars. The glass was so clear I could make out the scars mixed in with his tattoos. I tried to ignore the sheer power radiating from him, but the sight of so much muscle and natural weaponry threatened to bring up my meagre bowl of cornflakes.

He lowered to his knees with a sardonic smirk, the base of great, arching horns hitting my eye level.

My heart thundered, pounding like a fist against flesh.

The moment stretched taut between us.

Ashen lips peeled back, revealing vicious fangs in a cruel grin. "This is going to hurt."

Chapter 9

The monster struck, fangs sinking deep into my forearm.

My scream echoed off the glass. I'd braced for pain, but it was instant and all-consuming.

Acid raced outwards from his bite. My hand spasmed, and I crashed to my knees, clamping my lips closed, somehow staying aware enough not to rip my arm back.

I vaguely registered his low growl, the pulling sensation heightening as he gulped down my blood.

The initial shock faded, and I let the pain wash through me, accepting it rather than trying to fight it. A trick I'd learned long ago.

Pain was just my nerves firing messages to my brain. I could conquer this.

I breathed through it, studying the demon's reaction to distract myself.

His pupils had blown wide. The dark pits tried to swallow the glowing starbursts of silver that haloed them, the only light amid the otherwise pure black of his eyes.

White lashes fluttered shut in a look of bliss. His face almost pressing into the glass to keep his lips sealed to my flesh.

Six.

That was how many times I'd been bitten in my life. This was somehow more painful than all of them combined.

Granted, the others had been during fights. The adrenaline could have masked most of the pain, but I suspected there was more to it.

Was he a special subtype of blood demon? Or was he doing something else to make it hurt more?

A dizzying surge rolled through me.

"Enough, parasite," I hissed through gritted teeth.

Starred eyes locked on mine, somehow telling me to fuck off without words.

I lifted the remote, ignoring the heaviness in my limb. "Don't make me do it."

He growled, vibrating my forearm with a spike of agony.

But didn't stop.

This was the exact scenario I'd feared. I'd let a demon sink his fangs into me, and now I'd pay for my stupidity.

Images of my father's murder flashed before my eyes.

Of the demon yanking his head aside and ravaging his neck like a beast, spraying blood and bits of flesh to splatter me. The bloodlust and sick hunger in the demon's glowing eyes.

The light leaving my father's.

I pressed the button.

The demon choked, collapsing to the floor as he clawed at the device, crushing the life out of him with a metallic whine.

I jabbed the off button, horror filling me at the sight of such a familiar-looking demon writhing on the ground.

Warmth trickled down my arm, and I inspected the ragged punctures left by the demon, ignoring the way my stomach roiled at the sensation of fresh blood on my skin. The flow eased to a faint ooze as my body's natural coagulation response kicked into overdrive without the demon's fangs injecting a substance to stop it.

I frowned at the wound. I didn't remember it clotting so fast before either.

The demon panted on the floor, pushing himself up on arms that trembled ever so slightly. Blood ran from under the shiny collar. Within seconds, the metal had crushed his throat hard enough to split the skin.

He lifted his hard gaze to pin me in place. "You shouldn't have done that." His acidic tone was even lower than before, husky and deep.

The sheer audacity had my brows leaping up. "And you shouldn't have tried to kill me."

He smirked, the gesture filled with violent promise. "It's not smart to offer a vein to a hungry demon, especially a venomous one."

I sucked in a breath. "You tried to poison me?"

Panic bit me as hard as he had. No wonder it had hurt so much.

The demon chuckled. The sound carrying so much mocking it grated on my already frayed nerves.

"Aww, is the poor little huntress scared of the big, bad demon?" He looked far too confident for someone collared and half-sprawled across the floor of a prison cell. "It's not lethal, unfortunately, but I can make it...unpleasant."

There was zero remorse in his eerie silver eyes.

Of course I wouldn't find any. He was a blood demon. I might have met one who seemed half-decent, but that didn't mean the majority weren't monsters.

I stepped back with a sneer. "Classic demon."

He licked his lips, cleaning the last traces of my blood. Even with it gone, his lips held a faint pink tinge, adding a blush of colour to his grey-and-white appearance.

"Tasty huntress." He flashed his fangs, looking a breath from attack.

I observed him in the ensuing silence, watching for any unusual effects from my blood. Not that I'd expect any, but I had to be sure of the baseline.

Yay for science.

"Going to keep eye-fucking me all day?" he sneered, somehow making me feel small even from his position lounging on the concrete floor.

"In your demonic dreams," I scoffed, turning away.

To my irritation, warmth bloomed through my cheeks. What precious little blood I had left pooling somewhere utterly useless.

Ignoring the oppressive silence that descended, I made quick work of organising my notes, inputting today's observations into my notebook. I might have been half-arsing the other tests forced on me, but this time was different—I wanted results.

And the evil parasite in my lab was only making me more determined.

His attention traced my skin like the edge of a knife while I worked. I was tempted to find another room to finish up in, but that felt too close to letting him win.

The beast had chosen to hurt me more than he needed to. Sure, I was the reason he was caged, but whether he knew it or not, being my captive was better than the alternatives in this place.

I'd also fed the ungrateful bastard.

My eyes slitted as I worked myself up, letting anger wash away the traces of guilt and fear.

I had to come back and do it all again in two days' time. With poison in my veins.

"What's the point of all this?" he asked, raspy voice dripping condescension as he crossed his ankles, casually leaning back on his palms so his carved eight-pack abs popped.

The demon was bare apart from the standard-issue grey sweatpants he'd been given, leaving too much inked skin on show.

I narrowed my eyes, ignoring the irrational urge to take a closer look at his tattoos. "To save innocent lives."

"At the expense of innocent lives?" He quirked a brow, tugging at the two short spikes above its outer edge. "Judging by that cute little lab coat, aren't you meant to be smart?"

I snorted at his mocking tone, matching it right back. "You don't seem particularly innocent to me."

He bared his fangs in a violent grin. "Why don't you open this cell and find out?"

Shaking my head, I turned my back on him, tidying away my notes and heading for the door.

"I'll be seeing you, huntress." His voice was a dark promise that sent shivers of trepidation down my spine.

I switched the light off as I left, so the glare didn't strain his sensitive eyes, and immediately regretted the small mercy.

The bastard hadn't been worried about hurting me one bit.

Chapter 10

“You’re a pretty little thing...for a demon whore.”

The masculine voice held a familiar sneering that had me freezing just inside the doorway. Though its potency was nowhere near that of the prickly blood demon who’d bitten me a few hours ago.

My ex-fiancé leaned up against the silvery bars caging the back of the room, focus locked on the demoness trapped within. She might have fangs and claws, but apparently Leo was unconcerned by things like safety protocols.

If a demon got their claws into him and forced him to unlock the cell, it would put the entire compound in danger, not just one self-assured prick.

At least he dangled a hunting knife casually in his grip, the threat lying in wait.

He flashed a sharp grin at the captive demon.

Even aimed elsewhere, the sinister expression had a chill skating down my spine.

Harsh lighting glinted off the three pale slashes through his sandy-blond hair, extending from behind his ear to his temple. With his toned arms stretched overhead, showing off his bulky musculature, it gave him an aura of danger that my younger, naive self once found intoxicating.

Even though the muscles were pumped with a little chemical help, the danger was real. He didn't lead alpha squad for nothing.

I let the door slam behind me.

Leo glanced up at the noise, unfazed by being caught at whatever the hell that had been.

Taunting...? Flirting?

I grimaced. You'd have to be a little twisted to find a demon attractive. Then again, Leo wasn't exactly the most stable guy. Nobody in this place was.

Heat banked in his navy eyes, a look I recognised intimately. It used to set a fire blazing in me too, but now that heat was all rage.

I eyed the female behind bars, noting her blood-red hair and matching eyes. The witchy features were paired with short horns peeking up through the loose curls in an unlikely combination, marking her as a hybrid of major and minor demon breeds.

Sickly purple hues marred her cheekbone.

Something dark raked through my gut, and I fought back the urge to find whoever was responsible and see how well they could take a beating.

She looked startlingly human, and far too young to be here.

After my run-in with my new test subject this morning, I'd been stuck assisting Cara through lunch and well into the afternoon, trying not to vomit as the hours crawled by. She'd sent me here into the spare lab to fetch more dissection tweezers. Apparently I'd ruined the last set by simply touching the delicate ends against the workbench when I'd placed them down.

Was I still sabotaging her work on purpose? Maybe. But just because I wanted to stop demons from hurting humans didn't mean I supported all the twisted experiments the hunters ran.

Nobody should be here though. Not a demon or an idiot hunter.

I fought to keep my chaotic emotions tucked away. "What are you doing in here, Leo?"

A cocky smirk hooked one side of his thin lips. He lifted his blade, angling it to catch the light. "What? I can't have a little fun with the vermin?"

I made a snap decision. One I'd probably regret.

"No. Now get away from my subject."

His eyes narrowed, knowing me well enough to detect something was amiss. "We got this one in from the weasel just yesterday. How is it already yours?"

I straightened my lab coat, internally scrambling for a plausible lie. "She's a hybrid." I waved a hand towards her. "We've not captured one of her kind before."

There was a certain logic to it, at least in my mind.

My ex laughed, and I knew I wouldn't win that easily.

He lifted the set of keys he'd been hiding, grinning viciously at me. "Maybe I need to question it first. Get some intel before I throw it to your mercy... *Dozer*."

Anger flared at the nickname, joining my internal panic. It pissed me off when the other hunters called me that, but it was so much worse coming from him. And he had to know it.

He unlocked the door, easing the cage open.

The demon lunged for freedom, hissing as she swiped out with wicked red claws. "Big mistake, fucker!"

Leo slammed the door in her face, snickering as he hit her with the solid bars. She launched forward again, ignoring the blood now leaking from her nose.

Leo sliced along her forearm, forcing her back from the tease of hope.

"You're a naughty little thing too, huh?" He licked his lower lip, watching her blood run down his knife.

My stomach turned. What had I ever seen in him?

I couldn't let him do this.

Clearing my throat, I infused as much bite into my tone as I could scrounge up. "Do *not* interfere with my experiments. The work I do now is just as important as before."

A sneer twisted his features, but he didn't take his eyes off his prey. "Since when is playing scientist more important than killing demon scum? I'm saving people."

I swallowed the urge to scream. "*Playing scientist*, as you put it, is going to discover new ways to protect us."

At least, I hoped so.

He scoffed. "And to think you used to be fun."

My stomach churned at the reminder of all I'd done. The sins I could never atone for.

"Piss off, Leo. Let me get to work."

He scowled. "No. I'm going to get some answers out of this demon whore. You can play with what's left."

He swung the door open, and the demon bared her fangs with a hiss. The panic in her wide eyes betrayed her fear though. Blood rained from the cut on her arm, adding to the various splatters already covering her.

She wouldn't survive a *questioning*. Not from Leo.

I scrambled for a way to save her. I could probably take Leo in a fair fight, but he was always armed to the teeth.

Not that I'd get away with just attacking him unprovoked.

"Did you ever care for me?" I blurted the first thing I could think of.

Unsurprisingly, the violent brute could never handle talking about his feelings.

He swung around, incredulous, slamming the door closed again, even as his blade stayed angled towards the demon.

The relief was instant, even as I ripped open the scab on my wounded heart, offering my pain up instead of hers.

"What the fuck, Liliana? You're the one who ended things," he snarled.

Deep down, I longed to see some kind of pain cross his rugged features, but only anger simmered in his narrowed expression.

I'd broken up with him for many reasons. It wasn't just that he'd chosen to save someone else over me. I could write that off as her being in more danger. Maybe he'd believed I was strong enough to fight my way out.

The bastard left me for dead too, abandoning me amongst the bodies of our enemies.

But it was the memory of dulling sunshine eyes that struck me the hardest.

"Why did you even propose to me in the first place?" I asked the one question I knew would make him flee.

Because, deep down, I already knew the answer. I'd just never been able to face it before.

His jaw ticked as he locked the cell and strode towards me, aiming for the door at my back. "We're done. The fuck does it matter now, anyway?"

My throat tightened at his dismissal. I hadn't realised how much I needed him to admit it.

"Say it, Leo. I never took you for a coward."

He paused, inches between us, staring down at me like I was nothing.

The scent of too much woodsy cologne overwhelmed my senses, triggering a memory of the last time we'd been this close—when he'd dragged me back to my apartment, kicking and screaming, after I'd tried to flee this place.

His gaze met mine, unflinching. "Your. Uncle."

The two words hit me like bullets to the chest.

My controlling bastard of an uncle probably wanted to continue the family name. Breed his bloodline with other strong hunters, and nobody was stronger than Leo.

"To be the next hunter prime when he retires, right?" The words left numb lips as mere wisps of sound.

He scoffed. "What do you think?"

I'd wondered. Of course I had.

Each night he'd stood me up to meet his friends.

When he'd stiffen as I kissed him but was more than happy to fuck me from behind.

Every time I'd said "I love you" and he'd grunted "okay."

But I'd been so desperate for someone to care about me that I'd ignored the warning signs. I'd convinced myself that it was real. That Leo loved me. That he wanted to spend his life with me. Build a home. Start a family.

Was he only ever with me because he'd been told to? Had he ever wanted me?

What was so unlovable about me?

To my horror, moisture gathered behind my eyes, burning with the need to escape.

Leo smirked, like the slip in my composure was the victory he'd craved. Any self-esteem I might have had left was shredded.

I blinked furiously, forcing back useless tears.

He knocked into my shoulder, trying to break me fully as he stomped past. "Oh, and I was fucking Tia the whole time."

He might as well have reached into my chest and crushed my heart.

No wonder he'd chosen to save her over me. I hadn't even suspected it.

Rage flared, searing back the devastation until I thought I'd burn alive. Everyone thought it was okay to hurt me, and I was sick of it.

I turned to his retreating back with a mocking laugh, imitating the cruel demon who'd bitten me this morning. "I'll have to send the poor girl my condolences, then."

Leo paused in the doorway, brows furrowing as he glanced back at me before his expression twisted into an arrogant grin. "She wasn't the only one."

Chapter 11

"Yikes, that had to hurt." The demon's red brows lifted.

Pain drowned me, but I shoved it aside with a grunt. "At least he left you in peace."

Her blood-red eyes narrowed suspiciously. "Let me guess." She tapped her chin with a short claw. "Now you're done fighting over me like a prime cut, you're about to go all mad scientist on me?"

Her raspy voice barely trembled, and I silently applauded her bravery in the face of the nightmare she was living now.

Only weeks ago, I'd have thought it was necessary. Possibly even celebrated her capture with Leo and the others.

My mind shied away from the horrors of what I'd done. What I'd let happen.

I locked the dark memories back into the vault I buried deep inside and shuffled over to the reinforced bars caging the demon.

"I question my sanity daily, but I was trying to help you," I said, giving her another visual sweep. "As a test subject, the operational hunters should leave you alone."

In theory.

"Wow." She rounded her eyes, drawing my attention to her impossibly thick red lashes and mocking me with feigned hope. "I've always wondered what it felt like to be dissected. How did you know?"

I snorted a laugh, laced with bitterness. "It's letting me poke at you, or letting them torture you for information until they shove what's left into the fight ring upstairs."

She bared her fangs, giving an almost feline hiss, eyes burning with a rage that mirrored the one in my soul. "I get the feeling that walking STD you call an ex will be back to play his games."

My throat tightened. There was every possibility he would, and since I was a member of omega team, which comprised all the researchers and support staff, Leo far outranked me, despite who my uncle was.

If I wanted to protect this demon—something I'd have stabbed anyone for implying a few weeks ago—I'd need to get her officially assigned to my project.

Or pray for divine intervention.

I forced a smile, feigning confidence. "I'll keep you safe."

She quirked a crimson brow. "Or...you could just let me go." She stepped forward and strangled the bars separating us. "My name is Eve. I'm just another idiot who trusted the wrong bastard with her heart. Like you. I don't belong here. I've never hurt a single human, and I don't even want to, unless you count said bastard, who sold me out to you lunatics." She winced, as if realising the casual insult might have consequences. "No offence."

My jaw clenched at the desperation leaking from her every pore. There was every chance she didn't deserve this. Every chance she'd never hurt anyone.

But how could I know for sure?

Either way, I was in no position to save her. I couldn't even save myself.

My throat squeezed like the collar my uncle had on me was tangible. "I...can't."

Her brows furrowed. "Can't? Or won't?"

Guilt lathered over my skin, sticky like honey. I backed up a step, my breathing coming quicker as my conscience warred with logic.

"Standing by and letting it happen is as bad as holding the knife," she murmured, hope guttering out in her eyes.

Her words raked through my chest like claws.

She didn't understand though.

Terror iced my veins at the memory of speeding down winding country lanes with a 4x4 truck on my tail, gaining on me, praying to whoever might listen that nothing came the other way. The moment Leo's bumper slammed my rear tyre, sending me careening into a ditch.

I'd tried to escape in the dead of night, alone and with no sign I was going to run, and it still hadn't been enough. Leo had still hauled me from the wreckage, back under my uncle's thumb.

I swallowed hard, my voice coming out as a strangled whisper. "You might be the one behind bars, but you're not the only one caged."

Her eyes softened, making her look even younger. "Then come with me. If you can't escape the hunters here on earth, I can take you to hell. It's nothing like your stories of fire and torture. It's a stunning world, not that different from this one. My king will offer you sanctuary if you're a victim too."

But was I? I'd killed more demons than I could count. The chances that they all deserved their fate were slim. Statistics and probability called me an unhinged serial killer.

Even a retired hunter would be a target there.

"I'll come back," I blurted, turning from the sympathy I didn't deserve and taking the stifling guilt with me as I fled the room.

The long corridor stretched in both directions as I hurried back to Cara's lab, empty-handed. My supposed mentor was going to chew me out for forgetting her requested tools, but I didn't have the heart to face Eve again.

Cara's lab door was a plain white, as sterile as the walls trying to close in on me, interrupted by a small, reinforced window at roughly head height.

I didn't bother to peer in, just shoved the handle in and walked inside like I belonged. "I couldn't find those extra tweezers."

The lab was a carbon copy of all the others except for my tiny one with the parasite. A holding cell lurked at the back, shiny bars glinting. A workbench dominated the centre, and more counters and equipment lined the outer edges of the room.

Cara straightened in her seat at the table, pinning me with a stern glare. "Fine. You're lucky I had extra compounds to analyse today instead of sampling." She jerked her pointed chin at the demon bound to a steel table on one side of the room. "For your tardiness, feed it and put it back."

Tight smile in place, I nodded. "Sure thing, Cara. See you tomorrow."

A muscle ticked in her jaw at my use of her first name, but she'd given up on correcting me in the first week of my so-called training. Calling her Dr Smythe felt a little too close to respecting her chosen profession as a deranged sociopath with a penchant for torture.

She put the slide she'd been examining into the box with the others, clicking it shut and storing it in the temperature-controlled unit under the counter. Gathering her things, she swept out of the room, flat loafers clacking obnoxiously with each step.

The moment the door snicked shut behind her, I let out a relieved breath.

"So, Doc, what have you got for me today?" a hoarse voice asked.

I looked over, finally letting myself absorb the nauseating sight that was Cara's longest test subject.

Lavender skin stretched over bones, missing in numerous places to leave small craters of bluish fluid like some horrifying lunar landscape. Thin trails of blood overflowed, pooling underneath the body of a demon that should have died long ago. At least by human standards.

"Shit, Fane, what did that psycho do this time?" I hurried over, swiping up the gauze and antiseptic from the med kit under the counter as I went.

Fane hissed out a laugh, shaking his emaciated chest. "The usual." He shrugged, scraping a bony elbow spine against the metal table. "A little poky-stabby action and stealing too much blood and flesh."

"She doesn't need to hurt you," I snarled, squeezing the gauze in my hand as I struggled to get my rage back under control. I wanted to protect humanity too, but not like this. "I'm sorry."

Watery eyes met mine, filled with acceptance. "Liliana...free me."

A strangled sob lodged in my throat. First Eve, and now him too.

I shook my head. "They'll catch us."

They might not have cameras in here—the hunters wanted the general human population finding evidence of demonkind about as much as they wanted the beings here in our realm—but I still couldn't sneak a demon out past the layers of guards and security.

There wasn't a single moment of the day or night where a group of hunters weren't crawling all over this prison they called their headquarters.

"That's not what I meant."

His words punched through me.

"No. Don't give up. I... I'll find a way." I grimaced at the desperation in my voice.

After the demon with sunshine eyes had saved my life, I'd begun questioning whether they really were all monsters like I'd been taught.

Fane was one of the good ones.

He might feed on souls for power, but the elderly demon had explained that most of his subtype enjoyed animal souls, consuming more than just the meat when they hunted. He'd actually answered when I'd asked questions, despite the fact I was clearly with the people who hurt him. The demon had been patient and honest, telling me snippets about hell and his kind.

He didn't sugar-coat the bad stuff, but he helped me realise how little I knew about demonkind and how much was hunter propaganda, beaten into me from a tender age.

"There's no coming back from this." Dark blood leaked from the corner of his mouth, as if emphasising his point. "Save me, Doc. Let me join my family in the afterlife."

I stared at his abused body one more time, taking in every scar and cut and bruise, fortifying my nerve.

How could I deny him this? When there was no hope for any other escape. He was right. His body had taken on so much damage even a demon couldn't heal from it. Cara was balancing his life on a razor's edge, tending to the wounds she inflicted just enough to stop him from actually dying. I'd been trying my best to fix him, but I wasn't exactly a doctor despite his nickname for me.

Since the incident, the thought of spilling blood turned my stomach, but there was anaesthetic in the fridge. Enough to kill an elephant.

It would probably take twice as much to end a demon.

"Okay." I swallowed thickly, my voice coming out choked. "If you're sure about this. I'll do it."

Tears pooled in tired eyes. "Thank you. You've been the only bright spark in this darkness."

His praise sliced through me.

I was a fucking monster, actually, but it felt like a dick move to argue with the man I was about to euthanise.

Unable to hold his relieved gaze, I grabbed the vials from the fridge and swiped up a fresh needle from the equipment drawer.

My hands shook as I filled the syringe to capacity.

I wavered, hovering the needle over Fane's inner elbow. Countless track marks already bruised his lavender skin. The malnourishment and torture at my colleague's hands meant he'd not been able to heal even these slight injuries.

"Do it," he rasped.

My hands steadied as I slid the needle in and plunged liquid death into his vein.

A serene smile tugged at his chapped lips. "Thanks, Doc."

"Join your family, Fane," I whispered. "And be free."

His breathing slowed within minutes, eyes fluttering before falling shut.

I wanted to scream until my voice gave out.

Chapter 12

I drew in a steady breath and pressed the plunger.

It reminded me a little too much of what I'd done to Fane two days ago, and I had to swallow down the thickness narrowing my airways.

The chemical hit my bloodstream with a faint tingle, which I may or may not have imagined. I pulled the syringe from my scar-laden arm, ignoring the brightness of the tiger-lily tattooed on my wrist, and carefully disposed of the needle in the sharps bin.

"I hope that's poison," the demon sneered from his glass prison.

A smirk twitched my lips at the bite in his tone. I hoped so too. Just not one that would hurt a human.

Of course, my first suggestion to Cara and Martin had been garlic. Just to enjoy watching them share a loaded look and question my intelligence. Before they questioned theirs, since there might actually be a kernel of truth to the myths about it repelling vampiric beings.

I'd silently laughed as they debated the merits of garlic testing for almost an hour before I could make my escape.

I already knew demons could eat garlic, since last week I'd fed Fane my lunch of a cheap tomato pasta.

Neutral mask firmly in place, I turned to the snide parasite. It should only take forty-five seconds for the substance to circulate through my blood, but I waited an entire minute, watching my captive.

Since the demon had first bitten me, I'd been both dreading this moment and oddly eager to get it over with. Two days felt like an eternity.

He looked much the same as before, spiky and imposing. Watchful. Hateful.

So eager to hurt me.

I crossed the gap between us and unlocked the hatch in the demon-proof wall.

Understanding dawned in his silvery eyes. "So you *are* trying to poison me."

I pressed my forearm to the narrow slot, baring my wrist to him like before. "I'm not a walking buffet for kicks."

"And now why would I bite you after watching you play mad scientist?" he sneered, showing off a wicked fang.

He had a valid, and now embarrassingly obvious, point. It would have been smarter to inject myself in another room, *then* come in here to feed him. But after everything that had happened lately, I'd been a scattered mess.

I wanted to slap a palm to my forehead, but I already looked like an idiot.

Either way, it was too late now.

I matched his hateful expression. "I'm the only food you'll get, powered source or otherwise."

"So it's eat poison or don't eat at all?" he mused. "How very hunter of you."

I shrugged. "It probably won't kill you."

A derisive chuckle shook the demon's lethal shoulders. "So reassuring."

"Are we bitching or biting?" I huffed. "I've got better things to do than waste my breath on a fussy parasite."

"Oh, so sorry, am I keeping you from a vital cult meeting? Are you sacrificing a small child in a few minutes? Or is today just a mass bloodletting?" Sarcasm dripped from his raspy tone.

My jaw clenched hard enough to ache.

He could pretend to have the moral high ground all he wanted, but I'd seen what blood demons like him were capable of. He'd not exactly proved me wrong with his venomous bite designed for agony.

"Hurry up and bite me."

"So eager for more pain, hmm? What's a meek little thing like you even doing here? As irritating as you are, you don't strike me as evil."

His words had me shifting on my feet. I'd chosen to do this so I could protect people, but I was still being forced into it.

I said nothing, pointedly eyeing my exposed wrist instead. His bite wounds from before had fully healed, only two red dots remaining. I briefly wondered whether he'd go for the same spot or create a sea of wounds like I had some kind of contagious disease.

"Not feeling chatty today, hmm?" He stepped forwards, sinking to his knees with an indulgent smirk. "I suppose a little poison is worth it if it means hurting one of the hunters capturing and slaughtering my kind. How many demons have you killed? Are there others just like me trapped down here?"

My gut churned uncomfortably at the undoubtable knowledge that I was still the villain here, even though I'd done everything I could to escape the violence.

"Is there anyone just like you? I've not met such a bland prick before," I huffed. "Must be a one-of-a-kind parasite."

"I'm not a common subspecies," he sneered, raising his tail over his shoulder to show off the deadly spikes covering the heart-shaped tip. "But I am a dangerous one."

I already knew there were multiple types, or subspecies, of blood demon. Hunters just liked to group things into the generic categories of what they fed on. That way, we knew what type of attack to expect without overcomplicating things.

Given his monochrome colouring and spikes, he must be the same subspecies as my demonic saviour, but I couldn't face bringing him up.

"Sure you are," I muttered. "Besides, I don't *hunt*. Not...anymore."

Fane's dying eyes flashed through my mind. I didn't hunt, but I still killed.

My throat closed off with the memory. I wasn't sure why I was trying to defend myself to a demon I was about to poison, anyway. There was no redemption here for me.

The demon quirked a brow. "Oh, a reformed murderer, then? And when was your last hunt?" He leaned forward ever so slightly. "Whose life did you decide was over?"

I frowned, sensing he might be a little too interested in my answer. "If you must know, I was ambushed in a warehouse three weeks ago." My words came out carefully neutral. "I haven't hunted since."

"Did you shoot them? Or take a blade to flesh?" he hissed, eyes glowing with malice. "Did they die begging you for mercy?"

"Three demons surrounded me, and I cut down each bastard as they shredded my flesh and broke my bones," I snarled, hating that he was digging up my guilt and throwing it in my face.

Every detail of that night haunted me.

I couldn't talk about my saviour. His death was on my conscience, even though I hadn't wielded the blade.

"Good." The demon bared his fangs, pointy teeth glinting menacingly under the artificial lights.

I held my arm still despite the grating anticipation and rolled my eyes, more annoyed at myself for letting him bait me than the caged monster so eager to hurt me. "Get on with it, demon. I'm no stranger to pain."

He canted his horns, letting the pearly strands of his short hair fall aside to reveal the tapered tip of his elfin ear. Of course even his ears were pointy.

Glowing eyes bored into me as he seemed to consider something. "No... I suppose you're not."

I didn't like the way he looked at me, like I was some mouse he'd caught to play with before devouring me whole.

"I bet, in a place like this, they'd teach you all about pain. You're braced for it. Expecting it from every demon you come across." A slow grin showcased pointy teeth. "But you're not prepared for this."

He lunged, fangs slicing into my skin.

I hissed as the pain registered, but instead of the burning agony from before, a different heat swam through my veins.

A gasp cut off my exhale. My whole body responded. Heat travelled through my veins, pooling low in my abdomen. My core clenched in violent need, and I could feel the slickness at the apex of my thighs as I rubbed them together.

A strangled sound escaped me as I burned. The urge to slip my fingers into the waistband of my jeans was almost overwhelming. I clenched my fist, slamming it against the glass to stop myself as a fragment of sense returned.

"What the hell are you doing to me?" I squirmed on the spot, fighting the peak rushing closer.

Starlit eyes devoured me, vicious hunger transforming his predatory features as he pulled back just enough to snarl. "Break for me, poison."

He sucked hard on my wrist, igniting an inferno through my body.

"Fuck you," I hissed, but my body betrayed me, locking up tight as I pressed awkwardly against the glass. Core spasming around nothing as he shattered me.

The feeling of emptiness was almost unbearable, yet pleasured heat burst through me, tipping me over the edge into bliss.

The glass fogged from my rapid panting as I rested my head forward, struggling to recover.

A demon had just made me come.

Harder than Leo ever did.

My cheeks raged with a furious blush at the intrusive thought.

Plumped lips released my flesh with a lewd pop. A shudder ran through me as his forked tongue laved against my wrist in sinful strokes, catching the stray rivulets of blood.

I wished it were disgust.

I cleared my throat, adjusting my glasses and stepping back. Avoiding his gaze, I swiped away the last drop of blood he'd missed, thoughts scrambled.

There was no record of a demon having an orgasmic bite.

The thought of admitting how I'd found that out had shame coursing through me. Maybe that was why nobody else had fessed up.

A wicked chuckle rolled through the lab, coming from the evil incarnate trapped behind the glass. "You might be a murderous bitch, but fuck do you look pretty when you come for me."

My lips parted, gaze snapping up to his in shock.

He'd stood when I wasn't looking, now towering over me, forearms over his head, resting against the glass to show off the full expanse of his lean, muscled height. It was designed to intimidate as much as mock.

My eyes dropped to the carved abs across his middle, and even more shame burned through me as I grudgingly admired the strength in every line of his body. My gaze dipped further, tracing the clear outline of a thick length in the standard grey joggers all the captives were given.

The beast in his pants was at the same height as the open hatch.

My mouth dried up as that same stupid voice wondered what he would look like without the clothing. Would that thing even fit through the hatch on its widest setting?

Would he be able to soothe the empty feeling he'd created in my aching core?

I looked away, jaw clenching reflexively.

He was right.

Pain I could handle.

Pleasure was so unfamiliar I wasn't prepared to defend against it.

A horrible, oily feeling coated my insides.

"A pervert as well as a parasite, what an overachiever," I sneered.

I wanted to don my neutral mask and pretend I was just as unfazed by this as the last bite, but I was too thoroughly rattled.

Judging by the smirk on his carved face, the bastard knew it too.

My hand trembled as I pushed my glasses higher up the bridge of my nose and slammed the hatch shut, locking the sinful demon away more fully.

"That's just the start, poison." He loomed over me, eyes glowing with starlight. "I'm going to pleasure you, over and over, until you're hooked. You won't be able to come without a demon's venom lighting you up. Fitting punishment for a hunter, don't you think?"

A new kind of fear took root inside me, but I brushed aside his words as the empty threat they were. "One weak orgasm and you think you own my pleasure?" I clucked my tongue. "Interesting that men are all the same, no matter the species."

He grinned, the picture of demonic cruelty with the sharp edges to back it up. "I'm no man, poison. I'm all your past sins come back to haunt you. Your very own fucking nightmare."

Chapter 13

Exiting the secure basement level the following evening, I stepped into the chaos of the warehouse floor, bracing for the usual stench of violence. Unfortunately, it didn't disappoint. The distinct copper-pennies smell thick enough to lodge in my throat and choke me.

"Fucking savages," I muttered, adjusting my glasses as I hurried through the space, scanning for anything amiss.

A sizeable crowd sat around the brutal fight cage, heckling the poor souls battling for their lives. This evening, two hunters circled an injured demon like sharks.

I stilled.

It was *my* demon.

Cuts opened through charcoal skin, bleeding a bright red to smear pale tattoos and streak white hair. His bone-shard spikes were just as bloodied, even those tipping his poised tail.

Given the matching wounds across the newest delta team recruits, Roane and Harper, my test subject was holding his own. For now.

But training sessions weren't rigged in a demon's favour.

I should know. I'd been in that cage more than anyone.

A holding cell on the far wall held the other unwilling contestants for tonight's blood sport.

My gaze snagged on Leo, standing ringside, his focus wholly on me.

My ex smirked, lifting a snide, two-fingered salute. Rage sparked inside me, along with an unexpected dose of fear.

Before I knew it, I stormed towards him.

His smirk grew into a wide grin. "Hey, Dozer, got your other little pet in the cage tonight. You can play scientist with it after. If there's anything left."

I shoved aside the strange anxiety turning my stomach to lead and narrowed my eyes at the monster before me.

At least he was leaving Eve alone. I'd asked Martin to assign me a second official test subject for some bullshit experiment I'd made up for my non-feeding days.

"You can't do this, and you know it. You're ruining my experiment, and it's costing human lives." I shook my head, rage stealing my voice for a second. "For what, Leo? A little revenge? Last I checked, I'm the only one with a right to be pissed here."

"Pissed about the huge mistake you made?" Leo leaned closer, his breath slithering over my ear and causing me to shudder. He lowered his voice so only I could hear. "Drop to your knees and beg me with that talented little mouth of yours, and I might even consider taking you back."

I jolted as if he'd slapped me.

He'd cheated on me and left me for dead. Like I was disposable. Used-up and broken, only to be discarded on the floor.

Like I was nothing.

"Never," I hissed.

I yanked the set of keys from his belt, feeling the fabric loop give with a satisfying snap.

He leaned back, navy eyes darkening until I could barely see his pupils.

"Fine." He slid the shortest blade he owned from his pocket, holding out the tiny weapon in mocking, and raised his voice. "If you want your toy back...*go fetch*." He waved towards the cage, where the blood demon was barely dodging the two hunters and their long knives.

I paused.

Violence swirled higher in the air as the hunters nearby latched onto the drama unfolding. They scented fresh meat. A new victim to be sacrificed on their bloody altar.

How quickly they forgot.

I'd been forged in this cage, and others just like it, long before most of them learned demons weren't just scary stories meant to keep sinners in line.

My test subject got in another good hit, swiping his claws up Roane's arm. But Harper was already there, taking her price in blood with a long slash through his chest.

The demon hissed, jerking back with a ferocious snarl and a slight limp, favouring his left leg. Blood poured from a huge gash in the right, soaking the grey trousers somehow still clinging to him despite numerous cuts in the fabric.

He looked feral. Raking bloodied claws through the air. His spiked tail jabbing. Fangs bared.

The two newbie hunters were a little battered, but it was nothing the rest of us hadn't seen before.

The idea of holding a weapon, even the toothpick Leo offered, made my hands shake. They felt clammy, like blood already coated them, and I fought the urge to wipe my palms on my jacket.

But I couldn't let Leo kill my test subject. I owed it to the one project I was taking seriously. My last act as a hunter before I disappeared forever.

Maybe then I could sleep at night, without screaming myself awake in the early hours, drenched in cold sweat.

This was for science.

At least, that was what I told myself as I stepped up to the cage's secure door, shunning my ex and dropping my backpack and coat to the ground. I didn't like fighting in my glasses, but at least my long hair was secured in a messy bun.

The fighters paused, glancing at me suspiciously while trying to keep each other in sight.

"Get the fuck away from my demon." I cringed internally at the poor wording but kept a hard expression on my face.

He was mine in terms of *science*. That's what I'd meant.

The demon smirked, a cruel twist of his split lips. The dark-grey shade made them look hard and cold, but I knew what their soft heat felt like against my skin.

I shook off the weird, intrusive thought.

Harper shot me a look of disgust.

I lifted my chin, fighting back a blush. "He's my test subject," I clarified. "And I need him in one piece."

Harper snorted, wisely brandishing her weapon at the vicious blood demon, not taking her focus off him for a second. "We don't take orders from omega team." She raised her voice. "Boss, we ending this or what?"

"Kill it," Leo scoffed behind me. "We'll bring *Dozer* a new pet for her silly little games."

I clenched my jaw and unlocked the cage, ignoring Leo sniggering at my back.

"Last chance. Both of you, leave." I met Harper's and Roane's eyes, letting each of them see the cold, unflinching stare of my dark side. The one I'd needed to survive a lifetime of violence.

Harper laughed. Roane just shook his head.

"I don't know who you are, lady, but you're an idiot. You're not even armed," he said. "That beast is gonna tear your damn throat out, and we ain't gonna stop it."

Was it stupid to get into a fight ring with two armed hunters and a demon who hated you?

You bet.

But I stepped in anyway.

Adrenaline spiked, and yet my body loosened in anticipation of the oncoming violence. Calm clarity, which fighting always seemed to bring, slipped through me in a familiar wave.

I'd never admit it, but a part of me missed this.

Before any of the fighters knew what to make of me, I darted forwards, shoving Roane towards the cage door. He sliced out with his blade as he stumbled, and I narrowly avoided getting nicked before his face smacked into the metal bars.

I was on Harper in the next breath, kicking high.

My foot slammed into the side of her face, knocking her out cold before she hit the bloodstained canvas.

"Fuckin' bitch!" Roane snarled, rounding on me with a kick to my middle.

I took it on the shoulder, feeling the impact reverberate through my arm hard enough to numb but not do any serious damage. I pounded his kidney as I twisted into him and kicked his stomach, shoving him back before his blade could find a home in my chest. It sliced shallowly across my raised knee instead.

The fucker was trying to kill me.

But he'd forgotten about the bigger threat here.

The demon materialised behind him, a menacing beast of nightmares, but his silver eyes pinned me. They dropped to my knee wound, seeping blood down my jeans, and narrowed with a flash of something dark before leaping back to my face.

A cruel smirk twisted his lips, and my blood turned to ice.

He kicked forward, sending the unwitting hunter slamming into me before I could move. We went down in a tangle of limbs, my face throbbing as his elbow caught me. Years of brutal training had me rolling aside and popping back to my feet before my brain could process what had happened.

Roane wasn't fast enough.

The demon slammed his foot down on the man's face. Bone snapped. Blood gushed. Sickening wet sounds filled the air as Roane's head became a gory mess of pulp.

Hunters yelled obscenities beyond the cage, booing and jeering, but nobody interfered.

The demon's smirk widened into a full grin, painted with flecks of red.

My mouth parted in horror.

The yelling grew louder. But, really, nobody cared about a hunter who was too weak to defeat an already injured demon.

I stumbled back, half tripping over another body.

Harper groaned at my feet, pushing herself up to all fours. She stilled as she caught sight of her partner's mangled face.

The demon gave one last stomp and stared back at me, ignoring the other hunter waking to a nightmare.

"You killed him," I murmured, shocked by his brutality. I shouldn't have been though. Demons were violence given flesh.

"You weren't his to hurt." A low growl spilled from his throat, raising the hairs on my nape. "You shouldn't have stepped into this cage with me."

I swallowed thickly, tasting the metallic tang in the air. "Come back downstairs. Nobody else needs to get hurt." My voice came out steady, and I silently applauded myself for not devolving into a puddle of terror. He wasn't the first scary bastard I'd faced down.

But I wished he'd be the last.

The blood-smeared creature stepped over his victim, ignoring the other trainee hunter as she whimpered, scrambling back to the far side of the ring. Shaking, she hugged her knees to her chest and rocked back and forth, muttering something lost to the roaring crowd.

I couldn't look away from the monster stalking towards me in slow motion.

My back slammed into the bars, rattling whatever brain cells I might have had left. Heat ringed my neck as the demon's enormous hand gripped my throat in a blur of speed.

My chest rose and fell in rapid succession.

I supposed the reaper had a sense of irony about him. One blood demon had stolen my life from death's embrace, and now another was going to deliver me right back.

"You think I'll just come quietly, poison? That I'll let you lead me right back into your cage?" he purred, a low and deadly sound. Dark hunger glittered in starlit eyes. "I have a better idea, and it involves snapping your flimsy little neck right now."

"Go ahead, parasite. I fucking dare you." I bared my teeth, tasting the blood coating them from my split lip. "They'll execute you the second my body hits the ground."

He snarled, fangs gnashing inches from my face. He yanked me flush against his hard chest and slammed me into the bars again.

My head thudded painfully, but I choked down the urge to curse him out, instead letting a too-wide grin part my lips. "That's it, demon. Show us your true nature."

Maybe I'd been wrong to think more demons deserved to be saved. Clearly, at each one's core, was a vicious monster waiting to be set free.

He leaned close, running his nose along my throat until I shivered.

But not in the disgusted way I had with my ex this close just moments ago.

At this point, I was too stupid to live.

The crowd roared obscenities and encouragements, revelling in my imminent demise.

Lips brushed the shell of my ear, drawing another shiver through me. "Or perhaps I should return the favour, hmm?" He ignored my mocking and squeezed, cutting off my airway in an imitation of the scratched metal collar around his neck. My vision danced, and he released me just enough to suck in a ragged breath. "Every night I dream about choking on you, poison."

My brain must have glitched from the lack of oxygen, because I could have sworn he'd said "on."

His hand tightened again, and he pressed me into the cage bars. "Do you know how addicted I am already? Maybe if you're dead, I can stop fantasising about how you taste."

I frowned, realising I was just *letting* a demon manhandle me.

With a snarl, I jerked up my knee, aiming for his balls, but he dodged back with an infuriating smirk. Gore painted his carved features, giving him an even more sinister edge.

A low chuckle rumbled his chest, trembling the scant air between us. "That all you got, poison?"

His taunt had me swinging, feinting left before ducking right. I smashed my fist into his sternum, doubling him over, and darted back before he could get his claws into me.

His tail hooked my throat, stopping me short, and I choked hard on the living collar.

"Not so fast, huntress," he sneered, straightening to his full height.

I reached out and yanked further up his tail, tipping him towards me.

He wasn't expecting me to use his own body as leverage and staggered right into my waiting fist. Luck was on my side, because I hit his face just right, avoiding his horned brows.

His tail slackened from my neck as he dropped to a knee, spitting a mouthful of blood to join the rest splattered across the canvas.

The demon tipped his face up and smiled, teeth smeared a bright crimson. "Okay, poison, I'll let you win this round." He raised his claws in slow surrender, mocking me even though I'd rocked him. "Since you asked so nicely, I'll be a good boy."

Chapter 14

The monster climbed to his feet, taking his sweet time. Blood flowed down the muscular dips and valleys carved across his chest and arms.

I grimaced. He must be in pain, but he still moved with a fluid grace that spoke of strength, both body and will.

Maybe he really had "let me win." The thought made my jaw tick.

I gestured to the cage door. "Parasites first."

He smirked, giving me his back without hesitation. And I could see why.

The same bone spikes that topped his shoulders and elbows also ran the length of his spine, stopping inches from where his thick tail started. Tribal markings flowed along either side, almost glowing silvery white against his slate skin. My gaze dipped, taking in the firm shape of his arse even the sweatpants couldn't conceal. I bit my lip, yanking my eyes back up to the danger.

What was *wrong* with me?

A demon gets me off with some magical venom, and now I'm a complete perv.

I swallowed thickly, looking away from the nightmare male.

A bloody heap of flesh and bone lurked on the canvas floor. I stepped over Roane's body without inspecting it too closely, swallowing down bile at the evidence of the demon's viciousness.

At least the other trainee, Harper, was still alive. She rocked herself soothingly on the other side of the large fight cage, blinking too rapidly, but she'd survive.

Who knew, she might request a transfer to omega team, sick of the violence like I was.

The demon opened the cage door I'd left unlocked and stepped out onto the warehouse floor.

A chorus of boos rained from the crowd. I let their displeasure wash over me, fixing my neutral mask in place.

Swooping down, I collected my bag, stuffing my discarded jacket into it. A small black remote mocked me from the inner pocket.

I swallowed a curse as my stupidity hit me.

The control for the demon's collar was inside my bag. If I'd been thinking clearly, I would have brought the damn thing into the ring with me.

I didn't examine too closely why I was taking home the only defence I had against a demon trapped in the bowels of hunter HQ. Instead, I slipped it from the bag, gripping it tight.

The demon halted, and I almost walked into the deadly spikes protruding from his back. "Can I help you, blood bag?"

I stepped around the demon, already knowing what I'd find.

Leo blocked his way, a pistol aimed at the demon's chest. His pale scars shone as my ex's face flushed with anger, and I took a moment to relish his loss of composure.

Weighted gazes rested firmly on us, the crowd's murmured rumblings providing a backdrop to the air of danger.

I stepped in front of the demon with my chin lifted, despite the itch that formed between my shoulder blades to have the predator at my back. "You told me to fetch my subject, so I did. You'd better run along now and collect what's left of your recruits."

The hunters might think of me as nothing but a spoiled brat, yet I was the one walking out of the cage in one piece.

Leo's brows slammed low, a tick starting up in his jaw. "Your beast killed one of our own."

I quirked a brow, ignoring the frisson of anxiety in my middle. "You could have stepped in at any time. Don't act like I don't know the rules of the ring. I beat your arse in there enough times."

"But not anymore," he snarled, eyes blazing with more emotion that I'd seen when I'd dumped his traitorous arse. "And don't think I won't tell the hunter prime about this."

True fear bit me, closing fangs around my throat until I could hardly breathe. The demon stirred at my back, but he remained quiet.

"Go ahead." I snickered, infusing my false laugh with very real derision. "Tell him how you jeopardised the vital project that he assigned me."

Leo tried to hide a flash of uncertainty by holstering his weapon, knowing other hunters from the crowd would have theirs trained on the demon walking free.

My ex stepped in close, trying to intimidate me, but it was the low growl behind me that had unease prickling my nape.

Still, the bigger threat to my health was the man in front of me, not the monster lurking at my back.

"He hasn't forgotten about your...*unsanctioned leave*. If you think you can pretend it never happened, think again." He clucked his tongue. "Oh, the rage on his face when I told him what you'd done."

I ignored the terror icing my veins, keeping my mask in place. I shoved forward, knocking my shoulder into him as I passed.

The heat and innate sense of danger behind me signalled the demon followed.

I half wished he'd shoulder checked my ex as well. Those wicked bone shards would give Leo something to whine about.

The guards at the door let us through without incident, and I led the bloodied demon down the stairs into the sublevel used for labs and containment. The security door closed behind us with a loud slam, and I jumped at the sudden noise.

Silence swallowed us like we'd stepped into a tomb.

I glanced at the demon, watching him with narrowed eyes as I slowed, letting him descend a step in front so I could watch both his claws and spiked tail.

We were alone, and he was uncaged.

If I was going to murder my captor and make a break for it, now would be a great time.

Sure, I had the remote for his choking collar and he was trapped underground behind the reinforced, heavily guarded door. But he was fast, and could disappear down here to bide his time, rushing the door when they least expected it.

The demon took in my positioning over his shoulder décor with a smirk. "Nervous, poison?"

I snorted, bluffing a confidence that could save my life. "Of a demon with more blood outside than in? Besides, I have a little backup." I waved the remote at him with a sarcastic smile.

Cruel laughter filled the stairwell, bouncing off the concrete walls to echo loudly. "All this blood isn't mine, poison. Your friends pit me against quite a few other captives and frail blood bags before you showed up to rescue *your demon*."

Of course the bastard had heard me call him "my demon" as I'd stepped up to the ring to get him.

I grimaced at what Leo had put him through, hating the needless violence. Another reason I'd be leaving as soon as I could get everything into place. After I did this one good thing—finding a way to protect humans from blood demons like this one.

A tense hush fell as I led the predator into my lab, scanning my pass and gesturing him in. The monster ducked inside, curved ivory horns grazing the doorway with a harsh scrape.

I could feel his curious gaze roaming everything as we went. No doubt mapping his future escape route.

My mind shied away from the brutal reality that he'd never leave. Not alive, anyway.

The guilt that always lingered just below the surface rose to choke me, even though I knew what I was doing would save lives. I'd seen him stomp a person to death just minutes ago. He wasn't exactly innocent.

Neither was I.

"Take a seat," I blurted.

My cheeks flamed as the demon cocked a brow, shifting the mini horns lurking at its outer edge.

I clenched the remote tighter in my palm but gestured to his body. "I can treat the worst of your wounds."

He smirked. "A doctor as well as a mad scientist. Such a smart cookie."

Irritation surged at his mocking, but I'd already offered, so I reached under the counter to grab the first aid kit, flashing him a too-bright grin. "Actually, being frugal has taught me many skills. I'm sure your corpse-like skin will sew up just as easily as a split seam."

Fishing out the needle and medical thread, I prepped it with one eye on the demon.

I didn't mention that I had ample experience sewing up actual flesh. I used to just stitch my own, but nowadays I spent more time operating on wounded test subjects. Much to my colleagues' bafflement.

The demon's skin was an intriguing charcoal shade, dark and smooth. Accented with intricate tribal lines, white tattoos blended with a multitude of scars. He almost had as many marks as I did, a lifetime of violence exposed in the flesh.

Inked linework ran from his wrists up to his shoulders, slicing over his chest and running down his ribs. A sun took up one shoulder, and a moon took position on the other, both formed from the negative space of his tattoos. A spiked star wrapped one-half of his neck, reminding me of the celestial shape in the blackness of his eyes, haloing his pupils to glow through the sclera.

Cursive script curved over the muscle of one pectoral, and I hated that a part of me was so curious for a closer look.

The demon grunted, sliding onto the island in the centre of the cramped room. He was so tall, it was like watching a normal person sit on a chair.

I pinned him with a hard stare. "Try to hurt me while I'm stitching you up, and I'll have you gasping on the floor. Again." I flashed a vicious grin. "Then I'll activate the collar."

He chuckled, widening his legs and leaning forward to plant his palms either side of his spread knees on the table. "Come closer, poison, I won't bite."

"If only." I huffed, but stepped between his knees anyway, placing the kit within easy reach beside him, careful not to graze myself on the short horns topping each of his knuckles.

It was insanity to get this close to a monster, but something about him drew me in beyond logic. He was like the biblical myth of a demon, coaxing me to give into my reckless impulses.

I set the needle into the deepest cut on his chest, a ragged line topping his firm pec. With my skinny frame, the demon would probably fill out a bra better than I could.

Pushing metal through flesh, I began the gentle process that had become horrifyingly familiar. The demon didn't so much as twitch as I sewed him back together.

His attention warmed my face like the sun.

"What?" I poked him a little too hard on the next stitch, but I was the only one to wince.

He smirked. "You have freckles."

It was something my mother used to criticise, before she'd walked out of my life a year before my father died, pointing out how most men would prefer smooth, unblemished skin.

I'd never paid much attention to her little gripes about my appearance growing up. Fighting otherworldly monsters put things into perspective pretty fast. Besides, her opinions lost all value the moment she'd left me to this vicious life.

It was my turn to grunt. "And you're incredibly spiky. What of it, parasite?"

He pursed full lips as if in thought. "They're...intriguing. A shade lighter than your eyes."

I paused, an odd sensation squirming through me with the urge to blush. My eyes narrowed on his sharply angular face. "I can start on your gaping fish lips next."

He tutted, a smile tugging up one corner of his mouth. "Your bedside manner could use some work."

I clenched my jaw, refusing to look at the smug bastard as I jabbed the needle back through his skin.

The next gash sat just under the script on his left pec: "As I walk through the valley of the righteous, the shadow I cast is behind me."

I paused.

The words were tattooed in English. A human language, not one of their hellish dialects.

Their meaning resonated with something inside me. What righteous path was he seeking? What brighter future did he look for and what darkness did he leave behind? Did blood soak his claws like it burrowed under my nails and seeped into my skin? Was it in English for him to remember the human lives he'd taken?

I swallowed hard, unable to meet his gaze as I continued to patch him up.

Chapter 15

I looked away from the imposing demon, going about my routine, getting the latest compound Martin and Cara had cooked up for me to play guinea pig with.

Dosing myself up with the clear liquid, I exhaled a steady breath and approached the monster lurking in the back of the lab.

I hadn't seen my spiky lab rat since I'd wrangled him back into his cell three nights ago, throwing in a new pair of sweatpants behind him. My schedule said I should have fed him the very next day, but I'd skipped it, telling myself it was to allow him more time to heal after Leo had forced him into the fight ring.

The irritating demon had been on my mind ever since. The sight of his blood-smeared features haunted my nightmares. Almost as much as his pleasured bite consumed my dreams.

He looked as imposing as ever, curving horns reaching only a foot below the ceiling. The cuts that had littered his dark skin were fully closed, healing to pale scars that blended with his tattoos.

Starlit eyes glowed as they tracked my movements.

Unlocking the hatch, I shoved my arm against the slot. My teeth found my lower lip, worrying at it until it pinched with pain.

I waited for him to strike. For his fangs to sink in and inject liquid pleasure until I was wet and needy, coming for a demon and so embarrassed I could hardly look at him after.

Or for him to push agony through my veins until my legs gave out.

A dark chuckle rolled through the cramped space.

I glared up at the demon. The smug bastard thought he had the upper hand here, and I hated that a tiny part of me agreed with him.

I just hoped this compound knocked him on his stupidly toned arse.

"Get on with it, parasite."

"So desperate for your pleasure, poison?" He smirked, full lips curving up on one side. "No pathetic human able to meet your needs, huh? You need a demon to satisfy you."

I ground my teeth so hard my jaw throbbed in protest.

It would have been great to have someone even try to bring me more pleasure than a damned demon, but Leo had ensured no hunter would go near me. Not that I was particularly into vicious serial killers.

Anyone I dated outside the hunters would be drawn into my uncle's web, and he wasn't above threatening someone to get me to fall in line. Even a man I barely knew.

I rolled my eyes at the demon. "The only thing I'm desperate for is a rigatoni carbonara loaded with parmesan, and a pinot grigio that isn't from the sale section. Your little nibbles are a necessary evil."

"Nibbles?" His lips twitched into what could have been a genuine smile if he'd let it bloom. "Perhaps I should remind you just how vicious my bite can be."

I snorted. "Please do."

"You'd like that, huh?" He angled his horns aside, tapping his chin with a pearly claw. "What was it you said in the ring? That you wanted me to show you my true nature?" A low chuckle shook his muscular chest. "You want us all to be monsters, don't you? Does it ease that weight you're carrying, poison? The guilt of living with what you've done?"

I jerked back, arm dropping from the feeding slot. Was I being that transparent?

My hands fisted at my sides, nails digging into my palms. "You don't know the first thing about me, demon."

"Call me Sin."

He looked surprised by his own words.

I blinked at him, shock parting my lips. "What?"

The demon snorted, some of the tension leaving his frame. "I'm tired of you calling me *demon*. You might not believe it, but we're people. With names, and families, and lives of our own."

He had no idea how aware of that I was. It had cost me everything.

And yet not nearly enough.

"Liliana," I said, voice tight. Why I was indulging in this madness, I had no clue.

His pupils dilated as he took in my name, lips pursing like he could taste it.

"Sin...," I murmured, testing out his name on my lips too. I smirked as it sank in. "Is that your stripper name or something?"

"Short for Sinclair, actually. But if it's a show you're after...," he purred, claws hooking inside the waistband of his low-slung joggers.

"No!" I raised a hand to ward him off, heart pounding for an entirely different reason.

If I saw whatever little monster he hid in his trousers, maybe it would put me off and finally kill the shameful lust that had haunted me since his bite gave me the most intense orgasm of my life, five agonisingly long days ago.

Or it could give an edge of reality to the fantasies I desperately tried to ignore.

Ones I only had because of the unholy venom in his bite.

He chuckled, the rich sound far too warm for such a murderous beast. "I'm kidding, poison."

I scowled. "A demon with a sense of humour? Clearly, I've died and gone to hell."

He snorted, looking almost boyish despite the feral cast of his features. "Hell is much nicer than this shithole."

"I'm sure you think so," I snarked, pressing my wrist back to the gap in the glass.

He grinned, showing off wicked fangs a second before he dropped to his knees before me. I swore I could feel his heat through the glass.

Leaning forward, he rested his pearly fangs against my offered wrist in a faint prick, letting me feel their threat without breaking the skin.

Dread, and something too close to anticipation, had my body tightening.

I tapped a foot, letting the impatient patter fill the silence. I was already strung out from the rollercoaster of emotions I'd struggled through today. I'd been "helping" Cara all morning already.

"Come on, demon, your snack is getting bored," I hissed.

He spoke directly against my wrist, lips brushing my skin in a way that sent shivers down my spine. "Is that all you are, poison? Something to be consumed by others?"

His question dug sharpened claws into my mind. Was that all I was? Everyone just took from me. And what had I been doing about it?

His fangs sank in, pain flaring before heated pleasure soothed it away. I stifled a groan, clenching my jaw to hold back the breathy moan fighting to escape.

Heat and need flooded my veins, even as he drained them.

The column of his throat worked as he swallowed, taking a vital part of me into himself.

Along with potential poison.

I raced towards my peak, despite struggling to hold back. My core fluttered with the need to be filled. Pleasure coursed through me, radiating from my wrist to swarm my middle and sink lower.

The demon stilled, eyes widening, and jerked his fangs free with a spluttered cough.

Bright red splashed the concrete as he hunched over, bracing a hand on the floor. Strands of his pearly hair fell across his face.

Victory surged through me, twining with the lingering pleasure until I felt light-headed despite the denied orgasm.

"Sin!" I pressed my free hand to the glass, clutching the collar's remote tightly. Fear and anticipation twisted my gut. "What do you feel?"

Spiked shoulders trembled, and it took me a moment to register the familiar rumble of his cruel laugh.

He angled his face up, lips spreading wide. My blood coated his mouth, vivid against his dark lips. The abyss of his pupils rapidly swallowed the white starbursts of his eyes.

He'd never looked more demonic.

"You fucking bastard," I hissed, slamming my hand against the glass separating us. Frustration consumed me, channelling the lingering heat into anger.

"Delightful, thanks." He smirked, vicious mirth dancing in his eyes. "How about you, poison? I'd imagine the only thing worse than coming for your enemy is having them drive you to the edge and then being denied."

A frustrated snarl built in my throat. My thumb hovered over the button on the remote, tempting me to punish him right back.

My father's voice seemed to echo in my head—*'Never let them see you weak, Tiger-lily.'*

That violent side was the old me. I didn't want to live like that anymore.

I dropped the device into my lab coat pocket and wiped my bloodied wrist onto the stained fabric, ignoring the visceral unease as warm liquid smeared my skin.

My core still ached in need, but I ruthlessly smothered the desire.

I wasn't so desperate that I'd beg anyone, let alone a blood demon, to finish me off.

With a flat glare, I turned on my heel, refusing to let him bait me.

"Try not to miss me too much, poison." Cruel laughter followed me out, grating against my frayed nerves.

The familiar snick of the closing security door cut off the vicious sound.

He didn't know it, but the bastard had just started a war he had no hope of winning.

Chapter 16

Rubbing bleary eyes, I groggily tried to scrounge up the courage to knock on the polished office door and face whatever nightmare my uncle had in store this evening.

For the past two weeks I'd been playing juice box to the demon, and it was literally draining. Even taking iron supplements had done little to improve things. Eating more would have, but I could barely afford the microwave meals and ramen noodles I was currently surviving on.

Martin had fetched me from my daily horror show with Cara, summoning me for an impromptu meeting with the hunter prime.

It had been two days since I'd last fed Sin, meaning I was scheduled to see him after.

I wasn't sure which would be worse.

The demon had put me through a hellish two weeks of mocking taunts and denied orgasms already. He brought me to the razor edge of bliss and stopped right before I could tumble over the edge.

Not that I wanted a demon to make me come. But being denied over and over was getting to me.

I was hyperaware of his every move. Sometimes I swore I could sense him, even when I was working in another lab.

Combined with the unknown effects of whatever substances I'd been injecting myself with, who knew how long this game of poison Russian roulette could last?

But what choice did I have?

More than Rhia when she'd been murdered in a seedy alleyway.

With a deep breath, I knocked on the office door.

"Enter."

Even through the wood, my uncle's disapproval rang clear.

I grimaced, allowing myself a singular moment to feel the trepidation.

Had he discovered the...*side effects* from Sin's bite? Had Leo convinced him that rescuing my subject deserved punishment? Had Martin realised I'd been faking tests on the hybrid to protect her? Or maybe Cara had snitched on me for what happened with Fane?

His dying eyes sliced through my mind, merging with the sunny pair of my demonic saviour.

My list of miniscule betrayals was getting longer every day. An "accidental" overdose to one of our captives was probably the thing he'd be least angered by.

After all, the only good demon was a dead one. It was practically the hunter creed.

A terrifying thought occurred to me.

Had he found the money I was saving to escape him? Did my uncle know I no longer believed in the cause he killed for daily?

I carefully locked my emotions down, leaving nothing but the cold, brutal hunter he'd raised me to be.

I stepped inside, closing the door softly behind me.

There were no games this time. My uncle's full attention weighed on me the moment I crossed the threshold. Soulless grey eyes, leeched of anything colourful or bright, dissected me.

He nodded to the chair before his desk, and I dutifully took a seat on the creaking plastic.

"I assume you know why you're here?"

I froze, mask hardening in place. "No, Prime."

I waited for the axe to fall.

He frowned, the slight displeasure sending my pulse skittering. "You've been at this new project for weeks now, and not a single compound has proven effective."

I almost sagged in relief. Of all my supposed sins, this was the least punishable offence.

"I work through the compounds as provided to me by Martin." I met my uncle's gaze, tone level, as I stifled a smirk at throwing the blame onto my callous boss. "Results will come, but the timeline is out of my control."

"And how often have you been running these tests?" His voice turned deceptively soft.

He already knew the answer. Not much happened in this hellhole that he didn't know about. Or in my life, for that matter. It wouldn't surprise me if more cameras turned up around my apartment after this.

"Every other day." I fought the need to fidget under his unyielding scrutiny.

Doing so would only make me look guilty, and I'd done nothing wrong. That he knew of.

His thin lips pursed. "You will increase to daily feedings."

My lips parted before I could catch the gesture. "That will be...draining." I chose my words carefully, but his expression soured, and I knew I was about to regret my decision.

"You'll get a little tired? What about the hunters dying out on the streets every night to actually save people? They're more than just *drained*," he hissed, fist thudding on the desk between us. "We must sacrifice to rid this world of the evil scourge, Liliana. Now more than ever with this spike in demonic attacks. Your father would be ashamed."

His words had the intended effect, slicing through me to add to the shame that already festered within.

My uncle never missed his mark.

Disgust twisted his features. "If you're too weak for the job, I'll send someone to assist."

I swallowed down the panic. "No, Prime, forgive me. I can handle this. I won't let you down again."

His expression hardened into a chilling mask. "Perhaps some financial incentive will help."

My blood ran cold.

"When you get results, you'll get a bonus. Until then, you're on half pay."

I was already on minimum wage. Not that employment laws really concerned my uncle, given the other crimes his organisation committed. Crimes I myself was guilty of.

I could barely afford rent and two pathetic meals a day while saving for my great escape. Even if I stopped squirrelling away a pittance for a freedom fund, I was going to struggle to live on that wage.

And he knew it.

Dreams of being free burned to ash around me.

It wouldn't be cheap to leave the country discreetly, hopping around and leaving false trails until he lost me completely. Even then, I'd need to hole up somewhere remote, completely off-grid until he gave up the search.

I wanted to smash his face in with my chair. Not just once, but repeatedly. Until his smug face turned to pulp. To split flesh and gushing blood.

Maybe then I would finally be free of him.

But he was always expecting an attack. In my weakened state, there was no way I'd be able to hit him before he unsheathed a knife or gun and maimed me.

I stuffed the violent need deep down into the pit of things I couldn't deal with.

Instead, I nodded mutely, accepting my punishment like the obedient creature I hated. I knew how his mind worked. Any protest would cut my pay further or double the feeding schedule.

This wasn't my first time in hell.

"Get out." He jerked his chin towards the door.

I held my breath, rising on silent feet, exiting without a word. I made it all the way down the hall and into the bathroom, turning the lock behind me, before I made a sound.

A single sob clawed its way free. I braced over the sink, trying to breathe through the panic. My whole body shook, fuzzing my reflection in the vanity.

I blinked furiously, willing the tears back.

It wasn't the first time my uncle had starved me in punishment. One of his favourites, because, in his words, the psychological element would strengthen my resolve. I knew he preferred the physical abuse, but now and then, he liked to spice things up.

Plus, it would be harder to blame my cuts and bruises on demons now that I'd switched divisions. Not that anyone here had particularly taken notice of my injuries in the past, no matter how suspicious they were.

"I'll still have food," I whispered, gripping the porcelain for support.

Before I'd moved out of his house, he could take every crumb away if he'd wanted.

Someone tried the handle, making me jump.

"Occupied!" I called out, voice too shrill, but I doubted anyone on the other side would notice.

A low grunt sounded before the person stomped off.

My heart squeezed at the sight in the mirror. My face was bordering on gaunt already, with my pale skin and the sharpness to my cheekbones enough to rival a runway model, but not in an attractive way.

I ran a shaking hand through my mousy hair, smoothing back the wisps that had come loose from my bun. Dark brown eyes looked haunted behind oversize wire-rimmed glasses.

I had my mother's eyes. Their Asian tilt made me borderline exotic-looking for the small city of Riverside, but my father's British genes had come through with my chestnut hair and freckles.

I shoved my glasses up and splashed cold water onto my face, trying to erase the evidence of my near breakdown. Any hint of weakness was like a drop of blood in the water to these sharks.

The humans and the demons.

I eased out of the bathroom, heading for my one and only assignment left today. If luck was on my side, today's compound would be the one, and I could get my "bonus" already. Hopefully it would be enough to buy train passage to eastern Europe and the provisions to live off-grid for a few months.

Or at least keep eating this week.

Already, I was craving food. The thought of creamy pasta loaded with parmesan like a mini cheese mountain was making me salivate.

I shoved down the hunger clawing at my middle, and my constant longing for Italian food, swiping my pass and entering the lab that had become some twisted mixture of pleasure and pain.

As usual, the monster lounged on the floor at the back of his cell, forearms resting on his knees. Pale eyes waited for me, swirling with violent hunger.

"Ah, there she is, the only part of my day that matters."

Chapter 17

S in's words burrowed into me, bringing a strange mix of guilt and loneliness.

It was a sad existence when the only person who cared whether you showed up was the monster you fed.

I quirked a brow, but my voice came out flat, crushed by the heaviness sitting on my chest like a boulder. "What, you want a squeaky toy or something?"

He snorted, rising to his feet with an otherworldly grace. The three spikes topping each shoulder looked even sharper today, stabbing the air with every breath he took. Or maybe that was because everything seemed dire right now.

The demon closed the four steps to the reinforced glass holding him captive, assessing me with his usual intensity. "You'd get jealous if I had another plaything."

I tried to sneer, but even I could tell it was barely a twitch of my upper lip. "I'm not your plaything."

His presence was just as overwhelming as when I'd first seen him. Somehow, his powerful frame took up even more space than physics allowed.

He bared his fangs in a vicious imitation of a smile. "And yet when I get free, I'm going to toy with you until I finally grow bored enough to snap your tiny neck."

"Not when. *If.*" I shot him a flat look, but anxiety rattled me until it was hard to focus.

He chuckled, the gravelly sound breaking through some of the distracted haze. It shouldn't affect me, yet he'd dragged me to the edge of bliss too many times, that damned mocking laugh rumbling through the glass as he stopped just short of my salvation.

To say I was in a perpetual bad mood would be an understatement, yet I could almost *feel* his wry amusement. Despite it all, to my shame, seeing him made me feel alive in a way nothing else did. My days were in shades of grey, and facing off with the monochrome beast was the only thing that brought me colour.

I hated that seeing him somehow made me feel more like myself. Like I could leave behind all the masks and pretence at the door and walk into this lab without their suffocating weight.

I scowled at the demon, turning my back on him to go through the usual motions. Glare at today's notes. Grab the compound from the mini fridge. Prepare the syringe. Inject. Deep breath.

Face the demon.

"What useless chemical have you got in your veins today, poison?" he practically purred, leaning his forearm on the glass above his head, showing off the deadly elbow spike tipping it.

His presence sucked the oxygen from the room.

Need gathered at the sight of his dark form. How a demon could make my own body betray me was just embarrassing.

The bastard had conditioned me like Pavlov's dogs, but I was more than just salivating.

With my uncle's latest punishment bearing down on me, I couldn't summon the energy to care. If he knew what this demon did to me, he'd be furious.

A brief smirk tugged at my lips. I might not defy him openly, but even this small rebellion felt like the closest thing to freedom I'd ever get.

I closed the gap to my captive, running my gaze over him more fully as a twisted sort of curiosity sank its fangs in.

If you ignored the vicious demonic features, invoking fear in most sane people, he'd make an attractive man. Broad shoulders, thickly muscled arms and sharp cut abs. Sweeping tattoos marking his skin in intricate lines. His face looked carved from stone, all angular lines, but too masculine and rugged to be pretty. His white hair looked downy soft, just begging me to run my hands through it, even with the threatening horns nestled within.

All in all, if things were different, I might have considered it.

Or maybe that was the incessant need he'd built inside me without release. Even getting myself off in the privacy of my shower did nothing but frustrate me more.

And it was all his fault.

I levelled a steely glare at the demon as I slid the hatch open to the first click and shoved my wrist against the small feeding slot. "I hope you choke on it, Sin."

He grinned, sinking to his knees. "If you're good, maybe you will too."

I frowned, puzzling over his meaning before he struck, fangs piercing deep and stealing all rational thought.

Pleasure blinded me. A moan escaped my lips as I leaned heavily against the glass. Heat travelled from his bite through my bloodstream, lighting me on fire. Liquid need pooled at my core, building and building until I thought I'd explode if I didn't get the release that hovered closer and closer.

The demon slid his fangs free, my blood smearing his lips in a vivid splash of colour against his grey skin.

"You need to come, don't you, poison?" His mocking sneer only fanned the flames he'd ignited.

"Fuck. You," I gritted out, panting hard.

My body was on fire. Heat rolling through me in waves of need.

Was this what insanity felt like?

"Not yet," he drawled. "But I'll make you come if you get on your knees and choke on my cock."

His words hit me like a slap to the clit.

My lips parted in shock, quickly transforming to outrage. "Has this compound addled whatever pea-brain should be between those horns?" I hissed, yanking my bleeding arm back. "I'm not touching a single vile part of you."

The demon chuckled, pupils blown wide as he climbed smoothly to his feet. He pressed a palm to the glass, claws clicking against it. His hand was easily bigger than my face.

"Ah, my sweet poison with her bitter words." His evil smile was back. "I can give you exactly what you need, and I'll make you scream like no human ever could."

I sneered at him, but my legs refused to move. Pleasure stalked through my veins, hungry for an outlet.

Something warm touched my leg. I jolted as I noticed his long tail squeezed through the gap in the barrier. I tensed, watching as the smooth heart-shaped tip parted my lab coat, sliding under my dress to touch the bare skin of my thigh.

The smooth caress was like a fingertip stroking along my skin, only warmer, and soft like velvet.

Where were the spines that usually covered his tail's head like a porcupine?

I gasped as it climbed higher, running over the crease of my inner thigh. My body trembled against the glass, insanity and need intertwining.

The urge to do something reckless made my limbs burn. Everything was closing in on me, controlling me, boxing me in. But all I wanted was to feel free.

A plea sat on the tip of my tongue before I bit down on it. The sting helped clear some of the haze sucking me under.

"What the fuck are you doing, parasite?" I hissed, but the angry noise faded into a sultry gravel that sounded nothing like me.

"What does it look like, poison?" He smirked. "I'm going to break you."

Chapter 18

The demon slid his tail higher until he traced over my panties. I shuddered, my legs almost buckling under the onslaught.

He chuckled, husky and low. "You're soaked. Such a greedy little hunter. Is a demon making you too horny to think?"

My jaw ached from how hard I clenched it. I sneered, turning feral in the face of his mocking composure.

I wanted him as unhinged as I felt.

For once, I wanted to be the one stealing control, instead of everyone taking it from me.

Before I could process what I was doing, I shoved the feeding hatch to its widest setting, large enough for my spread hand to shoot through without brushing the edges.

I yanked the waistband of his sweats down. A hard length spilled out.

Saliva pooled in my mouth as a delicious citrus-and-musk scent hit me, and I swallowed hard.

Like everything about the demon, even his damn dick was made to intimidate.

His length was easily the size of my forearm, impossibly thick and covered in slight bumps, like domed scales. Or blunted spikes. They gleamed, almost pearlescent, like his eyes. Like gemstones embedded in the smooth charcoal of his skin.

They stopped short of the tapered tip, a mushroomed heart-shape that reminded me of his tail.

"Oh my god, did you glitter your dick just for this occasion?" I mocked, needing to regain the upper hand.

Pearly liquid dribbled from the pointy tip, running down his textured length in an obscene response.

A husky rattle joined in. "Aww, poison, do you think my dick is pretty?"

His tail slipped under my panties, brazenly stroking through my folds. A strangled moan lodged in my throat as I twitched against the glass.

He chuckled harder. "I bet this pussy is the only pretty thing about you."

"I bet your diamond-studded cock feels like fucking a cactus. No wonder you're so desperate for someone to touch you," I hissed, gripping the base of his length and squeezing.

I couldn't close my hand around it, inches still separating my thumb and fingertips.

He jerked his hips, rubbing himself through my hand as he groaned. The sensation was somehow both smooth and textured, causing a little shiver down my spine as I imagined what he might feel like inside me.

Not that this monster would fit.

"Not *someone*." His claws curled, scraping the glass. "You."

He slid his tail against me a fraction harder, and I cried out at the shock of bliss mixing with his ridiculous words. I was so close to shattering that I trembled against the glass, my grip tightening on his solid length.

"Get on your knees, poison."

"Make me, parasite."

A fire raged inside me, as hot as the pleasure pulsing through me as he slowly brushed his velvet tail over my clit.

He grinned, showing off fangs tinged with my blood. His tail pulled back and slapped against the back of my knees, buckling them. I yelped, releasing him as I fell, but he caught me under my arse, just short of cracking my knees on the concrete. The strength of his tail seemed impossible, but after all, he was a demon, capable of more than even us hunters knew.

He lowered me the last inch. The cold floor dug into my skin but did nothing to soothe the heat building through me.

His gentle movements were so at odds with the cruel sneer on his face that I might have imagined it.

I blinked up at him as if in a dream. Or, more likely, a nightmare.

He grinned wickedly, and broadened his stance, pushing forward until his cock slid through the widened gap in the barrier, separating us but doing nothing to keep me safe.

His tail trailed along my thigh before he pulled back. The heart-shaped tip hovered in front of my face, showing me the glistening evidence of my shame.

"So wet." He chuckled, the sound laced with mocking. "Are you embarrassed by how much you crave me?"

I snarled, anger heating my veins almost as much as desire. "That's what happens when I think of someone else. Someone human, and actually attractive."

The demon smirked down at me, a dark god straight from hell. "Liar."

His muscled tail wrapped my neck and yanked me forward. I gasped, and instantly realised my mistake as the head of his cock slid straight through the open hatch and between my parted lips.

My eyes widened as the taste of musk and mandarins burst across my tongue. I was allergic to citrus fruits, but the usual panic was absent as I savoured his unique flavour.

He embodied the forbidden fruit.

The sweetest sin.

Starlit eyes burned into me as he stared down at my face. "Fuck, poison. Seems your hot little mouth is good for more than just insulting me."

I scowled, but with my jaw wedged open by his monster dick, I must have looked ridiculous.

The expression caused my lips to tighten, and he groaned. His hips pushed forward to the limit until his heavy balls bumped the glass in an obscene display.

The tail collaring me pulled me forward, and I made an angry sound in my throat.

"That's it, poison." The demon snarled. "Pleasure your fucking enemy. Hate me while you get off on my taste. Feel exactly how I do every time you visit me."

The glow brightened in his eyes until twin stars shone from his dark features. "You might have me captive, but I promise you, one day I'll get free, and when I do, you're going to be so fucking sorry. I'll make you cry and scream and come so hard you'll black out on my dick."

I tried to growl again, my fists slamming against the glass on either side of the hatch. His heated length pulsed on my tongue, and I fought the desire to rub my thighs together to ease some of the desperate ache between them.

He growled back, low and menacing. The sound made my core flutter, like he'd conditioned me to respond to every demonic aspect of him each time he'd bitten me and drawn me right to the edge of insanity.

He pulled me further onto his length. The slow drag of each blunt spike across my tongue. My eyes watered as he forced my jaw wider with every inch he made me swallow. He hit the back of my throat and I choked, hacking a cough as I jerked back off his length, guided by the tail gripping my throat.

"You taste vile," I hissed, spluttering another wet cough. "Like bitter ash and sulphur."

I hated the fact that I was lying. He tasted divine, like citrus and musk, and I craved more.

His lips twisted into his favourite mocking sneer. "Good."

He yanked me forward with his tail, the heart tip pressing the corner of my mouth open so I had no choice but to welcome him between my lips.

His eyes burned like white fire. "You make me crazy, poison. Fucking toxic for you." He yanked me back and forth on his cock, forcing me to take him as deep as I could. Over and over.

My core burned with a pulsing ache as I sucked him down with wild abandon. I felt hollow and empty.

Yet my mouth had never been so full.

My hands crept up without my permission, wrapping the base that I couldn't get my lips anywhere near. Before I knew it, I worked him with my hands and mouth, his tail the only thing slowing my eager attempts to devour him right alongside his control.

He groaned, horns tipping back for a moment, before his burning gaze returned to meet mine as I drank in his rapt expression. His lips peeled back, baring fangs. A harsh whine sounded as his claws raked the glass barrier.

He looked unhinged. Demonic and feral.

I relished the sight. The sense of power I'd never taken before.

His tail unwrapped from my throat, and my pace quickened as I worked him harder, trying to steal whatever I could from him.

The pointed tip slid down my chest, circling my nipples through my bra before moving lower. He pushed under my dress, teasing the edge of my panties, and I almost choked in my desperation for him to touch me where I ached for him.

"Fuck, poison," he groaned. "When I get out of here, I'm going to fill this tight cunt up with so much cum you'll be dripping for days. My barb is going to lock us together so you'll mewl and scream but won't be able to escape me."

My eyes widened at the image he painted, fear and anticipation tightening through my body. I couldn't see or feel anything that might be a barb, so the threat lost some of its edge.

He pressed his tail into my entrance, dipping in just enough to tease but nowhere near enough to satisfy. I growled around his length, vibrating his textured gems that stroked the inside of my mouth so sinfully.

His tail shoved in fully, stretching me deliciously. I moaned, practically screaming around him.

He snarled, yanking his tail out and ripping my panties apart, leaving me exposed and achingly empty once more.

But he didn't torture me.

Instead, his slicked tail slapped my clit and began rubbing maddening circles. He pulled me apart thread by thread, and I took from him right back.

His face transformed into a mask of ferocity, eyes glowing white-hot. His fangs dripped a clear liquid, splattering the glass and running down like the tears tracking down my cheeks.

I kept going, working him into a frenzy, my hands slicked from my saliva and his addictive pre-cum. My tongue laved his thick head with every pass, and I bobbed harder and faster, building a rhythm as he matched my ferocity with his tail.

"Cry for me while I shatter you, poison. I want to see your make-up run down your pretty face until you're as ugly on the outside as you are inside," he snarled, shaking the glass with the force.

I squeezed him harder in retaliation and yanked myself off his length with a sneer. "No, parasite. You're going to break for me."

I swallowed him down my throat, as far as he would go, until my cheeks hollowed.

He roared, hips slamming against the glass as his length pulsed in my mouth.

His tail slapped me and buzzed wetly against my clit. I tipped over the edge, moaning around him as he shot searing pleasure down my throat.

I choked on his cum as he broke me apart. My body writhed as I knelt before him, sucking down his citrus-flavoured essence as I half screamed, half choked for him.

"Fuck, poison," he growled, breathing as ragged as mine.

I swallowed every drop, pulling off his softening length and licking my swollen lips. He spurted another thick rope against my mouth with a groan, closing his eyes briefly like the sight was too much for him.

I pushed to my feet, ignoring the twitches assaulting my body in the blissful aftershocks. His tail wrapped my upper thigh in an almost possessive hold.

I felt powerful. For the first time in as long as I could remember.

I met his blissed-out gaze, a vicious sneer on my swollen lips. "Disgusting."

He grinned back. "Seeing me is the only part of your day that matters too."

Chapter 19

The monster was watching me again.

He was always watching me.

Nothing escaped his notice. Not the vials I picked up, nor the way my hand shook as it hovered over the syringe. Nothing.

I skirted the bench, heading to the mini fridge that somehow made the sterile room feel more like a hotel room than a lab.

Was I walking weird?

It felt like I was walking weird.

What are you even meant to do with your arms while you walk? What is the optimal level of swing? Forty degrees either side? No. Surely it's more forwards than back, right?

I glanced over at the demon under my lashes, wondering if his heightened senses could somehow pick up on the internal panic threatening to make me fling my arms about like a marching soldier.

His starlit gaze met mine, arrowing straight through all the noise to pin me in place.

I stilled. My entire nervous system locked down for a drawn-out beat.

Then I blinked, breaking his spell and moving with purpose—and very little arm swing—towards the fridge.

Since the hate-blow-job incident, I was acting weird around him.

Of course, Sin was completely unfazed. Like he received hate blow jobs on the regular from people holding him prisoner and trying to poison him.

I'd fed him for the last week. Every. Single. Day.

He'd kept up his almost-orgasm biting tactic, and I hated to admit that it was working. Despite the...reprieve.

I was slowly losing my mind. Even though every night in the shower, I'd embarrassingly finish what he started. My thoughts betraying me with the image of his savage face and cruel smirk as I came.

I swore I could almost feel his twisted satisfaction in the act. Like he had some mystical demon powers and *knew* what I was doing.

The lack of food wasn't helping.

I'd resolved to continue saving money, but the cost was putting me on a bowl of cereal and a pack of ramen noodles as my only food every day. With the demon taking my blood, and valuable nutrients right along with it, I was starving. But that stubborn part of me that craved freedom refused to touch the savings I'd stashed in the flimsy wall of my apartment.

My stomach chose that moment to growl, as ferocious as any demon. I ignored the hunger pang, pretending it wasn't painfully hollowing out my middle, grabbing the day's compound as I prepared to inject it.

My hand shook too much to be of any use.

A wave of dizziness swept over me. I stumbled, dropping the syringe to the counter.

The world blinked.

I gazed up at a panelled ceiling. Roaring filled my ears.

My head throbbed. Nausea swam through my gut. My mouth felt thick.

The rushing sound cleared into words.

"Poison! What the fires are you doing? Get up!" a masculine voice snarled.

Booming thuds sounded, and I flicked my eyes to the source, struggling to focus.

A panicked demon slammed his spiked fists against the glass separating us. But he was the wrong way up.

I frowned. Why was I on the floor?

I pushed shakily up to sitting, and the demon blurred as I manoeuvred to press my back against a workbench leg, hugging my knees to my chest for support.

My hand shook as I pulled my wire-rimmed glasses off, noting the small crack spidering through the edge of one lens.

A low groan escaped my lips. There was no way I could afford a replacement pair.

"Poison... What the fuck was that?" the demon growled, chest heaving so deeply his shoulder spikes gouged the air.

I blinked at him, sliding my broken glasses back onto my face to bring all seven feet of pissed-off male back into focus. My chest burned oddly, like a hot coal sat beneath my sternum.

I swallowed thickly, trying to make sense of why I'd suddenly found myself on the floor. The throb in the back of my skull was a pretty big clue.

"I...passed out." I shrugged, as if it were no big deal.

The demon snarled, slamming his fist into the glass hard enough to rattle it. His spiked knuckles left four perfect indents into what should have been unbreakable, reinforced bullet-proof glass.

My every muscle tensed, but it held under his anger.

Why was he so pissed? I was the one who'd almost bashed their head in.

I eyed the corner of the stainless steel bench. If I'd have smacked my head just right, I wouldn't have been getting back up.

I pursed my lips at Sin and climbed to my feet. Clutching the edge of the table, I waited to see if weakness would surge through me once more.

The demon swallowed, tendons popping along the column of his throat as he seemed to restrain himself. "Fucking obviously," the demon snarled. "Why?" His question was a demand, filled with as much venom as his bite.

I huffed. "Don't worry, if I'm taken out by a rogue counter-top, I'm sure someone else will come in to feed you."

"That's not..." His expression shuttered. Every line of his exposed muscle had tensed, etching severe dips and valleys across his exposed upper body.

"I'm just hungry is all." I cleared my throat, flashing him an awkward smile. "Let's try that again, shall we?"

"If you inject that shit into your veins, I will rip out every artery in your wrist so fast you won't get a chance to press your little remote." He jabbed a pearly claw towards my face, scratching the glass between us.

I threw my hands up. "What the fuck do you want from me, demon?"

"Among other things, I want you to live, Liliana." Glowing silver eyes narrowed. "Apparently I'm the only one."

His words sliced down to my soul.

Ironically, he probably was the only one. Once again, my enemies cared more for my welfare than my family.

I felt a detached sort of pity for myself.

But that was why I saved up, even though it was starving me. Because in a matter of weeks, I'd have enough to disappear from my uncle's grasp. Forever. I could start a new life. With non-violent friends and a less hostile work environment.

I'd take up a gentle hobby, like crochet, and start a book club that involved too much wine and the smutty kind of story that would make me blush.

A girl could dream.

I crossed my arms, feeling too exposed. More so than when he'd ripped my panties off with his tail during the hate-blow-job incident.

"I thought you wanted to escape and *snap my tiny neck*?" I did my best impression of his mocking rumble.

"Well, I can't do that if you die from your own stupidity, can I?" His familiar sneer was back.

I rolled my eyes, but the movement triggered another wave of dizziness. I rasped in a harsh breath and grabbed the table, bracing to kiss the floor again.

"Poison," he barked. "Go. Eat something. Or you can tickle me with this collar all you want; I won't bite you."

I pursed my lips. "A demon on a hunger strike? Now I've seen it all."

"Stop deflecting. Leave."

"Fine," I snapped, irritation sinking its claws into my chest, along with a dose of fear. If my uncle found out that I didn't feed Sin today, I'd be punished with more than a little dizzy spell. "I'll be back."

"Looking forward to it," he sneered, back to his prickly self.

For a moment, I could have sworn he was worried about me. Of course, he'd just be worried about his one constant supply of food. He was my captive, for fuck's sake. Nothing more.

I already knew nobody would care if I actually died. It had been proven with empirical evidence the moment Leo and the rest of my team left me to die on the grimy floor of an abandoned warehouse.

With one last glare, I left the lab, heading off in search of the one place I could get food in hunter HQ.

I hadn't brought lunch in, down to just breakfast and dinner for the past couple of days.

I grabbed my purse from the staff lockers, stuffing it into my lab coat pocket as I hurried up the stairs, buzzing my pass to exit the underground level. The general bustle of people reached me the moment I pushed open the heavy steel door, along with the wordless judgement of two guards.

"Jorah, Tim," I said, nodding as I passed.

Neither returned the gesture.

I strode away, avoiding looking at the empty cage dominating the centre of the warehouse. I couldn't handle seeing the bloodstains on the mat today.

Scurrying to the only open doorway, nestled between a few stacks of empty crates, I slipped inside, bracing for the worst.

The canteen fell deathly silent.

Chapter 20

Three teams of hunters sprawled around long tables, laughter dying off as their beady eyes raked over me.

Fifteen sets of eyes would be intimidating enough, but every person here was a trained killer.

Even me.

I drew my shoulders back, ignoring the rising hostility, and made my way to the short counter, holding covered metal dishes under heat-lamps.

The scent of roast meat was like a punch to the gut. Hunger scraped through my middle, hollowing out the already empty space. Saliva pooled in my mouth, and I had to swallow thickly as I met the careful stare of the woman in charge.

"Hi, Belinda." I offered her a sheepish smile. "It smells delicious, as always. Can I have today's special, please?"

She was already shaking her head. "Sorry, dove, your uncle said you're not to eat here anymore. *Real* hunters only." Her upper lip lifted in distaste at the clear insult to us in omega team.

A few sniggers broke out behind me, but I kept my chin lifted, a fake smile bolted to my face. "Oh, I didn't realise they'd changed the rules today."

I knew for a fact that Cara and Martin had eaten here together yesterday.

There wasn't usually a big divide between the operational hunters and omega team. Those bloodthirsty lunatics usually saw our value.

I was just a shiny, new special exception.

The chef shrugged with an apologetic smile, but her attention wandered to the covered food as if she'd forgotten all about me already.

The urge to cry knifed through me.

I almost caved to the frantic need to rip off one of the metal lids and grab a handful of whatever was under it anyway.

But my uncle would not reduce me to a fucking animal.

I was already a leashed pet.

Turning from the feast I'd been denied, I made my way stiffly back out.

"What's the matter, *Dozer*? Heading off for another nap on the job instead?" a male voice called out, and laughter returned to the small canteen. "Or does the *princess* not only think she's too good for alpha squad but to even eat with the rest of us?"

Another male spoke up, "I heard she faked her injuries for attention, and that's why Leo finally dumped her."

"Tia told me he'd had enough of picking up the slack from having her in alpha," a feminine voice replied.

I glared over my shoulder, eyeing the mouthy bastards from gamma squad, and bashed into something hard, bouncing off before firm hands caught me around the shoulders.

I peered up at the last person I wanted to see.

"Whoa, easy there, Dozer." Leo's navy eyes scanned me from head to toe as he held me in place. "You look like shit. Maybe you *should* head back in there, put some meat on your bones."

At one point, I might have mistaken his words for caring, but the satisfied smirk on his lips outed them for the pure insult they were.

"I'm not hungry, but I am busy," I said curtly, hoping he'd take the hint and let me go without causing a scene.

Framed in the canteen doorway, we were in full view of the leering hunters.

"You sure? Nobody wants to fuck a skeleton, babe." He snickered, like it was just a good-natured ribbing between friends. "And you were pretty lifeless in bed as it was."

His words reached the rest of the canteen, and their laughter followed his. Hoots and catcalls piled onto my humiliation until my cheeks burned.

I gritted my teeth against the urge to slam the heel of my palm into my ex's nose and watch his blood arc crimson through the air. Maybe if I broke his face, I'd feel less anger over my broken heart.

My head still throbbed from bouncing it off the floor, and my limbs felt heavy enough to drag. It numbed me to the sting of his childish taunts. I was half starving to death, and the other half was being drained by an infuriating bloodsucker.

Ironically, it put a lot of things into perspective.

"Oh no, the two-pump chump thinks I'm bad in bed," I drawled with feigned nonchalance, shrugging out of his grip as his face purpled with rage. "Excuse me while I go cry myself to sleep over it."

I brushed past my ex, leaving the mocking hunters behind.

I needed to return to my lab.

But I couldn't face the demon who waited for me.

Sin.

He'd know. Somehow, my failure would be written all over me and he'd just know.

I didn't examine why that was such an issue for me.

Instead, I took the cowardly route, gathered my meagre belongings from the lockers, and fled the compound, heading home to the nutritious packet of ramen noodles that waited for me.

My uncle would hear that I'd left early—hell, he'd see it for himself on one of the many cameras he had watching me—but in that moment, I couldn't bring myself to care.

"You're not trying hard enough!"

My uncle's roar boomed through the tense office, scraping my brittle nerves.

I went rigid in the flimsy chair, knowing the slightest twitch could set him off.

He loomed over the desk, pinning me with an arctic glare. "Do you have any idea how many good men we've lost this week?" His voice dropped to a lethal octave that never boded well for me.

"Of course you don't. Too busy cowering in your fucking lab while the rest of us make real sacrifices."

I was borderline starving because of him and the vicious demon I fed daily. Felt a lot like sacrifice to me. But I bit my tongue, letting his disgust rake over me in silence.

I saw him move before I could do anything about it. Not that I would have.

The stinging slap echoed through the room, the acrid taste of blood blooming in my mouth as he knocked me from the chair. On hands and knees, I stared at the polished floorboards swimming in my vision, but at least my glasses miraculously stayed on.

Rotten memories swam up, offering me glimpses of past punishments.

Colourless eyes brimming with excitement, thick fingers woven into my hair to wrench my head back, exposing the fragile column of my throat as his other hand coiled around it like a steel vice. The hot brand of liquor-laced breath scorching my face as he leaned in with a cruel smile.

My ears rang as I blinked hard, trying to stave off the memories and the blackness flirting at the edges. I wasn't in nearly a strong enough state to take a beating right now, even though I'd caved last night and eaten my final semi-nutritious microwave meal.

He sneered, as if he could taste my weakness. "You're an embarrassment. Get. Up."

My cheek throbbed, tender and swelling with the bruise already forming. I could taste the coppery tang of blood, a bead running down my chin to splash the back of my hand.

The bastard had split my lip with my father's signet ring: the symbol of his position as hunter prime.

Hating the wavering fear trying to consume me, I rose to my feet, chin up, shoulders back, watching my uncle with a blank expression despite the useless rage burning a hole through my middle.

Any reaction except neutral strength would only provoke the beast.

His fist slammed into the same side of my face, whipping my head around with brutal force. I stumbled a step but managed to stay on my feet as agony lanced my cheek. Fresh blood flooded my mouth, thick rivulets running down my chin as my lip split wider.

An instant headache pounded my skull, but the pain in my cheek shrieked louder.

Clearly, I hadn't hidden my anger fast enough.

I worked my jaw, fixing my glasses back into place, before slowly turning to face my uncle. This time utterly devoid of emotion.

Beady eyes drilled into me, weighing, scrutinising. A frisson of fear slid through my veins as I wondered whether this was the time I didn't make it out of the room.

Shame swamped me.

I'd spent most of my life training to fight, yet when it came down to it, I was nothing but a coward.

His upper lip twisted in disgust, and he waved a hand in a shooing gesture, light glinting off my father's bloodied ring. "Go back to your damn lab, Liliana, and for once in your miserable life, stop shaming this family. You're meant to be saving lives, not wasting my time."

He'd been the one to summon me to his office this evening for an urgent meeting, which was apparently just an excuse to release some of his pent-up rage.

"Hunter Prime." I inclined my head, ignoring how the room spun behind the grizzled monster.

I left quietly, each step down the corridor stiff as I carefully locked away every jagged emotion. The pieces seemed to cut me from the inside out.

Finally reaching the small bathroom, I slipped inside and turned the lock with trembling hands. Leaning back against the solid door, I let my head thunk into the wood, squeezing my eyes shut.

My throat thickened, airway narrowing until each breath tore through in a panicked rasp that rang too loudly in my own ears. Black spots danced in my vision as I fought for control, for a single deep inhale past the tightness in my chest.

I clenched my hands together, rubbing at my knuckles where the constant ache lived. A bone-deep reminder of past mistakes.

Everyone says how hopelessness feels crushing, but it's the numbness that really gets you. My heart pounded with the typical signs of rising anxiety—shallow gasps, tremors, cold sweat prickling my skin. But emotionally, I felt...nothing. A hollow cavern, scraped bare.

I was so close to empty, what would happen when I finally reached the bottom?

Would I shatter and cease to exist?

Wetness leaked from my eyes, and I cursed under my breath, reaching beneath my glasses to wipe away the utter waste of hydration. I didn't have time for this.

I straightened, splashing cold water on my abused face and focused on evening out my ragged breaths, smothering the breakdown fighting to surface. I folded away the panic, embracing the numb to get me through as I methodically reconstructed my blank façade, ignoring the haunted look in my dark brown eyes.

When I finally emerged, the only outward sign of my uncle's fury was the mottled bruising purpling along my cheek and the split seam of my lower lip.

Not for the first time, I cursed the meaty ham hands of my uncle and headed for my assigned lab.

I swallowed back the tears, but they wedged in my throat as an unnecessary lump. I hated when emotions had physical manifestations instead of just lurking in the recesses of my mind, waiting to ambush me with a panic attack, like they were supposed to.

Without conscious thought, I paused outside the lab, staring at the smooth white door.

Whether I wanted to or not, I had to go in there and do my damn job.

"The cure," I murmured. "I can do this."

I drew in a deep breath.

One. Two. Three.

Released the air from my lungs in a controlled exhale and slapped my pass against the scanner. The door beeped in a familiar high pitch, and I pushed it open.

Like always, the monster from my nightmares haunted my days.

"Ah, she still lives." Sin's deep voice rumbled through the cluster of holes in his plexiglass containment cell.

He lounged against the far corner, a predator at ease. The devil's eyes tracked me as I strode inside, glittering with sadistic amusement.

The door clicked shut. The locking mechanism re-engaged.

Just me and the demon, trapped in a small room.

"Come to poison me once more?" His tone rasped like sandpaper over exposed nerves. "Or simply collapse again like the fragile human you are?"

I turned my back on him, unable to process any more aggression as I retrieved the kit from the mini fridge bolted to the wall. My hand quaked as I withdrew Cara's latest serum and placed it on the tray. The vial clattered loudly, rolling across the metal to collide with the waiting syringe.

Silence reverberated in its wake, the air charging with something indefinable.

The predator had scented blood. Weakness.

Would he finally escape and snap my flimsy neck like he'd promised? Or would he drink me down like my father's murderer?

"What's this? No scathing rebuke?" His words seemed to slither across my skin, each one a lethal caress. "No peek at that adorably vicious side you like to smother?"

My hand stilled on the tray as his rich chuckle washed over me, saturated in dark promise and anticipation. Finding some ounce of grit, I shoved the needle into my inner elbow and pressed the plunger, ignoring the cool rush down my arm.

Facing the demon, I almost lost my nerve at the sight of him right before the glass, an indomitable force of nature.

"No, I'm here to set you free for your all-you-can-eat human buffet," I snapped.

His lips twitched, but the smirk died off as his attention zeroed in on my mouth.

Notching my chin, I pretended not to see the storm clouds brewing in his eyes. Or feel the pit of dark need splitting my chest.

What did he have to feel violent about? The bastard just lazed about in his cell all day like a pampered pet. I was the one dealing with a hostile work environment.

"So," he murmured, voice deceptively casual. "What happened to your face, poison?"

A fist slamming against my cheek. A snarl of displeasure. Shame smothering me.

I cleared my throat, forcing my body to still rather than shifting on my feet. "Nothing."

His claws screeched like nails across a chalkboard as they raked down the plexiglass, the harsh dissonance setting my teeth on edge.

Looming like a monster, he uttered a single syllable, drenched in violence. "Who?"

For a moment, it almost sounded like he cared.

The idea was enough to crumble the fortress I'd rebuilt around my emotions. I was that desperate for someone to care about me.

So. Fucking. Pathetic.

No wonder my uncle tried to beat the weakness from me.

My father's callous voice echoed through my skull—*Never let them see you weak, Tiger-lily.*

"What does it matter?" I hissed, jutting my chin.

I was sick of being manipulated by everyone around me. My whole life was a lie. I'd committed atrocities thinking I was doing the right thing, and I could never remove the stains from my soul.

Now, the one time I could finally do some good, and even that wasn't simple. Even that caused suffering.

My life was an endless maze of grey. Every turn just led to more of the same. I was tired of the never-ending struggle, the meaningless sacrifices, the agonising existence that insisted on grinding me down until I was nothing but scar tissue and frayed edges.

"Look at me," the demon snarled, deep timbre rattling the glassware.

My gaze snapped up.

I'd never seen him this angry: glistening fangs slick with venom, broad chest heaving like he'd sprinted a marathon, shoulder spikes gouging the air.

But it was the churning darkness in his glowing eyes that held me against my will.

"You're mine, poison. Nobody else gets to lay a finger on you without me snapping it off."

A low chuckle bubbled up from the hollow pit in my chest, as bitter as the demon. "Yours to hurt?" I asked. "To kill?"

Sin's full lips curved into a slow, predatory smile that should have filled me with dread. Instead, heat whispered through my veins.

"Exactly," he purred, voice the darkest velvet. "I'll hurt you so sweetly, poison. Exquisitely. You'll never be the same again."

Something was fundamentally wrong with me, because it almost sounded like a sinful promise rather than the brutal threat he'd intended.

I shook my head, stifling a wince as it worsened the ache in my skull. How had things got so complicated?

I stuffed my wrist against the open hatch.

"Shut up and bite me, Sin."

Chapter 22

Fangs sliced into my wrist.

So familiar now I could time the second of pain before pleasure burned it away. It spread outwards, pooling warmth low in my body, straddling the line between delicious torture and forbidden ecstasy.

At least it distracted from my throbbing face.

Reckless desire tried to choke me into submission. I'd been ignoring the twisted longing ever since the demon had unravelled me with his sinuous tail.

Sin knelt behind the barrier, hooking me with starlit eyes. An intensity simmered in their depths, edging from bloodlust into dark, wicked things.

He pulled back before I could shatter, crushing my shameful hope right alongside it.

Self-disgust filled the void, and I turned from my captive with a grimace, but something warm snagged my leg.

I arched a brow at the shadowy tail coiling around my thigh. "What are you doing, parasite?"

The demon bared lethal fangs. "I'm not done feasting on what's mine."

My thoughts scrambled like I'd taken another hit to the face.

Before I could snap back at his ridiculous statement, he yanked me closer, his tail an unbreakable chain. My palms slapped the glass.

His sinuous tail slid down to my knee and lifted. I jerked forward, tensing my abs to stop from tumbling back. My lab coat parted, revealing the faded pencil skirt now riding up my hips.

The monster grinned, eyes brightening with a startling intensity.

My jaw slackened as I realised why.

I. Wasn't. Wearing. Underwear.

His forked tongue swiped over his full lower lip. "Were you hoping to need the easy access, poison?"

My eyes narrowed to slits at the mocking in his raspy tone.

If only that were the reason, but it was laundry day, and I was both cripplingly poor and half-starved. After getting home late last night, because Martin had assigned me some bullshit lab clean-up, I hadn't had the energy to put a wash on.

Warmth tinged my cheeks, but I flashed the demon a cocky smirk. "Yep. Most of the hunters are morons, but damn if they don't know how to fill out a compression shirt."

Sin growled, the deadly sound reverberating through the glass. His tail released my knee and lashed my waist, squeezing tight in a possessive hold.

I yelped as he lifted me off the ground, raising me in front of the barrier with preternatural strength. His hands shot through the gap, breaking the hatch to drop to its widest setting. Even so, the height cut off his movement mid-forearm, just enough for him to shove between my parted thighs and force them open. My knees slid up and out, trapped between my chest and the glass.

Wide hands squeezed my arse, claws pressing into the tops of the globes through my skirt, pricking my skin as he held me aloft.

My breathing came in ragged pants. In less than a blink, he'd trapped me, exposing my core to his hungry gaze. The remote to his choke collar weighed heavy in my pocket. The sly demon had left my hands free on purpose.

Another taunt.

I could stop him at any time, but a twisted part of me was desperate to see where this went. And the bastard knew it.

"I already told you how toxic you make me, poison." His words dropped to a husky whisper. The dangerous promise spoken close enough to my core that his warm breath teased over me through the hatch. "Anyone who touches you will die, writhing in agony as I tear them apart, piece by insignificant piece."

I licked my lower lip, tasting blood. Sin's intensity reached inside and tore me away from all the noise. I couldn't worry about trivial things like the ache in my cheek, the guilt that crushed me a little more each day, or the choice between food and freedom.

Sin robbed me of everything.

Until all that existed was him.

As he knelt before me, his eyes glowed with starlight. "If you're my addiction, I'll make sure I'm yours too."

His forked tongue darted through the gap, licking hard across the apex of my thighs in a lash of pleasure.

I moaned, core fluttering as delicious sensation rioted through me. The forked tips of his tongue teased over my clit, feathering across the needy bundle of nerves, the taunting caress driving me wild.

Untamed hunger transformed his features, making him look even more predatory.

"Fuck, Sin," I panted, jerking as he repeated the long, firm lick, like I was a treat he couldn't get enough of.

The demon growled, vibrating his tongue as he continued to taste me. "Your arousal tastes even better than your blood, poison. So damn sweet I could devour you every day, and never get enough."

His words teased my lower lips, and I widened my knees to my shoulders, desperate for more.

The demon rewarded me with another trace, an almost sweet caress of his wicked tongue as he toyed with me.

My hands spasmed against the glass. With nothing to hold on to, I felt cut adrift. Completely at his mercy. His claws dug into my arse and his tail hugged my waist. At any second, he could drop me. He could reach up and slit my femoral artery with his claws.

He could slide the spikes out of his tail and rake them across my throat.

There were a million different ways Sin could kill me.

Instead, he knelt before me and pleasured me like I deserved his worship.

He drew his tongue through my folds, growling like a starved beast. The pace became urgent, Sin feasting until I was dizzy with bliss and racing towards ruin.

"Sin, please," I whimpered, intoxicated by the sight of such a powerful monster on his knees for me.

Even my ex-fiancé hadn't spent this long going down on me on the rare occasions he had.

"Say my name, Liliana. I love hearing you beg," he snarled against me, and I writhed in his hands.

Claws dug into my arse, and I knew he'd drawn blood, but I didn't care. My hips rolled, adding to the sting as I tried desperately to increase the pace, the pressure, the maddening friction.

Only he could undo me like this.

"Sin...," I moaned, eyes fluttering shut for a moment before I glared down at him with a snarl on my lips. "If you don't get that creepy monster tongue back in my pussy this second, I'm going to fucking choke you."

Glistening obscenely, his lips spread wide to flash ivory daggers.

The dark demon had crawled from hell to devour my soul. And I was giving it to him gladly.

He didn't know it was a battered, tarnished thing.

I grinned back as the vicious side of me came out to play. The one that only he seemed to coax out nowadays.

I grabbed the remote from my pocket, lifting it to the glass.

And pressed the button.

Starred eyes gleamed with menace. He lunged, biting down on my pussy.

Tingling heat exploded through my core and I screamed, breaking apart as pleasure swallowed me whole.

His fangs slid out, and I writhed uncontrollably. The hazed sounds of coughing and spluttering reached me, and I had just enough mental capacity left to jab the stop button as I came undone.

Something thick pushed at my entrance, and I moaned, blinking open eyes I didn't know I'd shut.

The thick head of his tail notched at my entrance in a sensual threat. Twin drops of blood ran from the puncture marks on either side, combining with my dripping arousal.

Sin's charcoal tail contrasted my pale skin as he disappeared inside me. The size of it stretched me in a vicious burn, mixing with the toxic heat of his venom pulsing through my core.

"I fucking hate you, poison. Now come harder for me," he snarled.

He shoved all the way in. I screamed, slamming my palms against the glass and thrashing in his claws as pleasure tore me apart in an all-consuming light.

Waves of bliss smashed through me, dragging my pleasure on and on as I struggled to hold on to something. Anything. My hands curled into his tail at my waist, the steady band keeping me upright when I slumped back, breathless.

I panted hard, blinking rapidly as small, whimpering sounds escaped my lips.

My vision cleared, and the sight would forever be burned into my mind.

My sinful demon waited on his knees, lips glossy with my pleasure and smeared blood, starlit eyes locked onto my face with rapt cruelty.

He was every dark fantasy I didn't know I had.

A familiar, cruel smirk carved his striking features. "Disgusting."

I grinned back, and it was all teeth.

Chapter 23

Late the following night, I slipped into my assigned lab, bracing for insanity. I'd been delaying this moment for as long as possible, and now I'd run out of excuses, as well as time.

At least I wasn't the only person staying late for once. The other scientists were all here somewhere, whipped up into a tizzy about a breakthrough by one of the other lab teams, much to Martin's aggravation. I steered clear of anything to do with them. Always had. Capturing and experimenting on mages, a human-looking minor demon breed, was more than I could stomach, even if their magic could aid the hunter cause.

To my horror, anticipation lit embers in my middle, and I fought to stomp them out as the security door clicked shut behind me. An odd warmth sat in the middle of my chest.

I hadn't been able to stop thinking about Sin. The things I'd let my enemy do to me. Again.

I sucked in a ragged breath.

His cell was empty.

My heart leaped into my throat as I scanned the tiny room, but there was no sign of the demon anywhere. The glassware and equipment were exactly as I'd left them yesterday. Even the reinforced plexiglass wall that formed his cell looked untouched, apart from the gouges he'd made when I'd passed out.

So how had he escaped? And, more importantly, where the hell was the demon who'd promised to kill me?

A loud boom rattled the glassware, and I spun, expecting him to be right behind me like in a horror film.

It took my mind a moment to connect the sound to a great thundering coming from upstairs.

I frowned. Demon attacks had spiked lately, giving rise to a heightened need for security. With so few operational hunters left, it was ridiculous for them to be carrying out their sadistic battles, pitting demons against one another for sport or lethal training.

"No…" The denial slipped from my lips unbidden.

Surely he wouldn't have.

Leo liked to pick the most ferocious demons for those match-ups. Given how I'd insulted him in the canteen, and my reaction to him taking Sin last time, a sinking feeling weighed my gut.

A shrill beep cut the noise. I leaped back, sliding instinctually into a fighting stance even as fear clutched my chest.

The door swung open.

Martin stepped inside, and a sigh of relief escaped me as I straightened.

"There you are," Martin huffed, thick brows low. "A word, Liliana."

Clearly, he was mad about something, but my mind was spinning out of control, wondering where Sin was.

Thumping and banging seemed to escalate from above.

I frowned, glancing at the panelled ceiling. Normally, you couldn't hear anything down here. The labs were practically soundproof. A necessity when each was a glorified torture chamber.

Martin looked up at the next thud. His concerned gaze met mine before he seemed to dismiss the worry. "What in the blazes are those meatheads up to now?"

I cocked my head, straining to listen. "Something's wrong."

My uncle had mentioned the attacks on our squads were getting more frequent, more violent. The unshakeable brute had seemed...concerned.

The noises continued, punctuated by sharp retorts that could only be gunfire.

I chewed my lower lip, thoughts racing as I evaluated my options.

Where's Sin?

"We have to go." I strode for the door, but a moist palm clamped my wrist.

I quelled the urge to wrench my arm free and slam my fist into his face.

Martin scowled. "You're being dramatic, Liliana. Again. It's just idiots being idiots." He released me to wave a dismissive hand.

"We're under attack." My voice came out flat. Instinct screamed that we were all in danger.

"By who?" He scoffed. "We're perfectly safe here."

I jerked my arm free. "Come with me now or stay here and die."

I wouldn't waste my breath trying to convince a haughty sociopath to save himself.

Now would be the perfect time for me to flee. I could get a head start. I had enough money for the first train ticket to continental Europe, and then I could figure out the rest from there.

If we were under attack, my uncle's focus would be pulled. If luck were truly on my side, they'd assume I'd been killed.

Hope filled me for the first time since the incident that ripped my life apart.

A bang sounded outside the room. Something slammed against the door again.

I backed up, anticipation stretching the moment taut.

"Get behind me!" I shoved Martin back, watching the only way in or out of the tiny room.

Another boom vibrated through the door.

"W-What is it?" Martin's voice ended in a terrified squeak.

The door flew open with a crash of sound, the outside world pouring in as screams and gunfire assaulted my senses.

A figure roared in the doorway, eyes glowing blood-red from a narrow face.

I flinched at the disorienting sounds of war but kept my fighting stance. Adrenaline flooded my veins, heightening my focus on the danger.

One of my old test subjects, the skeletal fear demon, licked his lips, eyeing me like his next meal.

He took a step forward, and I tensed to attack, but he jerked still. Something burst from his middle. It took a second to recognise the spike-tipped tail protruding from the groaning demon.

The tail yanked back, and the demon crumpled to the ground.

A horned figure waited, silhouetted in the doorway. Spikes decorated broad shoulders, and a familiar sneer sent my pulse fluttering in panic.

The living shadow stepped over his victim into the lab, a look of triumph on his bloodied face. Bright splashes of red covered him from head to toe, along with deep lacerations through charcoal skin. No scratched metal ringed his throat.

His eyes glowed white-hot as his gaze clashed with mine.

A cruel smile twisted split lips. "Hello, poison."

Chapter 24

"S in," I croaked.

He was free.

And I was about to die.

"So good of you to wait for me, poison. Oh look, and you finally brought me that squeaky toy you promised." The demon grinned, all teeth and bad intentions.

He darted forward, and I threw a jab, but too many days without proper nutrition had made me slow. My knuckles brushed the side of his cheek as he dodged the sloppy attack and stepped past me like I posed no threat at all.

A scream pierced the lab.

Something warm wrapped my throat, pulling tight. I grabbed the heated rope as I stumbled back.

No, not rope. His *tail*.

The smooth heart-shaped tip, dripping warm blood, came to rest against my cheek. I watched in horror from the corner of my eye as pearlescent spikes slid back out from the entire mass, pricking my skin in warning.

I stilled, unable to move. Hardly able to breathe.

A low tutting sounded. "No, no. Squeaky toys are higher pitched. Let's try that again."

Martin shrieked behind me. The shrill bleat shot terror into my heart.

Dark spots patterned the edge of my vision, covering the gleaming spikes in my periphery. My hands spasmed around Sin's thick tail, fighting to keep some tendrils of air squeezing through my throat.

Another wave of dizziness crashed over me, but whether it was from the choking or the starvation, I couldn't tell.

Ironically, Sin's hold was the only thing that stopped me from falling.

"Better." A dark chuckle haunted the room.

With a sharp tug, Sin's lethal tail twisted me to face the violent scene.

Martin dangled from Sin's grip, legs kicking uselessly as the demon choked him with a single hand and impossible strength. My boss's arms drooped oddly inside his lab coat sleeves.

"Let him go," I croaked, voice barely audible over the scientist's distressed gurgles.

"Another dead hunter…" Sin smirked up at his thrashing victim before eyeing me over his spiked shoulder. "You look good collared for me, poison."

"Sin," I hissed. Fury loosened the shock holding me captive. "Don't do this."

I hated Martin—for all he'd done to the beings trapped here—but I still didn't want to watch him suffer like this.

The demon drew his prey closer, baring his fangs.

He shoved his thumb under Martin's jaw, snapping his neck to an unnatural angle. Martin fell limp like a marionette with its string cut.

"But it's so much fun." Sin's smirk was pure evil, malice dripping as thickly as the blood from his wounds.

With all the damage etched into his flesh, he should have bitten Martin. The fresh blood would have helped him heal.

So why didn't he?

My eyes narrowed on the demon.

I supposed his eating habits didn't matter to me anymore, since I was about to become another mad scientist with a snapped neck.

I wanted to rage at the injustice. Freedom was finally within my grasp, and Sin was going to take that from me along with my miserable life.

But for all the things I'd done, maybe I deserved it.

Dread curdled my stomach, but I tightened my grip on Sin's tail at my throat as I prepared to fight until my last bitter breath anyway. "Fuck you, parasite. If you're going to kill me, get on with it."

"Ah, my sweet poison. You're not getting away from me that easily." He smirked, drawing me in with his tail until a mere whisper separated us. "I made you a promise. I'm going to toy with you endlessly. You're not allowed to die until I let you."

He yanked me flush against him. Solid heat radiated through my clothes to warm my skin. My chest brushed his with every rapid breath I took.

Nothing could have prepared me for being this close, no safety glass between us.

He towered over me, easily twice my width, a dark nightmare stacked with muscle and natural weaponry, highlighting how weak and thin I was. Power rolled off him in waves, the heat and vitality of the monster before me overwhelming.

The scent of leather and mandarin filtered in over the tang of blood. Usually the alluring citrus scent shoved me into high alert, but for some reason, on my enemy, it made my mouth water.

"Parasite...," I murmured, unsure where he was going with this.

Starlit eyes dipped to my parted lips. "Yes, poison?"

"What the hell are you doing?"

He grinned. "Finally taking what I want."

His mouth crashed against mine, all feral need and punishment. He nipped my lower lip, and blood bloomed through the kiss, metallic and dark, matching the ferocity with which he dominated. He lapped at the slight cut, adding to the sting.

A groan shook his chest, vibrating through mine. He forced his way inside, sweeping past my defences. I startled as the forked tip of his tongue tangled against mine. The heady taste of him scrambled all thoughts.

He ripped away, leaving me panting and dizzy and more confused than ever. Glowing eyes seemed to search my face, though I had no idea what the psycho might have been looking for.

A familiar sneer curved his lips, slightly swollen from the fierce kiss. "Even your lips taste like poison."

I scoffed, "Fuck you, Sin."

His tail tightened at my throat, eyes flaring with dark promise. "Not yet."

Dizziness had me slumping heavily against his chest as my breathing shallowed. Blackness swam over me, fuzzing out the world.

"Liliana!" Sin's urgent voice filtered through the rushing in my ears I hadn't noticed.

I blinked, realising my face was pressed against his charcoal skin, smeared in blood. For a second, I worried it was mine, but a hand on my shoulder eased me back until I was gazing up at the familiar face of my enemy.

Something like worry creased his features, but it was gone before I could fully identify it. Instead, narrowed eyes told me he despised the weak creature before him.

"Stop passing out." His sharp words were designed to cut.

I snorted, instantly regretting the action as another wave of dizziness hit me. "Pretty hard when you're half-starved and being forced to feed a parasite."

"Pathetic." His upper lip curled in disgust. "I'd have liked to drag you out of here by your tiny neck, but I suppose I'll have to carry my frail captive instead."

My lips parted to snipe back, but before I could get a word out, his arms hooked under my back and knees, lifting me bridal-style. His strength engulfed me, making me feel tiny as he cradled me against his chest. For some bizarre reason, being surrounded by all his pointy edges left me feeling safer.

The fear his kiss had stolen came rushing back as I realised what he intended.

He was *leaving* and taking me with him.

"Put me down!" I hissed.

This was not how I thought I'd escape my uncle. A body bag would have been more likely.

Sin stepped heavily over Martin and the fear demon, like the men he murdered were nothing but litter on the street. He carried me out of the lab, limping slightly from the wounds across his legs.

Reality pressed down, and I thrashed hard. Never go where a demon wanted to take you.

I'd probably end up in hell.

"Sin, you vile beast, put me down!" I snarled, knocking my glasses askew as I fought his hold.

The bastard grinned down at me viciously, not pausing his long strides. His arms tightened, squeezing me against his chest.

We weren't alone in the hallway.

The long lilac hair and matching purple eyes were a dead giveaway. The young woman gawking at us was a mage, but she looked healthy enough that I knew she wasn't another captive.

"Thanks for the rescue," Sin grunted, barrelling past the startled witch. "Sorry I couldn't stick around for all the fun!"

He raced up the stairs, and the stench of blood hit me before we reached the top. Snarls and growls layered through the cavernous warehouse, pierced by the odd scream.

Hellhounds and hell-mutts, their half-canine offspring, battled in a sea of black fur and colourful flames. Carnage reigned. Bodies littered the concrete. Human. Demon. Hound.

"Fuck." The curse fell as a strangled wheeze.

Sin broke into a run, holding me tight as he skirted the violence, snarling at anything that came too close.

A hell-mutt the size of a Shetland pony leaped for me, jaws headed right for my face.

I opened my mouth to scream, but Sin's spiked tail slammed into the beast, knocking it off course with a canine yelp.

My hands fisted in my lab coat, arms trapped to my sides by the monster smuggling me through the chaos.

We reached the back of the compound and burst out through the mangled vehicle shutters, like some giant beast had torn through it.

Moonlight bathed the remains of hunters littering the parking lot, and I looked away before I could recognise any severed heads.

I had enough nightmares.

Sin breathed deep, squeezing me tight against his chest. "Ah, finally free." He peered down at me trapped in his arms. His signature cruel smirk sharpened his expression. "But you're not."

Chapter 25

"Bad demon, put me down!" I hissed, thrashing in Sin's iron hold for the hundredth useless time.

He grinned, wicked fangs looming in my vision. "No."

Sin had run through the shadowed streets of Riverside for what felt like hours, leaving behind the industrial estate and skirting the city centre to plunge into the quieter housing districts.

He carried me like I weighed nothing, despite the deep lacerations in his torso that had long ago seeped through my lab coat and top to soak my skin.

Clearly, the demon was in a terrible state, limping slightly and everything, but he hadn't so much as grunted in pain once.

Stubborn bastard.

"You'd better not be dragging me off to some dingy lair," I muttered.

He scoffed. "I don't just take any captive to my lair."

I snorted, immediately annoyed at myself for finding anything about him amusing. "So you have no idea where you're going, then?"

The steady cadence of his quiet footfalls tried to lull my exhausted body into sleep. Since the adrenaline from the attack had faded hours ago, I had nothing left keeping my eyes open except fear and determination.

I would *not* take a nap in my enemy's arms.

The hunters already called me Dozer.

My heart squeezed as questions plagued me. What had happened to hunter HQ? Had anyone else survived? Was Leo dead? My uncle?

Guilt churned my gut. I wouldn't mourn either of them. What kind of callous monster did that make me?

I supposed I had bigger problems than my faulty moral compass.

Like being kidnapped by a demon.

Plus, with dawn peeking between the detached homes, a charcoal-coloured demon covered in spikes and blood was bound to draw a few raised brows from anyone unlucky enough to glance out their windows.

"Sin, you can't be seen like this," I said, trying to keep my tone level. Maybe if I pretended I wasn't a frail captive, he'd treat me with more respect.

The general population couldn't know about demonkind. Not yet. And not like this. It would create mass panic, and so very many deaths.

On both sides.

He shot me a glare before going back to aggressively ignoring my wishes in typical Sin fashion. The demon ran for another few minutes with me in his arms, scanning the suburban street.

I craned my neck, trying my best to copy him. After all, he wasn't the only one with people out to get him.

"What are you even looking for?" I asked, caving under the tense silence.

"That's not your concern, poison." His attention snagged on something up ahead, and a smirk curved his lips. "But it's about to be."

He sped up, and I clung to his arms as best I could in case he was planning to drop me. He turned off the pavement, heading up a long driveway towards a generous detached house with a for-sale sign pitched outside.

Skirting the brick structure, he took us right up to the side gate. His tail shot out, punching the lock. A bang sounded as the fence door flew open, but his tail snapped up to catch it. I winced at all the commotion, but there was nothing I could do as Sin strolled into someone's manicured garden, weaving through a patio laden with rattan furniture, heading for the back door.

"Sin… What are you doing? You're not about to kill some innocent family, right?" I hissed, a very real fear settling deep into my bones.

I'd had my fill of bloodshed, but I wouldn't stand idly by and watch him tear apart whoever had the misfortune of living here. Adrenaline flooded my veins as I thought about trying to fight him unarmed, my body weak from starvation.

He might bleed from multiple wounds, but I was the one closer to death.

The demon eyed me for a moment, lips pursing in mock contemplation. "And just what would you do if I was, poison?"

"You wouldn't live to find out," I sneered.

But we both knew I was at his mercy. The smug bastard fucking loved it.

"Ever the fierce hunter," he taunted, unfazed by the threat. "Now shut that pretty little mouth of yours before I find another use for it. I already know how good you feel. Don't tempt me into another round just yet."

I almost choked on my tongue, covering the slip by baring a feral grin. "Try it, parasite. You're not the only one with teeth."

He smirked. "Promises, promises."

I narrowed my eyes but kept quiet, straining to hear any movement from inside the darkened house.

Everything was silent, but at the crack of dawn, most people would be tucked up in their beds, safe and sound.

Sin eyed the wood-grain door, peering through the glass panel, then scanned the surrounding area. His tail dived under the mat, flipping it to reveal a brassy key.

"Humans," he scoffed, tail scooping it up and passing it into his waiting hand.

As if I weighed nothing, he transferred me to one arm as he unlocked the door, opened it, and stepped into the open-plan kitchen.

I listened for any hint of someone being home, but the place was as silent as a tomb and perfectly clean. No dishes waited by the sink. No splatters of sauce on the cooker. Not even a stained tea-towel hanging from the oven handle.

Sin strode through the house, passing through the corridor and up the stairs. I peered into each room we passed, holding my breath for signs of life but coming up mercifully empty.

He strode into the first room, and the sight of the king-size bed made me squirm in his hold once more. My heart thudded as I evaluated the space, looking for anything that might help me fight back.

A door sat ajar in the corner, revealing the glimpse of an en suite. Double-glazed windows dominated one side of the room, showing the oncoming dawn in warm shades of pink. An enormous built-in wardrobe covered the opposite wall, but the neatly made bed dominated the space—a soft, inviting trap of cotton sheets and fluffy pillows in a gentle sage, complete with a Jacquard silk throw that screamed luxury.

At least nobody was currently sleeping in it for Sin to murder.

The demon set me on my feet, my side pressed against his front. Dizziness gripped me for an embarrassing moment as I leaned heavily into him, locking my legs to keep from collapsing.

He tipped his horns towards the bed. "Get in."

My lips parted. "What? I'm not getting into bed with you."

He quirked a pale brow, a smirk playing at his lips. "Poison... You don't make the rules anymore. You're my captive now, and I'm telling you... Get. In. The. Fucking. Bed."

Each word was punctuated with the sway of his deadly tail over his broad, spiked shoulders.

I swallowed thickly, feeling the implied "or else" right down to my tarnished soul.

But I'd had enough of domineering men telling me what to do.

I lifted my chin, staying rooted to the spot.

Sin chuckled, a low sound that had no right to do the things it did to me. "You don't want to bait me right now, poison. I'm not exactly in the best state. My patience is slipping."

Clearly, I had faulty self-preservation instincts, because I just couldn't resist.

I quirked a brow. "This is you being patient?"

He bared his fangs and lunged.

I had a second to throw an elbow towards his face, but my weak body betrayed me, barely grazing his cheek before he shoved me back onto the bed. The world spun as his weight settled on top of me, pressing me into the mattress.

He gripped my wrists in one hand, lifting my arms over my head to shove against the pillow.

A snarl contorted his features, sending a jolt of fear through me.

"Do it, parasite. Stop fucking about and do it," I hissed. "You want me dead, remember?"

I was so damn tired of waiting for the blow to come. I'd lived most of my life waiting for the next hit, and I refused to do it for a psychotic blood demon now.

Anger lit his features. "You have no idea what I want."

His tail flattened against my cheek, shoving my face aside along with the confusion. Thankfully, his spikes had disappeared again.

"You should know…" His lips pressed against the delicate skin of my throat, drawing a shiver from me. "When a blood demon feeds on the same person over and over, a connection can start to form," he whispered. "A special kind of attachment with the one person who could be their everything. A blood bond."

I went rigid at his words. At the implications of what I'd unknowingly started. I'd never heard of a blood bond. What did it mean? What did it do?

Before I could voice my racing thoughts, he continued. "Even though it's not fully formed yet, I'll always be able to find you, poison. No matter where you run off to. You're mine."

He gave me a single second for his warning to sink in.

Fangs pierced my bared throat, the sensation so familiar, yet so different. Having all that powerful male on top of me as he bit my neck was too intimate. Heat rushed through my veins.

I braced.

But it turned to a soothing warmth, not the pain I'd have expected now I was fully at his mercy. Now I was his prisoner instead of him as mine.

"What are you…?" My voice trailed off, slurred even to my own ears.

The exposed ceiling beams blurred, making me dizzy.

Fangs quickly left my flesh, and his forked tongue traced the marks, oddly gentle.

Soft lips ghosted against the wound he'd inflicted. "Sleep, poison. You're safe."

For now.

It was the last thought I had before drifting off.

Chapter 26

The smell of cooking bacon roused me from sleep, rather than the usual echo of my own cries.

My mouth watered before I'd even cracked my eyes open, and my stomach growled so fiercely a hellhound would have tucked tail and run.

A smile played at my lips before a yawn robbed the expression.

"Mmm." I snugged deeper into the blankets wrapped around me, relishing the rare treat.

Leo never woke up before me, if he even stayed the night, and he'd certainly never cooked me breakfast before. As annoying as I found his insistence on traditional gender roles, he claimed he wasn't a great cook, anyway. The gesture this morning was unexpectedly sweet.

Birds chirped, singing a happy little song to complement the best start to a day I'd had in...I couldn't even remember how long.

Wait. Birds?

I lived in a shitty high-rise that took me too many floors up with no balconies for there to be nesting birds... And I'd dumped that betraying bastard weeks ago.

My eyes flew open. I bolted upright, taking in the slightly blurry unfamiliar room. Memories of yesterday came crashing back.

The attack on hunter HQ. Sin saving me from a demon. Him killing Martin. Capturing me. Being carried through the streets. Breaking into an empty home.

The demon forcing me into bed. Fangs in my throat.

My heart pounded in time with my racing thoughts.

I had to run. Get away from the psycho demon before he could kill me.

After what I'd done to him, I couldn't blame him for hating me. Even if there was some unnerving heat that flared between us, and whatever possessive insanity that was driving him to.

My glasses rested on the nightstand, though I didn't remember taking them off before passing out. I quickly shoved them on, ignoring the slick crack through one side as the room sharpened into focus.

I threw the covers off and breathed a sigh of relief. My clothes were perfectly intact, the long knit dress tangled around my thighs.

My blood-splattered lab coat was folded on the snug arm-chair, and I didn't know what to make of the idea that the vicious demon had taken it off me while I slept.

I shoved on my sensible trainers, waiting neatly for me on the plush carpet, and hurried to the window, pulling open the curtains to reveal the low-slung sun, illuminating the rosebushes that bordered the garden.

It was either dawn or dusk, and I prayed for the former. The thought of any amount of time unconscious and vulnerable to the demon left me on edge, but an entire day was unfathomable.

Why would he have left me to catch up on sleep? Or even kept me alive and unharmed this long?

I didn't trust it one bit.

I eased the window open.

"If you think to jump out of the window, poison, know that I'll be fangs-deep before you've taken a single step onto the grass."

I stilled at the masculine rumble coming from downstairs. I was all too aware of how fast demons were. Sin wasn't being cocky. The smug prick could back up his threat, and I didn't want to give him an excuse to hurt me.

He had enough already.

"Demons and their fucking spidey senses," I muttered, slamming the window closed.

Years of training had meant I'd moved in near silence. Had he really heard me from a different floor of the house? Or was it down to whatever *bond* he mentioned last night?

It didn't matter what bloody connection he thought was forming. I was already on the run. A demon wasn't going to chase me any further around the globe than my controlling uncle.

Once more, I sent up a silent prayer that the grizzled bastard was dead.

Taking one last look at the freedom beckoning me outside, I left the room, running my fingertips over the soft sheets one more time as I passed the bed.

I quickly searched the other rooms I passed down the corridor, holding my breath in the hopes I wouldn't find any corpses. The other three bedrooms were cosy, holding cute knickknacks on tidy bedside tables and framed art on feature walls. You could feel the warmth in the plush throw pillows and scented candles already burned part-way.

A pang of longing hit me so hard I could barely breathe.

Each room appeared lived in but empty, and just as neat as the master bedroom I'd slept in. Whoever owned the house must be away, and I let out a relieved exhale. Some innocent human family had been spared.

I made my way downstairs, ignoring the smiling faces watching from photo frames along the stairway. Claws raked at the hollow longing I was desperately trying to smother.

Depending on how long I'd slept, today should have been my wedding day.

If Leo weren't such a colossal arsehole, would I have ended up in a gorgeous home like this? Would I have started my own family, in a haven away from the violence of hunter life? Would we all be smiling at a camera, radiating enough joy to choke strangers?

The happy pictures blurred, and I blinked rapidly, shoving down the emotions trying to leak out. With every step, I rebuilt my armour, donning the blank shell and hardening it into place.

I followed the tantalising scent of food into the modern kitchen. My stomach grumbled, reminding me that the last time I'd eaten was over a day ago.

I stilled at the bizarre sight.

A familiar grey demon stood in profile, a line of vicious spikes running along his vertebrae. The same bony weapons protruded from his shoulders and elbows, warning me not to approach.

Low-slung joggers hugged his hips, straining around powerful thighs and stopping short mid-calf. His tail poked through a slit cut just under the waistband. It should have looked ridiculous, but if anything, it only highlighted the sheer size of the monster.

The wounds from yesterday were practically healed, only thin pink slashes interrupting the white tattoos covering his muscular torso.

But it was what he *did* that rendered me speechless.

Sin held a pair of tongs in one hand, casually turning pieces of bacon in a frying pan. A steel pot rested on the cooker, small flames licking its base as something simmered inside.

Not bothering to look up, he tipped his horns aside, pointing to the dining table I'd yet to notice. "Sit down before you fall down, poison. It's almost ready."

For a moment, I considered launching myself at him while his back was turned, and finding out whether a steel pan was tougher than that square jaw. The wicked spikes jutting from his spine were a warning that he was deadly from all angles though.

His tail curved upwards, snagging my gaze. The heart-shaped tip was a slightly darker shade than the rest of his charcoal skin, and it pointed to a chair, silently repeating his command.

I rolled my eyes but grabbed a seat at the polished oak table, watching the demon in fascination. "Am I dead? Is hell watching the most irritating demon cook for himself?"

Sin turned, showing off his angular features in the soft light that streamed through the windows.

A smirk graced his pouty lips. "No, poison, but I'll take you as close to heaven as a sinner like you could get."

I crossed my arms, lacing my tone with a heavy dose of scepticism. "Since I've never had a real home, I'm sure heaven would involve me waking up in my dream house"—I gestured around the luxurious kitchen that would be wasted on my paltry culinary skills—"but it sure as hell wouldn't have a monster lurking inside."

Pity flashed across his features before he gave me his back once more.

Bands squeezed my chest as I realised what I'd just admitted. He probably thought I was even more pathetic now.

The demon lifted the cooked bacon from the pan, chopping it into pieces before adding it to the larger saucepan.

A stoneware bowl waited on the counter beside him, and he stirred the pot one last time before serving up whatever was in the pan, broad frame blocking my view.

My stomach growled again, reminding me I wasn't dead yet. Though watching a demon cook and eat while I slowly starved would be its own form of torture.

Or poetic justice.

Sin returned the pot and carried the bowl over, setting it before me.

My lips parted as I stared down at the food he'd brought me.

But not just any food.

My *favourite* food.

The demon had cooked me a rigatoni carbonara, complete with crispy bacon and a mini mountain of parmesan.

My heart kicked in my chest, something akin to panic lancing through me. "I... You... What the fuck is this?"

Pale stars twinkled with mirth as our gazes clashed. For some horrifying reason, my eyes burned as a mix of emotions bubbled up.

He quirked a horned brow, lips twitching. "And here I thought you were meant to be smart."

His verbal jab pierced the overwhelming feeling, and I shot him a flat look, secretly grateful. The demonic bastard would never cease baiting me.

"Why is there a bowl of pasta in front of me?" I drew the words out, like slowing them down might help him understand why this was a valid question.

"To eat." He drew his out too, loaded with even more mocking.

I frowned, trying to examine his stupidly carved features for any hint of motive.

He huffed, grabbing the fork he'd placed beside my bowl and aggressively spearing a rigatoni tube before taking a bite. His hard jaw worked and the long column of his throat bobbed as he swallowed.

I couldn't have looked away, even if my uncle was roaring at me with a cocked fist.

The demon stared at me with enough scrutiny to make me blush. "Just because you're poison doesn't mean everything else is."

I glanced away, unable to handle his intensity. Instead, I took the fork from his hand, ignoring the brush of his fingers against mine, and dug in to the food.

A moan slipped free with the first mouthful. Creamy perfection. Soft pasta with a little crunch of bacon and pure cheesy goodness.

Sin inhaled sharply before fetching himself a bowl and returning to sit opposite me. For my own sanity, I mentally blocked him out and enjoyed the first proper meal I'd had in weeks.

It was everything I'd been craving.

And a *demon* had cooked it for me.

Not just any demon. One I'd kept captive, tried to poison, and been far too intimate with and that had now kidnapped me.

Silence settled between us as I inhaled the food, polishing it off too quick when a meal this good deserved to be savoured.

The dangerous company should have robbed me of my appetite, but who knew when I'd next get to eat?

And I loved carbonara enough that I could easily devour it for breakfast.

"You know, this isn't usually a morning meal for humans," I said, finishing the last bite with a mournful look at the empty dish.

"I'm aware," he drawled. "Your kind has always fascinated me, and I was in the process of moving here when I was unwittingly volunteered as your lab rat."

My brows hit my hairline.

Sin was trying to live here in the human realm? The idea of him owning a home like this and dressing in a suit to commute to work seemed absurd. More than likely, he'd be some seedy crime boss in a villain's lair, somewhere on the bad side of town.

A dark chuckle smoothed over me, distracting me from the bizarre mental image. "Plus, it's the evening. You've been asleep for over fifteen hours. I even had time to pick up groceries."

Without comment, he grabbed my empty bowl and swapped it for his.

A lump formed in my throat as his words sank in alongside his actions. Not only had he left me to sleep all day, but he'd gone out and somehow bought supplies. For my favourite meal.

Thinking back, it was the only food I'd mentioned in front of him.

I struggled to make sense of that information. Why would a demon I'd been trying to poison care about feeding me at all, let alone feeding me something I'd love?

Everything about the situation bugged me.

I scowled. "How would a demon even know what pasta is?"

Another one of those husky, mocking chuckles filled the kitchen as he eased back in his chair. "We do eat food in hell. You think we haven't taken some of the good things about humanity for our own?"

Even as hunters, we knew hardly anything about their realm or culture. Until recently, my life had revolved around how to kill demons, not cook for them. I'd learned a few snippets of information from Fane but nowhere near enough.

Nagging curiosity itched at my brain.

"Tell me about hell," I blurted the words before I could think better of it.

The demon considered me in drawn-out silence, and I fought not to squirm.

"You eat, I'll talk." He jerked his chin at his full bowl sitting before me.

It had been a long time since anybody had tried to feed me. If anything, I was more used to being purposefully starved.

I stabbed a tiny piece of bacon, lifting it to my mouth in silent acquiescence.

"Hell is a wilder version of your realm. Forests dominate, but we also have rich seas, barren deserts and vast grasslands. Most live in one of the many kingdoms, usually forming cities with a single type of demon, but there are hybrids too." He shrugged. "Life is chaotic and cruel, yet beautiful at the same time." His eyes raked over me with unexpected heat. "I'm starting to realise there might be more of that here than I thought."

My gaze dropped at his flirtatious insinuation. I'd stopped eating to listen to him talk, and I carried on with my meal, making quick work of his food as I searched for my voice.

"If hell is so great, then why would you move here?" I asked, surprised at how much I needed the answer.

His fingers reached up, massaging at his left shoulder, the one that held the depiction of a sun. "Family."

I looked away, an oily sensation turning my stomach. "Aren't you hungry?"

His lips twitched. "I am, but since I've just fed you, I'm sure you'll return the favour."

I almost choked on my pasta.

Chapter 27

Reality seeped into the surreal domestic scene. I eyed the demon seated across the dining table, his corded arms draping the backs of the fragile chairs on either side of him.

"What are you doing, Sin?" I carefully lowered my fork. "Why did you take me instead of killing me like you threatened so many times? Is it your weird bond thingy?"

A familiar, cruel smirk graced his features. "Whatever sorry excuse for a life you had is over. You're mine now."

I scowled back. "So you thought you'd take your food to-go?"

His shoulder spikes stabbed the air in a shrug, the casual gesture infuriating. Was my life always going to be worth so little?

I squeezed the fork, letting the metal dig into my palm. "Developed a taste for poison? Is that it?"

"Not all poison. Just the bitter nectar running through your veins," he sneered.

In a burst of movement, his hand fisted my hair and dragged me off my seat. His tail lashed around my middle, yanking me over the dining table. Porcelain shattered as bowls knocked to the floor.

I stabbed with the fork, but he batted it away before it could sink into his bicep.

The demon sprawled me across him, and I gasped, barely catching myself on his chest instead of impaling my hands on his shoulder spikes.

He yanked my head aside until my scalp ached from the strain.

Laughter filled the kitchen, as sharp as the claws grazing my skin.

The monster dipped to my exposed throat, lips hovering over my racing pulse.

"Sin...," I whispered, afraid to trigger the predator trapping me in his cruel grip.

"Yes, poison?" He pressed a kiss to my neck, causing a shiver to run the length of my body at the threat lurking behind the softness.

"What are you doing?" I squirmed in his grip. The feel of his heated body beneath me was overwhelming, and I longed to put him back behind the glass of my lab.

He was too real now. Too warm. Too strong. Too dangerous.

His arm hooked around my lower back, bringing me up to straddle his lap fully. Hardness pressed right against my core, shooting my eyes wide with alarm. My breathing turned erratic at the feel of him, of his monstrous length that I knew far too intimately, considering he was a *demon*.

Even sitting on him, I had to tip my head back to meet his piercing gaze. The stars around each of his pupils shimmered, trying to mesmerise me as much as the feel of his body.

I was completely at his mercy, and although I hated it, part of me begged to see where this wild ride would take me.

That part was a dumb, horny bitch.

"Sin," I warned. "Whatever you're planning...don't."

He smirked. "Since you ate my dinner, it's only right I eat you."

He lunged, fangs sinking into my throat with a sharp sting as familiar as breathing. Pain melted into bliss, warming my veins with liquid pleasure that dripped straight to my core.

"Oh, fuck, Sin," I moaned, unable to stop my hips from rolling, pressing my core against the hardness he offered.

Hands tightened in my hair, adding an ache to spice the pleasure of his bite.

His fangs slid free, and I instantly mourned their loss.

"That's it, poison." His words feathered across my throat. "Take your pleasure while I take you."

I moaned as his forked tongue trailed up my neck, catching the blood running down my skin. His hot mouth returned to the bite wound, sealing against it and pulling more of that reckless pleasure through my veins.

I couldn't catch the needy little sounds that fell from my lips as I writhed in his lap. The steely length of him rubbed against me in the most maddening way. I hated how much I craved the sensation.

His hand splayed across my lower back, encouraging me with claws pricking through my dress. He growled, and the vibrations somehow rumbled right down to my clit.

Just as I thought he'd let me shatter, the demon pulled away, mouth hovering just far enough that I could feel his warm breath teasing my skin.

I hissed a sharp sound of frustration, reaching up to tug on his smooth horns, but his face didn't budge.

"Sin, you cruel bastard. If you're going back to this teasing bullshit, I'll find a new way to choke you to death."

I felt his smile against my sensitive throat, and his words peppered my skin. "I wanted dessert too."

Before I could process his meaning, he lifted my hips, setting me on the dining table. His long tail held me in place as he tore my dress down the middle with a loud rip.

He yanked my soaked panties off next, throwing them aside and baring my heated core to his hungry gaze. Sharp claws dug into my thighs as he spread me wide.

I blushed, chest heaving as I watched the demon expose me. "Sin..."

Starlit eyes met mine. A cruel smirk played at his lips, and I knew I was in trouble. "You wanted to choke me, poison? Drown me with your sweetness. If I die, at least you'll be the last thing I see."

He attacked in the next breath. Leaning forward in his chair and spearing me with his forked tongue. Hot and thick and everything I needed.

The monster feasted on me at the table like a man starved.

My head fell back as he tongue-fucked me, thick length thrusting deep and writhing like a damn vibrator. The flexible base rubbed wetly at my clit with his upper lip, driving my hips off the table as I bucked and writhed.

He growled inside me, and I screamed, shattering apart on the kitchen table. He didn't stop, snarling as he devoured me whole. The dangerous edge of his fangs against my skin only driving me higher.

Pleasure roiled through me in waves, spilling unintelligible noises from my lips. My hands slid through silken strands to find the cool ivory of his curved horns. I pushed him away as my orgasm waned, leaving me twitching on the table, hyper-sensitive from his attentions.

He growled, giving my pussy one last firm lick that wrung another moan from me.

The screech of a chair had my eyes flying open.

Sin loomed over me, eyes raking my bare flesh. They glowed white-hot, framed by pale lashes that matched the silvery strands falling into his face. Bared fangs dripped clear venom while my pleasure glistened across his full lips.

He'd laid me out on the table like a sacrifice on his altar.

And I wanted the devil to take me.

"Is that all you've got?" I chuckled, low and husky from screaming my pleasure. "I thought you were meant to be a demon."

If I was going to play with demons, I might as well truly sin.

He tipped his horns back, cruel laughter giving the darkening kitchen a sinister edge. "Oh sweet poison, you have no idea what you're asking for, but I can't wait to make you regret it."

He shoved his trousers down, kicking them aside as he freed the monster I'd been craving ever since that first taste.

His jewel-studded cock jutted forward, already seeping pearly liquid for me. The thick length was easily the size of his forearm, and apprehension swirled through the bliss and hunger.

My core clenched in vicious need at the formidable sight.

He lined himself up, pointed head notching inside my entrance. Just that alone stretched me enough to suck in a gasp. Part-fear, part-need.

He hooked his claws under my thighs, digging in sharp enough to draw a hiss from me.

But he didn't thrust inside me like I needed.

His eyes bored into me, instead, seeming to reach deeper than should be possible, until something *more* passed between us.

That one look unnerved me more than all the venomous threats he'd delivered before. That heat in my chest returned, burning like coal beside my heart.

I sneered, desperate to break the strange tension. "Fuck me like you hate me, Sin."

He smirked back, just as vicious. "I do."

The demon yanked me down onto his length, and I screamed.

The stretch burned my core in the most delicious way, pain flirting with pleasure. He gave me a single beat to adjust, his sharp features transformed with a look of pure rapture.

My reprieve was over in an instant.

He drew back, and thrust in, sliding me across the table with the force. Stinging claws curled into my thighs and his tail strangled my waist, holding me down as he unleashed his fury on my body.

The hot drag of his textured cock against my inner walls was like nothing I'd felt before.

Sensation overwhelmed me. Heat from his venom still flooded my veins, burning me from the inside out. But his pre-cum was like liquid fire, coating my inner walls as he pounded into me.

I moaned as he fucked me like a beast, urging him on.

He snarled, lifting one of my legs over his forearm to deepen the angle. I hissed at the feel of him bottoming out inside me, my hands finding his arms to scratch at him, punishing him back even as I was desperate for more.

His claws raked the wood beside my face, and he growled, fucking me harder and faster.

The table shook with force.

"Take. It. My. Little. Slut." Each word was snarled with a thrust of his hips.

Pleasure drenched me, saturating every part of my being until I could hardly think through the bliss.

"Is. It. Even. In. Yet?" I hissed back.

His unhinged laugh slithered between us, and he upped his ferocity.

My brain rattled from the onslaught, but I couldn't care less as I moaned and cursed him in equal measure.

He leaned down, and his fangs sliced into my breast, either side of my nipple. Fire shot through my chest in a blinding line of pleasure.

His smooth tail slid from beneath my waist, gliding over my stomach and hips to rub at my clit.

I moaned, overloaded with sensation. The feel of his cock knocking all sense loose as I raced towards something immense.

"More!" I slammed my nails into his back, clawing at him like a beast.

The monster obeyed.

Sin bit harder at my breast, rubbed faster at my clit and smashed his cock so deep he punished my cervix.

It was everything I needed.

"Liliana," he snarled against my nipple. "Break for me."

I detonated, pleasure exploding through me in a violent torrent. Screaming registered, but bliss hazed the world as I thrashed, body bowing for him.

His cock swelled, pulsing heat as he roared. Cum filled me in heated lashes I felt like a brand inside me.

Something pressed into my front inner walls, and my eyes shot wide. I gasped as his movements slowed to a rocking motion.

He throbbed inside me, more hot liquid filling me up, but he stayed lodged deep, something...*extra* holding him there.

"Oh my god," I slurred, remembering his threat from before. "Barb!?"

He grinned down, vicious and cruel, even as he panted just as hard as me. "Yes, poison. I made you a promise, didn't I? My barb is going to make your pussy strangle my cock while I fill you up."

I swallowed thickly. My core clenched reflexively, and the barb pressed forward. His cock pulsed, and I moaned as another wave of pleasure took me under.

I writhed on his cock, laid out over the table as he braced his hands on either side of my face, rocking into me hard enough to slide me across the table until my shoulders hit his tattooed wrists.

"Fuck, Liliana. Your pussy milks my cock so well. Are you desperate for more of my cum, pretty slut? Are you trying to make me mate you? Breed you?"

That cut through the haze.

"Are you fucking serious?" I hissed. "A demon can get a human pregnant?"

Why hadn't I thought of that before? I was such an idiot.

"Of course." He smirked, giving me a shallow thrust. "We are a compatible species, much to the devastation of your delicate hunter sensibilities, I'm sure."

"Get that monster dick out. Right. Fucking. Now." I sneered, swinging for his dumb face.

He dodged my fist with ease, mocking me with a low laugh that ended in a strangled groan as the sudden movements triggered another wave of bliss for us both. His cock throbbed, pumping even more heat into me as I fluttered around his textured length.

"My barb can only lock us together if you were a willing potential mate. The blood bond forming between us is proof of that. You're a scientist, you should know the biological purpose of fucking," he purred. Leaned down, he brought his lips to my ear. "And I'll let you in on a little secret, poison. I wouldn't pull out of your tight cunt even if I could. Our offspring would be both adorable and vicious, like you."

My elbow connected with the side of his fat head. "You bastard," I hissed. "If you get me pregnant, our poor child is going to be raised without a father, because I'm going to murder you."

But a secret part of me wondered what it would be like. I'd always wanted a family. Of course, I'd meant a *human* family. With a stable man who didn't threaten to snap my neck.

He growled, rocking deeply as more jets of cum spurted inside me. I moaned, cresting another orgasm as the sensation of being hot and full overwhelmed my shocked irritation.

I blinked, realising he was licking the blood dripping down my throat from his earlier bite.

He purred against my skin. "Say that again, poison. Promise to have my child in the same breath you threaten me."

"I didn't promise anything. You are fucking deluded," I snarled. "Now shut up and let a girl ride a dick in peace."

He chuckled, a husky, mocking sound that had me shivering. "You're not in charge anymore."

He yanked back so hard his barb popped free. I hissed at the sting, but the slice of sensation accompanied a rich gush of heat.

It pushed me right over the edge.

I writhed, vaguely aware of Sin wrapping his cock with his tail, stroking himself with it as he held my legs wide open beneath him, eyes raking over my body to rest at my spasming core.

Hot ropes lashed thickly against my lower lips as he came, roaring his pleasure loud enough to shake the table beneath me.

I whimpered, exhausted and spent as the world blurred lightly behind the dark demon looming above.

I should have been alarmed by his possessive declarations, and the fact he was apparently into breeding me, but I couldn't think about anything. Only feel. Bliss slipped through my veins. My body felt boneless as I relaxed under the demon, relishing the deep sense of satisfaction.

Sin cupped my face, forcing me to meet his glowing eyes as his clawed thumb stroked my cheek. "I'm going to turn you into a fucking addict. Just like you've done to me. Toxic doesn't even begin to describe this nightmare between us. You're mine, poison, and I'll never let you go."

Chapter 28

Great. It was less than twenty-four hours since I'd been kid-napped and I'd already fucked my captor.

Did Stockholm syndrome even work that fast?

Sin leaned down, covering my bare front with his, holding his weight up just enough to avoid crushing me. The press of his heated skin was decadent. Apparently he didn't care that his solid abs were now resting between my spread thighs, which he'd covered in his cum.

I panted, embarrassingly out of breath as I came down from the high Sin had shot me to. "You are such a parasite."

The demon's low chuckle vibrated through me where he pressed me into the table, face hovering inches from mine. "And yet you come so sweetly for me."

My tongue glued to the top of my mouth.

He dipped closer until his lips brushed my ear. "And I can't wait to prove it to you, over and over."

He would very literally be the death of me.

And yet I'd just lost my mind because of him.

"Go fuck yourself, Sin," I whispered, the ends of his pearlescent white hair tickling my lips.

He straightened, looming over his prey left sprawled on the dining table. Masculine satisfaction carved his striking features.

The pink scratches through his charcoal skin had now healed white, blending with the intricate strokes of his tattoos.

Because of what I'd let him take from me.

The blood donation had probably added to whatever bond bullshit he kept mentioning too.

Anger flared bright enough to eclipse all logic.

I crunched up and slammed my elbow into his cheek, feeling it connect with a thud that whipped his head aside.

My grin was feral. "You might have me, but not willingly."

In slow motion, he turned his face back towards me, a cruel smirk playing at his lips. The deliberate movement saturated with chilling threat. "And what makes you think I care?"

Right. *Demon*. Of course he didn't.

I narrowed my eyes on his smug face, wishing evil looked ugly on the outside rather than the deceptive package of the alluring monster trapping me. I'd sworn off violence, but somehow he brought out the vicious side of me I was trying to forget.

I braced for retaliation. There was no barrier to keep me safe now. No remote and collar.

"If you keep up with foreplay, poison, you'll make me late for my evening plans." He grinned, the violence in his putting mine to shame.

A measure of hope blossomed at his words. If he left me behind, no doubt chained up, at least I'd have a chance at escape.

Silence lingered as I gave him a neutral mask. The one I'd perfected over years of my uncle's idea of training.

The demon quirked a spiked brow. "Nothing to say to that, hmm? Or can you not trust yourself to speak in case those pretty lips start begging for more instead?"

My jaw clenched to hold back the scathing retort bubbling up in my throat.

He smirked, and from the cruel glint in his eye, I already knew I was going to hate what he did next. "Let's get ready then."

His arm slipped behind my lower back as he straightened, keeping me wrapped around his front and taking the tatters of my knit dress with me. He strode through the house with me pressed intimately against his rock-hard length. I was sensitive from the orgasms he'd ripped from me and dripping the evidence of both our pleasure, but I refused to let him see how easily he could make my body betray me, just like I refused to think about the unholy stamina he must have to *still* be hard.

"Put me down!" I hissed, trying in vain to thrash my way out of his unyielding arms.

His husky chuckle only made me fight harder.

The demon stalked into the bedroom I'd woken up in and unceremoniously dumped me onto the unmade bed.

I landed in a soft heap of sage blankets.

"What the fuck are you doing?" Scrambling free with a snarl, I fully ignored the fact my tits were out.

He quirked a silvery brow, eyes dipping to my chest briefly. "Giving in to your demands."

"I should have choked you more when I had the chance," I huffed, pushing my hair back from where it had fallen into my face and straightening my glasses.

He shrugged, those imposing shoulder spikes stabbing the air. "Probably. Now, get dressed. I got you an outfit so you don't draw undue attention."

Disappointment hit as I realised he intended to take me with him. But perhaps I could work with this. If he had plans, he might become distracted enough for me to slip through his claws.

He reached into the wardrobe and plucked out one of those posh, glossy bags made of cardboard. On the rare occasion I bought myself anything, it only ever came from somewhere doling out cheap plastic.

Sin dangled a scrap of material, the dark hue of lifeblood, from a pearly claw. "Put this on."

I bared my teeth, feeling more demonic than him. Until now, my life had consisted of nothing but bloody violence and bowing to demanding men. I was starting to realise I'd resort to a lot of the former to prevent the latter.

"Fuck you, Sin. I'm not doing a single thing for you."

Brute strength wouldn't save me though. If I wanted to live, I had to outsmart my captor.

I'd accepted going with him for a chance to escape, but it would look suspicious if I gave in to anything too easily.

We might have caved to the wild heat between us, but it changed nothing.

His lips twitched in that cruel way of his. "If you don't get yourself into this outfit, poison, I'll be doing it for you."

The thought of him dressing me, his hands all over my bare skin again, had me blushing and spitting mad in equal measure.

My upper lip curled. "I'd rather feed a hundred blood demons than have you touch me again."

Thunder clouded his expression, transforming with a deep well of rage he usually hid better than this.

Sin leaned down, pressing his spiked hands into the bed on either side of me, caging me in with his strength and every sharp point jutting from him. His face drew level with mine.

An intensity sparked in his eyes. "You. Are. Mine. Nobody else will know the taste of you."

Of course the only possessive man in my life was a demon after my blood.

"Fine." I snatched at the material trapped under his hand and he let me take it with an indulgent smirk. "But get out. I need to shower off all your disgusting juices first, and I'm not putting on a show for a demon."

"No?" He chuckled. "Yet you'll still scream for one like a good girl."

He caught my fist before I even knew I'd thrown a punch, and dropped it with a cluck of his forked tongue.

"You can shower, poison, but I know you'll be dripping my cum all night," he purred, flashing me a victorious grin.

Taking his sweet time, he finally trailed out. His heart tail waved almost sarcastically as he left me with my rage and the scrap of material.

With a huff, I ditched my torn dress and eyed the skimpy fabric like it might sprout fangs and take a bite. I made quick work of showering in the en suite, a pang of envy hitting me as I borrowed someone's fancy shampoo and matching conditioner. Some snooty French brand I definitely couldn't pronounce.

I couldn't remember the last time I'd actually conditioned my hair. The cheapest two-in-one combo had been ruining my hair for years now. It was the little luxuries you had to sacrifice if you wanted your own apartment and food.

Of course, if I'd moved back in with my uncle, he'd have given me all the meals and comfort I wanted.

Until he didn't.

Shoving down the urge to hug myself and sob in the shower like the broken creature I was, I quickly got out, drying off with the fluffiest towel I'd ever used and blowing out my pin-straight hair.

I glared at the outfit Sin had given me. It was the rich crimson of blood from a fatal wound, seeming to mock both my value to the demon and my dreams of safety.

A matching lace thong lurked in the bag he'd discarded at the foot of the bed.

Instead of chucking the whole thing out of the window, I took a calming breath and slipped it on.

A complex system of straps and lace made up the outfit, and it took several minutes of shimmying before I stepped to the mirrored wardrobe for inspection.

A familiar purple-green smudged above my cheek. Oddly, the bruising gave me a heady sense of relief. My uncle had taken his frustrations out on my face, but it might have been the last time. It had only been two days ago, yet it already felt like a lifetime.

My attention dropped to what I was wearing.

It barely reached the tops of my thighs. The built-in cups pushed my tits up to give the illusion I had more curves than I really did. Thick straps crisscrossed over my slender body like I was dressed in luxurious ribbons, with lace panels helping cover the gaps and obscuring most of the jagged lines scarring me. The dress made the delicate orange tiger-lily tattoo on my wrist pop even more.

"Sin!" I snarled, rage flooding my veins and overriding any embarrassment I might have felt.

He sauntered into the room, a cocky smirk already loaded.

A weak part of me took notice of the way his white tattoos graced the carved muscles of his bare chest and arms like art. How black slacks slung indecently low on his hips so his tail could poke out and a pair of matching dress shoes gave him the air of a sexy mafioso. He must have showered too, because his hair had turned silver with the dampness clinging to it, making his ivory horns look even taller.

His eyes devoured me right back, taking in every inch of my body revealed by the joke of an outfit.

The bastard had dressed me in blood-coloured lingerie. The damn thing was tight-fitting and see-through enough to leave zero to the imagination.

I'd have felt less exposed naked.

"Where the hell are you taking me that *this* would blend in?" I hissed, gesturing down at myself.

His smirk bloomed into a full, wicked grin. "Ever been to a demon nightclub?"

Chapter 29

I tugged on the dress's hem, cursing Sin with every fibre of my being.

"Stop." He slapped my hand away, tempting me to return the favour on his smug face. "You're meant to be my human plaything. You'll look suspicious and get us kicked out."

"Oh no," I deadpanned. "What a shame if I don't make things easy for my kidnapper to complete his nefarious plans."

"It would be a shame if I had to prove you're mine in front of all the other demons to save them from figuring out you're a hunter who likes to experiment on demons." He flashed a pointy grin. "I will make you scream for me in a room full of people, poison."

My teeth snicked as I clamped my mouth closed on the next verbal jab. Sin was threat personified. I wouldn't put it past him to toy with me anyway, in his own little form of revenge.

After making me dress in this ridiculous lingerie, he'd given me a pair of surprisingly comfortable strappy heels to match, somehow exactly in my size. He'd also grabbed a long coat for me to fend off the chilly British summer.

Despite the temperature, he was topless, which I supposed must be normal for him, given the vicious spikes across his back and shoulders.

It turned out, before his capture, a witch in another city had glamoured him with magic. He could walk amongst the humans, and all they'd see was a normal person. No fangs, claws, horns, or spikes in sight.

It made calling a ride to the seedier part of Riverside a lot less stressful. The man hadn't batted an eye as we'd hopped in, whisking us away in tense silence before dropping us outside a run-down pub on a narrow street.

All hunters had spelled charms created by captured mages so we could see through glamour. Mine was a citrine stud earring disguised among other gold piercings that I never removed.

Hence why I saw the monster beneath the lie.

"It's just down here." Sin guided my steps with a hand on my lower back. I resisted the urge to shove him away, letting his warmth invade me with gritted teeth instead.

I was British. It was practically a law that you didn't turn down free heat.

A smirk twitched his lips in my periphery. The evil bastard knew just how to get under my skin and was clearly loving every moment.

"Remind me again why you have to drag me with you? You know anyone who survived the attack will be after us both, right?" I eyed him as we walked, wondering whether he knew who my uncle was.

If he didn't, I definitely wasn't telling him. Whatever tenuous use he apparently had for me as chief juice box would dry up the second he found out I was the only living relative to the leader of the Riverside hunters. In theory, I'd be a strong contender to take over the chapter as hunter prime once my uncle retired, but I'd never wanted that position.

Sin huffed. "Those cultist morons are always after demons in this realm, despite how few of us actually harm anyone." He shot me a considering look. "I already know they'll be trying to find any hunters whose bodies haven't turned up, but why would that worry you? Don't you want to be found, poison?"

Only years of practise kept me walking casually, my face a neutral mask as I realised my error. "Of course I do." I flicked my long, now silky-smooth, hair over one shoulder. "I just thought you should know that whatever you have planned will ultimately be for nothing."

His eyes narrowed, silvery lashes eclipsing the stars in his eyes. "You're hiding something."

I scoffed. "I'm not hiding anything. You just don't know a thing about me, Sin. There's a difference."

He arched a brow, tugging at the small horns edging it. "Like your obsession with Italian food? Or how you lift your chin right before you're going to cut me down? That you struggle to bury your delightfully violent side?" He grabbed my wrist, smothering the tiger-lily tattoo and turning me to face him. "Or how you were being slowly starved? How the other hunters were cruel to you? How you were being forced to work there? How someone high up beats you and everyone turns a blind eye?"

He was practically snarling by the end, his bare chest rising and falling too fast as his eyes flashed with starlight. His hand tightened on my wrist, solid and warm, grounding me when I felt completely untethered.

My lips parted, mask cracking along with my strained voice. "How...? You can't possibly know that. You were caged in a lab."

My emotions spilled out, scrambling my composure.

Even Leo had been oblivious to what I'd been going through all these years, let alone the past few weeks since the incident that tore my carefully controlled world apart.

"I was, and you were my everything. All I could do was watch you, learn about you, and hope to one day use all my knowledge to get what I want." His lips spread into a feral grin. "I made you a promise, poison, and I'm going to keep it."

Pain lanced my chest. He was studying me to find information he could use against me. Obviously.

I'd slept with the enemy and was somehow surprised that he still wanted to hurt me. Nothing had changed though. I'd been the one dumb enough to take things that far.

Sometimes I thought I was so desperate for someone to actually care about me, that I deserved to get hurt for it. Like when that first idiot decides to go outside and investigate the strange sounds in a slasher movie.

"If you're going to snap my neck, just fucking do it already," I hissed, lifting my chin to bare my throat. The constant threat of his presence was like a splinter I couldn't cut out.

"Don't tempt me, poison. There's nothing I'd love more than to wrap my hands around your throat." He leaned in close, bringing his lips to my ear. "It's a great way to hold you down while I make you scream."

I inhaled sharply, freezing up at the bolt of desire.

Was he...*flirting*? Of course Sin's idea of seduction was as deadly as the rest of him.

He straightened with a devilish grin, showing sharp white teeth. "Now stop wasting time and come along."

He yanked me behind him, an unyielding grip on my wrist. We turned down a narrow street in the darkness, and I strained to make out the details in the gloom as we approached an unmarked door. He knocked, a booming crack of spiked knuckles against the blackened metal.

It creaked open, revealing a hulking monster bathed in artificial light. Curved horns and bright-crimson skin made him look like a cartoon devil.

The demon scanned us both, solid black eyes narrowed tight with suspicion. "Haven't seen you before, bloodsucker. Who the fires are you, and who's this bitch?" He jerked his flat chin in my direction with a sneer.

So not a polite welcome, then.

I wanted to grab his horn and slam the door into his sneering face repeatedly, until his nose gushed blood and his lips split like overripe plums.

Wouldn't want to come across as a *bitch* though.

Sin smirked, unfazed by the rude male. "I'm Sinclair, and this is my lovely little toy." His tail slid up my arm, wrapping around my throat like a collar. Loose enough to rest gently against my skin but a threat to behave myself nonetheless, like he could sense the violence brewing in me. "You're not fit to even breathe the same air as her. If you so much as look at her again, I'm going to slice open your arteries and bathe her soft skin in your warm blood, then lick it off her."

I swallowed thickly, unsure whether I needed to throw up or fan myself at that vivid imagery. From Sin, I could believe every word. It was strange, having someone defend me. I could almost convince myself it was more than just a demon protecting his food source, but Sin was giving me emotional whiplash as it was.

One minute, he claimed there was some mystical bond growing between us, and the next, he threatened to make me scream.

The bouncer laughed, his suspicion melting away into a shared look of mirth. "Ah, little possessive, are we?"

Since when did a threat melt the tension? Demons were odd.

He opened the door fully, stepping back to usher us inside the lit foyer. "You'll have your claws full trying to keep her all to yourself. It's wild in here tonight. We're celebrating the destruction of those cultist twats."

I almost rolled my eyes at that but kept my expression into what I hoped was a too-stupid-for-self-preservation look. Sin slipped the coat from my body, throwing it haphazardly into the packed cloakroom off to one side.

The devilish bouncer hacked out a low laugh like he was choking on smoke. "Oh yeah, you're going to get bloody tonight, big lad."

Sin turned, claws flashing as he lunged for the other male. Blood sprayed across my thigh, catching the hem of my dress and blending in perfectly with the colour he'd chosen.

Sin snarled. "What the fuck did I say?"

The bouncer sniggered, backing up with his hands raised in surrender, even as blood gushed down a deep set of claw marks in his chest. "Couldn't resist a quick peek."

Sin growled, a low, rumbling threat, and then eyed the speckles of blood across my bare thigh with a look of hunger I recognised intimately.

I jabbed a finger towards his stupidly carved face. "Don't even think about it."

<h1 align="center">Chapter 30</h1>

I knew that when Sin had said we were going to a demon night-club—with me in this outfit—that it would be bad news.

But this was something else entirely.

We stepped into a seedy club, complete with dancers in raised cages and several demons getting intimate onstage beside a horned DJ responsible for the sensual beat thumping from towering speakers.

The razor edge of danger scraped against my nerves.

The sheer number of demons living in Riverside without hunter knowledge was terrifying. A sea of them gyrated with humans on a sunken dance floor, red strobe lighting flashing over them through a haze of smoke.

A few were moving a lot more intimately than was legal in public.

My brows shot up. "You brought me to a demon *sex club*?!" I hissed, glaring at the psycho collaring me with his velvety tail.

Sin chuckled, the sound lost to the bass-heavy music, and stepped in so close the heat of his bare skin seared through the lace covering me. "Why, are you blushing, poison? After everything you just did to me on the dining table? This isn't even where the real action happens."

I shot him a dark look, choosing to ignore his comment about earlier for my own sanity. "These humans had better be here by choice."

He bared his fangs, practically glowing white in the semi-darkness. "You think I'd stand idly by while people were abused? You know me better than that, poison."

Did I though? He was a vicious blood demon who, in some sick joke from the universe, made me feel wild and reckless and more alive than any shot of adrenaline. But what did I really know about him as a person? And why did that thought have curiosity winding through me?

He must have seen the scepticism on my face, because he huffed a low grunt. "They look it, don't they?"

I scanned the crowd, hunting for any hint of someone in need of a hasty rescue. From the looks on their faces, most people seemed drunk or high, but huge smiles lit their expressions as they pressed themselves up against demons, just as eager as the monsters pawing back at them.

Nobody looked afraid, which, if you asked me, was the normal reaction to getting up close and personal with a demon. Glamour or not, most people seemed to have some instinct that warned something predatory was looking back at them.

Sin tugged on his tail, lightly drawing me onwards. "Come on, poison. I need to speak with someone."

Glaring at his broad back, I followed behind him, trying not to trip in the ridiculously comfy heels he'd given me.

Eyes seemed to rake over, an almost physical scrape across my exposed skin, but Sin hadn't been wrong about fitting in. Most people wore skimpy clubbing outfits, everything from straight lingerie to latex bodysuits and chains.

Sin headed for the bar, easily weaving through the crowd with his towering height and intimidating physique. The lighting tinged his white tattoos and short hair red until he looked painted in gore like some hellish god. Only a few other demons had spikes like him, and not nearly as many.

Even amongst demons, Sin was a walking weapon. Danger personified.

The press of so many demons had panic racing through my veins faster than the pain of Sin's bite. I was unarmed in a room full of predators. Ones celebrating the death of almost every hunter I knew.

What would they do to me if they found out I'd been one of them? The things I'd done to their kind.

Sin stepped up to the bar, hauling me to his side. The demon slung an arm around me, trapping me between the counter and corded muscle. The warmth against my back had a dumb part of me singing at the contact.

He bowed his head, whispering in my ear to be heard above the bass-heavy music, "You look afraid, poison. Did you think I'd let the other monsters have you?" He ran a claw along my collarbone, dipping between the straps of my dress and drawing shivers in his wake. "You're all mine."

His husky voice promised pain and pleasure, just like his bite.

"Sinclair." A bright feminine voice pulled his attention away, letting me breathe.

A demon waved at Sin from behind the bar, giving him a toothy grin as she threw a towel over her shoulder. "Glad to see you're still in one piece."

He grinned back, lacking the malice he usually threw my way. "Can't get rid of me so easily, Aurora."

I almost mistook her for a human until her heart-tipped tail waved over her shoulder and she stepped close enough for me to spot the fangs and claws. With her bronzed skin tone and lack of horns, wings, or spikes, she looked like a watered-down demon, possibly a blood or lust feeder, but it was always hard to tell which subtypes were which.

I studied her with a hunter's eye, ignoring the weird pang in my chest as Sin's dark expression lightened with her sparkling presence.

Full, glossy lips pouted at Sin. They matched the tips of her ombre hair, which bled from black roots into the paler shade obscured by the red-tinged light. Large cat eyes glowed a UV pink under the dim lighting, slashed through with slitted pupils and framed by stunningly long lashes. A shimmery dress looked painted on but covered more skin than most in the club, which made sense, since she clearly worked here. She looked like the demon equivalent of a swimwear model, all lush curves and captivating features.

I didn't want to be jealous of another woman's beauty; I wanted to be in awe of her and encourage her, but I couldn't help but feel a little inadequate. Since Leo had thrown his affair with Tia in my face, I wasn't exactly bubbling with self-confidence.

The fact I was practically a walking skeleton covered in scars and bruises wasn't helping my look. When I finally escaped all the violence, I was going to find a cute goth guy obsessed with Halloween.

Sweat beaded the small of my back, the humidity of the club pressing closer.

A patron called out to Aurora, but she ignored them, eyes tightening as she leaned over the bar, bringing her lips closer to Sin's ear. "Like I told you before, I haven't seen him, but meet me out back in ten minutes and I'll tell you what I know." She glanced in my direction before turning back to Sin with a raised brow. "And those bruises and scars had better not be your doing, or I'll make sure you feel each one as I copy them onto your flesh."

My brows shot up. A *demon* was defending a human against their own kind?

I'd learned more about them tonight than I had in my last ten years as a hunter.

Sin grunted, waving her off with a dismissive hand. "I wish they were from me."

She giggled, eyes bright. "You're a terrible liar."

Reaching beneath the bar, she grabbed a frosted glass already half-filled with a dark-red liquid and lifted a bottle of whisky from the back.

"No." Sin shook his head, eyes darting to me for a second. "Straight for me."

She quirked a brow. "Something you want to tell me about you two, hmmm?"

He shrugged with false innocence, deadly spikes drawing my attention.

She pursed her Cupid's-bow lips but didn't press, swapping the likely blood-filled glass for an empty one before upending the bottle for a generous free pour and expertly sliding the drink to Sin. I'd have slid it right off the edge of the polished counter and smashed the glass.

"What'll it be, killer?" Her oddly warm gaze met mine.

I startled for a moment at the nickname before realising she couldn't know what I used to be. Sin snorted, hiding a smirk in his drink beside me.

Swallowing nervously, I considered my options before deciding a little booze couldn't hurt. Who knew what I'd need to do to escape Sin's clutches. Liquid courage might be necessary.

"Sloe gin and tonic, please," I said.

She turned, nimbly fixing my drink before placing it before me. Her claws were only a fraction longer and pointier than human fingernails. She'd painted them a black lacquer with fanged smiley faces that had my lips twitching.

"It's on me. You'll need it with that grumpy bastard." She beamed at Sin. "Pay up, fang face."

He rolled his eyes, handing over a few notes from his pocket before tugging me along by the tail collar as we plunged back through the crowded club. I sipped my drink, welcoming the fizz on my tongue before it burned sweetly down my throat.

A slender demon in a pinstripe suit stepped up beside me, eyes glowing as he took me in. Curved claws raked out. Before he could so much as scratch me, Sin was there, gripping the male's wrist hard enough that I could hear the crunch of bone over the bass-heavy music.

Adrenaline lit my veins, sharpening the scene. I knew his type—a fear demon—just like the bastard test subject Sin had saved me from when he came back to kidnap me.

"Leave," Sin growled. "Before I rip that hand off and gift it to her."

The other male didn't back down, ignoring the pain he must be in, along with Sin's threat. "You into sharing, gorgeous? I can pay. I bet that little slut looks good on her kne—"

His words cut off with a choking sound. A line of red opened along his throat. Blood poured down his neck, staining his open dress shirt. Sin flicked his hand, splattering the hem of my lacy dress, mirroring the droplets he'd left from the bouncer.

The male collapsed to the sticky floor, hitting his knees and pitching forward.

A human squealed as the body smacked into their legs. His eyes widened on Sin, and he backed away, palms raised.

"You... I... What...?" I blinked at the dead body, now bleeding out on the raised edge of the sunken dance floor.

Sin tugged me behind him with his makeshift collar around my throat, leading us towards a corridor while I impersonated a fish.

I swallowed, finally finding my voice in a shouted whisper as he brought me into a quieter section. "Did you just commit literal *murder* on the dance floor!?"

A few couples lined the walls, making out and doing...other things.

Sin's eyes locked on me like prey. He backed me up against the wall, caging me in with his body until he was all I could see. His tail unwound from my neck, replaced by his hand, the clawed tip of his thumb stroking over my skin until I shivered.

The scent of mandarin and leather, sweet yet masculine, invaded my senses, blocking out the nightclub's cocktail of sweat, alcohol, and blood.

"Yes, poison. I killed a man for trying to touch what was mine. And I'd do it again, in a fucking heartbeat."

Before I could process his words, his lips slammed against mine, taking my mouth in a rough kiss.

Vicious. Claiming. Sinful.

Chapter 31

S in ended the kiss, his sharp fangs dragging over my lower lip in sensual threat. The moment he pulled back, dizziness slumped me against the wall. I fought just to breathe in the wake of his intensity.

The pearlescent stars in his eyes glowed. Hunger and anger twined through his expression. His arms caged me in, keeping me trapped against the corridor wall with the heat and strength that radiated from him.

His tail flickered, swaying back and forth behind him, the sharp spikes on the heart-shaped tip glinting with menace.

The way he kissed me and threatened to kill me was sending some serious mixed signals.

Possible red flag.

Gaze never leaving mine, he knocked back the last of his drink and set the empty on a ledge beside me.

He smirked, jerking his chin at the glass I clutched in my hand. "Finish it, poison. Maybe when I sip from you later, I'll get even more high off you."

I obeyed, downing the rest of my gin and tonic. Not because he'd told me to but because I needed something to quench the thirst Sin had left me with.

"What are you doing here?" I blurted, curiosity getting the better of me. My cheeks warmed as he raised a horned brow, but I ploughed on. "Any survivors will be coming for you. For *us*. If you were smart, you'd be on the next flight out of here, or jumping through the nearest portal back to hell."

A muscle feathered in his jaw. "I'm looking for someone."

I frowned, the puzzle pieces sliding together in my head. "So that's why you were captured? You let them take you so you could look for a particular demon at hunter HQ?"

He blinked, obviously not expecting my response.

I snorted. "Don't look so surprised, demon. I'm meant to be smart, remember?" I threw his words from earlier back in his face. "Obviously, they weren't there, or you wouldn't be in a demon nightclub trying to get a hot tip."

His eyes narrowed on me. "It wasn't easy getting information inside your torture den, since all the demons are constantly being killed, but at least I could rule out him being there while I was."

I nodded, filing away the information for later use. At some point, Sin would make a mistake. One that I'd use to escape him. I hadn't spent years trying to get away from my uncle just to be captured by a demon when I'd finally been given a real shot at freedom.

Sin had done me a favour by taking me with him. Hopefully, my uncle was either dead or thought I was.

Now I could leave behind hunters and demons and violence altogether. Carve out a new life like a regular human.

I'd have to start off-grid, probably in the remote forests of eastern Europe, but after a few months, maybe I could find somewhere that reminded me of my hometown, with its rolling countryside hills and lush forest edging a bustling city.

Even as a dumb part of me grieved the loss of vividness from a certain monochrome beast, the desperate fantasy crystallised inside my mind.

I just had to survive playing with demons long enough to get there.

"Come on, before that big brain of yours gets you killed." Sin smirked, flashing the sharp tip of a fang. "By me."

"Yes, almighty demon overload." I snorted, rolling my eyes at him despite the very real threat he posed to my health. Living in constant fear had a way of skewing your reactions to it.

He chuckled. "Careful, poison. I might like you playing the obedient little toy for me."

I flashed him a sarcastic smile and brushed past him, avoiding the three spikes on his shoulder.

Something warm wound around my wrist. His tail circled me, velvety smooth skin so dark compared to my anaemic paleness.

His heat covered my back. "I'm not letting you go anywhere without me, poison," he whispered in my ear. "Someone might try to touch what's mine again."

He strode past me, tugging me along.

His tail on my wrist felt oddly like holding hands, intimate in a way that nothing should be between a hunter and a demon.

I glowered at his broad back but let his caveman bullshit slide. The more compliant he thought I was, without raising suspicion, the easier it would be for me to run when the opportunity arose.

We walked down the corridor, and I fought a blush as a demon used her tail creatively with a woman who moaned extra loud right as we passed. The demon shot me a wink as she caught me staring.

I edged closer to Sin, ducking my head and chasing him through the door at the end of the corridor.

The cool night greeted me, a welcome breeze tousling my loose hair and soothing my clammy skin.

The club had been filled with too many sweaty bodies, and the fresh air was an instant relief despite how little I was wearing. I adjusted my glasses and drew in a breath, ignoring the stale tobacco scent.

Fake grass waited for us in a bright smoker's area, loosely penned in with short planters and dotted with benches.

"So good of you to bring us another human snack, brother."

My heart shot into my throat. A grinning blood demon stepped from the shadows of the building, joining us in a pool of white cast by the club's security lighting.

Behind him, a second demon leaned against the bricks. He sucked on a cheap roll-up while he held a smiling young woman against the wall, a hand pinned between her tits so her satin dress bunched under his wrist. She looked barely old enough to be here but pretty enough to get in regardless, her doe eyes rimmed in dark kohl and big curls tumbling to her trim waist.

Stark lines of blood trickled down her throat.

Both demons looked similar to mine, with grey skin, white horns and a long tail, but that was where the similarities ended.

Neither had Sin's bony spikes, making them seem tame in comparison. Where Sin was packed with lean muscle and a cruel streak wider than his broad shoulders, the pair eyeing us seemed thin and sly. Even their tails lacked Sin's heart-shaped tip, tapering into nothing instead.

Sin edged in front, pulling me closer. My chest brushed his forearm with each rapid breath.

The thought of their fangs sinking into my flesh was terrifying.

Yet that instinctive fear had somehow vanished when it came to Sin. The realisation shocked me out of the growing dread.

"I'm not your brother. This is *my* human," Sin sneered, the expression so familiar that it was almost comforting at this point. "And you're leaving that one with me too."

An oily sensation coiled through my middle. I frowned at the idea of him drinking from someone else, then instantly berated myself for being a colossal idiot.

The smoker pushed off the wall, helping the giggling human along with an arm slung across her shoulders, coming to stand beside the other demon. "How very greedy. Don't worry, we'll share ours with you too. We just wanted a taste of yours. We won't hurt her."

"Oh? But I'll hurt you." Sin raised his tail, releasing my wrist as his spikes slid from the heart tip in eerie threat. "Leave the girl and go back inside. This is your final warning."

The woman blinked sleepily, and her head lolled aside, bumping the smoker's bicep. She might be smiling, but she was also *dying*.

I stepped from Sin's shadow, readying to fight. I might be unarmed, but I wouldn't let another person die by fang while I did nothing.

"We aren't bones for you rabid dogs to growl over." I borrowed Sin's favourite sneer. "Keep your fangs to yourself. All of you." I shot a pointed look at the demon towering beside me.

Before Sin, nobody had ever protected me. But I'd been raised to kill demons. Not knowing how many innocents I'd executed would always haunt me, but some of them had deserved their fate.

Like these bastards if they tried to slurp any more from their juice box. She was past consenting at this point, and I'd seen enough bite victims to know she was flirting with oblivion.

I caught Sin's cruel smirk in my periphery.

"Jealous, poison?"

"Shut it, parasite."

The smoker released his victim, and I didn't spare a moment to wince as she collapsed on the fake grass. I launched myself at him, ducked grabbing claws as I weaved aside, and kicked out the back of his knee.

He grunted as the joint caved, dropping him with a solid thud that sounded like karma.

The lack of short horns edging his brows like Sin gave me a free shot at his face. I slammed my knuckles into his temple, leaping aside before his jabbing tail could find me. His eyes rolled back, and he crumpled beside the woman.

A pained whine filled the night.

Behind me, Sin had created a bloody mess of the other demon, but starlit eyes were locked onto me.

"And you call me the vicious one?" He chuckled, dropping his latest victim.

My brows shot up. "I only knocked the fucker out. Yours looks ready to go into a Bolognese."

"Oh my g-god, what did you do?" the now anaemic woman slurred, sitting up to gape at the bloody scene.

I opened my mouth, but Sin beat me to it.

"You let them take too much." His expression was stern, as unyielding as his tone. "When you start feeling sleepy, you stop. Go home and rest. Don't feed another demon for a week."

The crack of authority in his voice was something I hadn't heard before. He'd been cruel and mocking, husky and seductive, gleeful and violent, but this side of him was new.

Was this the real him? Did he work in some kind of law enforcement or high-ranking position? I could easily picture him delivering violent punishments, but the rescuer side of things threw me.

Her plump lower lip trembled. "But... But he was going to blood bond me." She gestured at the smoker I'd downed.

Sin quirked a horned brow. "No, he wasn't. A blood bond is a form of mating amongst demons, like marriage for humans. The slimy fuck wouldn't be asking to feed on anyone else if he'd started bonding you. He would be so obsessed with you that all other blood tasted like ash."

I jolted, eyes widening.

Was he saying he didn't want to drink from anyone but me? Why would he keep biting me if it would only strengthen such a bond? What would happen to him when I left?

I avoided his penetrating stare. Hopefully, the possessive bastard liked the taste of ash.

The other woman swallowed thickly. "Oh." She pushed to stand on shaky legs, wobbling for a moment in her heeled boots. Then kicked the unconscious demon in the ribs. "Sleazebag."

I chuckled, and she shot me a grin. "Cheers for the rescue."

"Us blood bags have to stick together," I snorted.

She gave Sin a timid smile in thanks before shuffling back into the club, thankfully steadier with each step.

The demon I'd knocked out stirred, and I readied myself to kick his face in if he so much as twitched wrong.

Sin threw his whimpering victim at mine. They crashed together in a clack of horns and flesh.

He snarled at the tangled pair. "Leave. Now. Before you can't."

"You'd better listen to him, boys. He's already killed one guy for propositioning his lady friend tonight." The demon bartender we'd been waiting for stepped around the corner of the building, vaulting the low bush to join us with a bright grin.

The breeze toyed with her long hair, a dramatic black-to-pink ombre without the club's red haze obscuring the colours.

Sin huffed, reaching behind him to tug me flush against his side, easily guiding me between the sharp points at his elbow and spine. "Yeah, well, let's just say I went through a lot to get her."

I flipped him off behind his back, and Aurora caught the gesture with a saucy wink.

The sleazy pair climbed slowly to their feet and backed away, one considerably slower and bloodier. The one I'd knocked out gave me a final, hungry once-over, and they disappeared into the club.

A shiver ran through me, and Sin held me tighter against his side, almost like he might be trying to reassure me.

The bizarre thought snapped me back to reality. We were enemies. He was defending his food.

The bartender pursed her lips. "I know you're looking for Silvanus, and as I said, I haven't seen him in over a month. The hybrid king massacred the Riverside hunters last night. He might have freed Silvanus. Heard that nutter monarch declared an open invite to live in his kingdom too." She shook her head with a small smile on her lips. "People are saying it's actually safe there."

Sin quirked a brow. Apparently as sceptical as I was that anywhere in hell could be considered "safe."

She continued on, "I happen to...er...know one of his generals." She waved her painted claws like it could dispel her fumbled words, bronzed cheeks turning dusky. "If you want, I could find out if Silvanus went with them?"

My curiosity had been piqued, but I kept my mouth shut. Who was I to judge if she was in a complicated situation with whoever this general was? I had enough of my own drama.

Deep furrows carved between Sin's pale brows. "I doubt he's gone back to hell, but I'd be grateful if you'd speak to your contact."

Aurora huffed, pouty lips twitching. "He's not exactly the chatty type, but I'll see what I can do. It might take a while though, so you should check with some of the hunters that I heard escaped. I'm sure they'll tell you anything if you ask nicely."

A hysterical laugh bubbled up my throat, and I coughed awkwardly to prevent the mania spilling out. She didn't realise Sin had already checked with the hunters. He even had his own captive.

Not that I was particularly useful, given I'd stayed as far as I could from the main holding cells. I couldn't face the shame of seeing so many people slated for death, and being unable to save a single one.

Sin eyed me, before turning his considering look to Aurora. "I was there, and he wasn't, but you're right... Perhaps I need to question some hunters more. Thoroughly."

She grinned, a viciousness peeking through her pretty pink eyes. "Stab one of those bastards for me, won't you?"

Sin chuckled, attention flashing to me again. "Oh, don't worry, I know just how to punish naughty hunters."

Chapter 32

The door shut behind Sin, sealing me back into our borrowed home.

Apparently I was living some twisted parody of domestic bliss. With a demon.

For years, I'd longed for a real home. A safe haven to start a family and live a normal, happy life. After being raised in violence, I craved the idea of regular problems like running out of fabric softener or deciding what colour to paint a nursery room.

No more worrying about whether the blood would even wash out of my clothes, or whether my uncle would evict me from my apartment for some perceived slight.

I headed straight for the stairs, wanting this night to be over with. If I could somehow get Sin to leave me alone, maybe I'd be able to think clearly enough to form an actual plan to escape him. Yet a small part of me wondered what life would be like if I stayed.

What if Sin and I explored this unpredictable bond growing between us? Would he cook for me every night? Would I feed him right back until we burned with passion? Did he want a quiet life, too? A cosy home? A loving family?

I squashed the silly notion.

After all, it was only a matter of time until he snapped my neck, blood bond or not.

Sin shackled my wrist with his velvety tail, halting me on the bottom step. "I have a few questions for you, poison."

I stilled, turning back to face him and willing my heart rate to steady despite the contact. I'd been expecting him to ask me about the demon he was searching for the entire ride back from the club, but only a tense silence had lingered between us.

"What do you want to know? I think I'd remember if I met someone called Silvanus," I drawled, locking my jaw against a yawn.

A few good meals weren't enough to counter weeks of mal-nourishment, and years of pushing myself past limits I shouldn't know.

"Do you get every demon's name before you kill them?" His voice was deathly soft, and I felt the first stirrings of unease.

I hadn't been afraid of Sin in a long time.

The reminder of how deadly he was shouldn't have been necessary, but apparently I'd let myself become weak since leaving active duty as a hunter-slash-genocidal-killer.

"No." I met his silky darkness head-on. I might have sworn off violence, but I was no coward. "It's also been over a month since I killed a demon who didn't ask for it."

"And who would ask to die?" Scepticism dripped from his tone like blood.

My lips peeled back into a snarl. "Fane was being tortured, so I freed him in the only way I could."

He watched me, face an unreadable mask.

I notched my chin, refusing to bow under the strained silence.

The bastard could judge me all he wanted for my past sins, but I'd done what little I could for the elderly demon forgiving enough to speak with a hunter.

Sin's lip hooked into a familiar sneer. "Even your mercy is violent, typical hunter."

I stifled a flinch. His words struck a little too close to the truth, and I crossed my arms like it could ward off any further blows. "Your real question?"

"Back in your lab, you said you'd never met a demon like me... Are you certain? Think hard, huntress. The male I'm searching for looks similar to me. Only a touch shorter, with yellow eyes instead of white."

My entire body locked up.

Sunshine eyes that ripped apart my life. A kind smile. Gentle hands tending mortal wounds.

Sin was looking for the demon who'd saved me.

The one I'd got killed in return.

Only a lifetime of mortaring the cracks in my façade with blood and pain stopped me from giving myself away.

I mirrored his sneer, shoving down the panic screaming at me to strike first. "All you parasites look the same to me."

He rolled his eyes. "Such dramatics, poison. I'm guessing that's still a no then."

Curiosity burrowed into my mind.

Who was he? The demon who'd stolen me from the reaper and changed my life completely. They looked so similar, they had to be related. Had I killed his father? His brother? His son?

Anything I asked would only raise suspicion.

And if he discovered what I'd done, he'd finally kill me.

Whatever ridiculous kernel of hope planted in my heart withered. A foolish part of me had felt something beginning to grow between us. It was twisted and toxic, but there nonetheless.

An addiction to how he made me feel.

A dumb hope for something different. Something more. Something real.

I feigned disinterest with a shrug. "Can I go to bed now, demon? Or do you want to stay up and talk about our feelings?" I taunted, channelling every ounce of the insufferable hunter I was trained to be.

He flashed fang in warning but tipped his horns towards the staircase. "Come on then, poison."

The demon somehow slipped his bulk past me on the carpeted stairs, using his tail to tug me along behind him.

My attention was riveted to the lowest spike on his back as he prowled up the stairs. The bony point weaved slightly as he moved, jutting several inches long from the charcoal skin hugging the base.

I concentrated on the lethal tip, refusing the mocking call of the family photos along the wall as we passed. Their joyous smiles loomed sharp in my periphery, like they hid something sinister just beneath the surface.

Sin led me into the luxe bedroom I'd slept in the night before.

My thoughts churned, flipping from blaring intensity to static hollowness.

It was more important than ever for me to escape. The demon had more than enough reason to want me dead already. If he found out what had happened, he'd snap my neck in a blink.

I'd seen the casual brutality he was capable of.

He swivelled to face me, eyes glowing like starlight. My breath caught at the sight of him, brighter than the slash of moonlight through the windows. A vicious god made of starlight and shadow.

Why did my potential murderer have to be so damn alluring?

Because life was unfair, and I had terrible taste in men.

His spikes retracted, leaving the barest tips across his shoulders, as shallow as the ones edging his brows.

I blinked rapidly, mind blanking. He'd never once shown me that.

"Did you think I just stabbed every bed I got into?" He smirked.

I bared my teeth in a rough approximation of a smile. "Funnily enough, I hadn't given much thought to the bed habits of a parasite."

He tutted, shaking his head with a devilish grin. "Liar."

I dropped his gaze like it burned, ignoring the rush of heat to my cheeks. He wasn't right, per se, but I might have had more than a few inappropriate thoughts about the demon I was meant to hate.

"Think what you want, demon. I'm tired, so get out." I pointed at the door as if treating him like an obedient pet might make him act like one.

Sin quirked a silver brow. "You think I'm going to let you sleep in here alone? How stupid do you think I am, poison?"

Disappointment weighed my shoulders, but I'd already half expected him to have some cruel trick up his sleeve. The need to flee burned stronger than ever though.

"Now get in and move over." He smirked, a wicked twist of his full lips. "You'd better not snore like last time."

My lips parted. "Last time?"

His smirk bloomed into a full, vicious grin. Before I could back away, his tail shot out, wrapping my neck.

I braced for the suffocation to follow.

But none came. Just his warm skin resting against mine.

My muscles refused to unlock, knowing to wait for the strike to come.

Sin closed the gap between us, crowding me back against the bed. "Don't think I'm not aware of all those little plans running through your pretty head, poison. You'll be gone the second I turn my back." His claw pressed under my chin, forcing me to meet his starlit eyes. "I will collar you until you realise you're mine. Now get into bed so we can sleep, unless you want to stay up for other reasons?"

The hunger in his gaze told me exactly what he meant by that.

I swallowed thickly, the weight of his intensity bearing down on me. A reckless part of me craved a repeat of earlier. The feel of him was carved into my skin, scarring my flesh until I could never get rid of him.

But if he knew what I'd done to his kin, he'd never touch me in that way again.

Because he'd murder me.

I was so fucked.

Without a word, I threw back the fluffy sage duvet and moved to slide under the sheets, but he halted me with my living collar, stopping me on the edge of the bed.

"Your shoes," he grunted.

The monster dropped to his knees and hooked his claws under the delicate straps holding the comfy heels in place. Warm fingertips brushed my ankles as he worked. I stilled, afraid to shatter the fever dream that must hold me as I witnessed such a large predator kneel for me. My hands itched with the urge to run my fingers through the white silk of his hair, tumbling messily between his horns to brush the tips of his lashes.

A blush stole across my cheeks. It wasn't the first time he'd knelt for me, and thoughts of his wicked forked tongue tasting me through the lab's glass barrier had me punishing my lower lip.

I cleared my throat. "You know, you're meant to *undo* the straps, not destroy them."

An indulgent smirk claimed his features. "Don't worry, poison. I'll buy you new ones."

I cocked a brow. "With what money? I'm broke."

Sin chuckled, the sound cut through with his usual mocking. "What? Being a mad scientist doesn't pay well?"

"Most scientists aren't paid well," I sniffed. "We sacrifice for the greater good."

I'd wanted to taunt him, but in the process, I'd sounded a little too much like my uncle. The thought made me want to vomit in my mouth.

The demon scoffed, "Spoken like such a human." A wicked grin sharpened his expression. "But I meant with *our* money. I was moving to the human realm, remember? I already have ID to match my glamour and enough funds for us to live on comfortably for years."

My eyes practically bugged out of my head. Not only was the demon richer than me, but I didn't have any ID myself. My uncle had my passport and driving licence—just another way he kept me under his thumb.

But Sin had also spoken as if his money was *mine* too.

I didn't know how to feel about anything. I was emotionally and physically drained.

Leaving on the ridiculous lingerie dress, I pulled away from Sin and settled fully under the covers, turning my back on him. There was no chance in his home world that I was taking off the last barrier between us, however flimsy it was.

His sinuous tail moved as I did, not once choking me.

I froze as he slid in behind me with a low growl. Heat enveloped me as he wrapped his arm around my waist, thawing me a little as he pulled me back against his firm body, propping his chin on top of my head.

I hated that some of the tension left my body with him holding me like this. Like I was safe. I was being spooned by a monster, I should be spitting and clawing till my last breath.

He shifted even closer, and a hard length pressed against my arse.

"W-What are you doing?" I squirmed, embarrassingly both nervous and needy in an instant.

"For security," he whispered, wrapping me tighter in his intimate embrace until I felt like he touched me everywhere.

"Security is your dick poking me in the arse?" I hissed, trying to twist around to face him, but he held me fast.

"Keep your enemies close and all that." His low chuckle vibrated through me. "Though, if you want me to take your arse next, all you had to do was ask."

My eyes shot wide. "That's not... I didn't..."

The bastard had me too flustered to even string together a coherent insult.

"Sleep, poison. If you keep enticing me, I'm going to think you want to be fucked by a demon." He leaned down, and his forked tongue flicked out, tracing the shell of my ear. "Again."

Chapter 33

Sunlight filtered through the paned windows, haloing the monster.

The demon of shadow and starlight perched opposite me on an upholstered chair at the ruined dining table, making both look comically small. Sin leaned over a ceramic bowl of porridge, a tiny spoon clasped between his ivory claws.

I couldn't look too closely at the furrows carved into the polished wood without blushing.

Last night, I'd slept in the arms of my enemy. Somehow, I'd woken peacefully instead of my usual routine, with pleas for mercy on my lips. Sin had kissed my hair and slipped from bed, disappearing downstairs to bang around in the kitchen while I pretended to be asleep like a coward.

The tiger-lily tattooed on my wrist had felt heavier than usual, a constant reminder of my father's last words—*never let them see you weak, Tiger-lily.*

I'd dragged myself out of bed pretty quick after that, showering and changing into someone else's clothes from the wardrobe. Thankfully, I'd found a belt to cinch their smallest jeans in tight, since I resembled a stick more than a person lately.

"Finish every bite for me, poison. I'd hate to watch you collapse like a dusty skeleton again." The demon sneered at me over the clawed-up table, his malice as familiar as breathing. "Though I suppose this time, I could at least catch you. Wouldn't want you to accidentally kill yourself by hitting your pretty little head on something," he mused, vicious expression gentling into a cruel smirk.

I deserved his hatred, now more than ever, since I'd got someone important to him killed. But it still pissed me off.

Just another sin to add to the list. I probably wouldn't be getting any presents from Santa this year.

"Let me guess." I waved my spoon at the demon, pulling a sour face. "Because my death is yours to deliver? Your demon is showing."

He chuckled. "See? Such a smart little human."

"Har har." I threw a sarcastic laugh back but shovelled another spoonful of porridge into my mouth.

Who knew demons were so bossy?

To say I was surprised to find the demon cooking for me again was an understatement. Sure, it wasn't a carbonara, but he'd made me a nutritious breakfast of porridge, complete with honey and fresh berries.

No man had ever cooked for me, and the thought that the demon who wanted me dead was treating me better than my ex-fiancé would be hilarious if it weren't so tragic.

But the pity party could wait until I was finally free.

First, I had to survive Sin.

"So what nefarious plans are you involving me in today?" I asked before enjoying another comforting spoonful.

Sin's lips curved into a wicked smirk. "We're going hunting."

I nodded, keeping my mask of indifference in place. "For hunters."

It was the logical next step for him in his search for Silvanus. Assuming he'd already searched this area, likely the last place he'd been spotted.

The demon he searched for had, in fact, died nearby at the hands of hunters. I just couldn't tell him.

The secret burned in the pit of my stomach like acid.

Starlit eyes raked over me, assessing. "You seem unconcerned by the fact I'm going to capture your friends and torture them for information."

I arched a brow. "Who said they were my friends?"

He shrugged. "Fine by me if you want to play pretend. But remember who holds your life in their very sharp claws." He grinned, holding up his hand so the sunlight streaming through the kitchen window glinted off the pearly claws tipping his fingers.

I pulled a sour face at his dramatics. "How could I forget? My captive is now my captor."

He smirked. "Exactly. And since you've finished your breakfast…"

My spoon clattered into the empty bowl. I leaped from the chair and sprinted through the kitchen, instinct driving me on.

Footsteps pounded behind me, followed by a villainous laugh. "Oh, playing a new game, are we, poison?"

I made it halfway to the front door before something warm lashed my wrist. I snarled as Sin whipped me back to face him, knocking me off-balance. He slammed me into the corridor wall before I could recover, trapping me with his body.

"A smart person would know not to run from a predator," he purred, vicious delight glowing in his eyes. "We always give chase."

I snarled at the sadistic demon, "Fuck you, Sin."

He gripped the lower half of my face, muffling my lips, and forced my head aside. "Later, if you promise to take my barb like a good girl. I can't stop thinking about stuffing you full of my cum again. But I'll make you come right here like the fang-addict you are, poison."

He struck, sharp teeth piercing my neck.

I screamed into his palm, trying to bite him back as he drank from me, flooding me with heated pleasure like he'd poured it down my throat.

I was wet and needy, and I hated him more than ever for making me feel so good when I knew I'd never have this again.

He was right to call me an addict, because I didn't want him to stop. Even when he wasn't biting me, a secret part of me craved the wild ecstasy of it. The forbidden act that could take me to either heaven or hell.

Ecstasy set me on fire, shattering me with startling intensity.

"Sin!" I moaned for him, writhing against the cage of his body even as my mind fought it.

His fangs retreated, and his forked tongue laved across the wound. I jerked hard against him. It felt like he'd licked somewhere much more intimate.

"You are fucking delicious," he murmured against my throat. "I will never drink from another vein but yours, poison, because I want your life for my own, in every way I can get it."

I panted hard, coming down from the high as his lips left my skin and he dropped his hand to run his spiked knuckles over my collarbone in a lethal caress.

Anger replaced the floating bliss. I was making this far too easy for the possessive demon.

Starlit eyes mocked me as much as his smirk.

"I hope you choke on your breakfast," I hissed.

He chuckled. "Aw sweet poison, don't tempt me to choke my breakfast." He stepped back, letting the mild air flood between us, and tugged on my wrist with his tail. "It's time to hunt."

"This is dumb," I said, eyeing Sin with a frown.

We'd left the cosy house we were officially squatters in and driven into the city centre, Sin forcing me to drive the SUV he'd commandeered from the garage.

I really hoped whoever that family was, they were on a very extended holiday. Who knew what Sin would do if they came home to find us living there.

Apparently we were all on borrowed time.

By some miracle, I'd found parking, despite it being almost nine a.m. midweek. Most people would have been there to run errands or going to work, not chauffeur a demon into the shopping district so he could parade himself about waiting for hunters to miraculously appear and try to murder him.

It shocked me to realise I actually trusted Sin not to snack on random innocents. After all, he'd claimed the blood bond forming between us meant he only wanted to feed on me. I hated the possessive satisfaction that ran through me.

Sin rolled his starred eyes. "How else will I find the rats scurrying around the city? They've just had their base raided and their numbers depleted. They should be in hiding. So it would take an extra juicy bait to draw them out." He tugged me along behind him, large hand gripping mine in a strangely intimate act. "What could be more irresistible than you, sweet poison?"

He smirked, lifting his tail to wrap it around my throat in a warm velvety collar I was becoming sickeningly used to.

I narrowed my eyes, giving it a sharp tug that did absolutely nothing to dislodge him. My own helplessness lit embers of rage in my middle. At least he had his tail spikes sheathed. For now.

His smirk split into a wicked grin. "They'll eventually spot me dragging you around and jump in to save you from the evil beast."

I bared my teeth, annoyed at being controlled so easily. As usual. "You overestimate my value."

Sin growled, pulling us to a stop as some darkness blazed in his bright eyes. "And you underestimate it." His jaw feathered as he looked away for a moment. "Why wouldn't they save you? You might be their last surviving scientist."

Humans parted around us like we were rocks in a stream.

I huffed, not bothering to correct his mistaken assumptions. If his whole science staff were killed, my uncle would put out an open invitation to other hunter chapters, seeing if anyone wanted to transfer to Riverside once he was back up and running.

The hunter network was a mishmash of bloodthirsty zealots, but it was organised.

If Sin thought I was useless to his plans, though, he might actually kill me on the spot.

His warm skin at my throat felt tighter than a second ago.

"Maybe." I shrugged, looking away, pretending to study the shopfront as I resumed our slow walk.

Sin allowed it, his arm brushing mine with every step.

I'd brought him to the city's main street: a long pedestrian road lined with mismatched shops on either side.

Small cobblestone side-streets branched off, hiding the more boutique stores specialising in everything from unique buttons to artisan chocolate.

Riverside was a melting pot of old and new, the quaint village having rapidly expanded a few decades ago when a railway was built alongside the town.

"So where do you want to go first?" Sin asked, scanning the oblivious crowd bustling past us.

He stood out like a knife in a bouquet. Everything about him sharp and dangerous, a weapon honed. A feral predator among unsuspecting prey.

I tore my gaze off him and tried to assess my options. Sin wasn't stupid enough to let me out of his sight.

At least he'd been feeding me. I could already feel the strength returning to my body after how weak my uncle had kept me.

But how could I turn traipsing through the city to my advantage?

I flashed him a full-wattage grin. "I hope you brought your credit card."

Chapter 34

I dragged Sin around Riverside for two hours before my stomach rumbled, fiercer than a hellhound.

I'd prodded him into buying me things all morning, practical items I'd need for living off-grid. Everything from thermal leggings and hiking boots to a power bank and flint lighter. He'd even got me a firewood hatchet, muttering about how he knew exactly what I was doing.

The strangest thing about walking around with a monster was the feeling of safety it came with. I mean, who would attack me with death strolling beside me? Probably just him.

Until hunters actually found us.

Then my uncle would beat me bloody for disrespecting the organisation and bringing shame to our family by letting a demon get the better of me.

I crossed my fingers as I walked towards another shop.

Hopefully, the old git was dead.

My stomach let out another snarl as we passed a boutique restaurant. The scents of garlic and parmesan called to me like a lover.

I eyed a man's pasta through the window with longing, even though I'd eaten more in the two days since I'd been kidnapped than I had last week.

Sin's low chuckle rolled over me. "If you're hungry, you can just say," he mused, lips twitching with the first hints of a real smile. "Wouldn't want my food source to keel over. Again."

I flashed him a sickly-sweet grin. "Yes, wouldn't want you to lose your shit. Again."

His features flattened into a dark mask. "You haven't even begun to see me lose it, poison."

The threat hit harder than it should have. With my betrayal looming in the back of my mind, I was living on borrowed time.

It was a race between Sin finding answers and me escaping them.

I'd need strength for whatever came my way.

I strode towards the upscale Italian, calling over my shoulder, "I hope you have money left in that account."

"Of course." Sin stepped up beside me, reaching for the door first like he was some civilised gentlemen. "I can provide for your every need, poison."

I cocked a brow and walked through the open doorway but didn't remark on the strange act or even stranger comment.

Inside was cosy, and surprisingly intimate, with a rustic pizza oven throwing heat from the corner and only a handful of tables, draped in fine cloth. Everything was muted warm tones that made me feel instantly welcome, despite the prices I'd glimpsed on the menu a while back.

Sometimes I liked to torture myself by looking at food menus for places I could never afford. Last year, when my uncle had starved me for another imagined slight against the family reputation, I'd seen this new restaurant opening, and couldn't help myself.

A waitress immediately hurried over, eyeing Sin up and down with blatant interest.

I wanted to shake her. If she knew what he really looked like beneath whatever magical image she saw, she'd be screaming, not winking.

Or maybe not. Sin might be a monster, but even I could admit he was a stupidly handsome one.

Clearly, Stockholm syndrome was real. And I was an idiot.

At least he was wearing a shirt today, so I didn't have to stare at his glorious tattooed abs. Even though he could retract them, his threatening spikes tore through the tight material at his shoulders and back.

"Table for two, please," Sin said, like he'd done this a thousand times.

I frowned. Now that I thought about it, he was at complete ease in my realm. He'd gone grocery shopping and cooked me an entire meal that first day while I'd slept. Apparently he'd spent enough time here to know how the little things worked.

If I went to hell, I'd be a lost, vulnerable little lamb. The thought irked me.

The waitress beamed and led us towards the back, past several filled tables. I scanned them all, praying not to recognise anyone.

A toddler in a highchair squealed in excitement, throwing her stuffed dinosaur in the air as we neared a busy table. Without missing a beat, Sin snagged the bright plushie before it could hit me in the face.

His lips quirked, and I sucked in a panicked breath as he turned to the small child. My limbs burned as I readied myself to intervene.

The toddler looked up at the demon and shot chubby hands out in a grabbing motion.

Sin smiled, a gentle look of indulgence on his features as he handed the toy back to the little girl. "Here you go. You have a very cute friend," he said.

Of course Sin would think a bloodthirsty, overgrown lizard was *cute*.

My heart melted as the girl smiled shyly, cuddling the toy to her front as she peeked up at the demon.

Her mother cooed beside her, giving Sin a grateful smile. "Sorry about that. Go on, Annabelle, say thank you to the nice man."

I wasn't sure I'd call Sin a "nice man," but I also wasn't sure what to make of the expression on his face. On anyone else, I might even call it broody.

The thought struck me harder than my uncle ever had.

Did Sin want children of his own? And why did the idea of that take my breath away?

That odd warmth in my chest was back, stronger than ever, nestling right beside my heart.

"Ta-ta," the little girl said, hiding her face in the dinosaur.

"You're most welcome." Sin pitched forward into a regal bow and the girl burst into a fit of giggles before Sin nodded to the mother.

The waitress looked how I felt, as if her ovaries might burst from the cuteness. I shot her the side-eye I wanted to give myself, and she blushed, quickly leading us further into the restaurant.

"We'll take this one." Sin pointed to a table in front of the vast windows.

My eyes narrowed. Would he insist on the tail collar while I ate? If he didn't, any hunters watching would think I was complicit in my capture.

Nobody else would have just sat there opposite a demon and peacefully eaten lunch.

"Of course, sir," the waitress said, a slight breathy quality to her voice.

I felt the first stirrings of a tension headache and massaged my temples as I followed Sin to his chosen table.

He dragged my chair out for me, positioning it closer to him.

I raised a brow but sat. Apparently the collar stayed.

Great. Who didn't want to be lightly choked at lunch?

The demon joined me at the table, flashing me a wicked grin like he'd read the thought on my face.

"Would you like anything to drink?" The waitress asked brightly, having followed us over.

Sin's attention dropped to her throat, and I tensed. Surely he wouldn't just leap up and sink his fangs in? Right here in front of a restaurant full of people?

Sin showed off a fang as he smirked at me. "A bottle of pinot grigio. If you have it, please."

I scowled at the demon. Another little titbit he'd remembered about me. The fact that he was so polite set me even further on edge.

What kind of bloodthirsty monster said "please"?

The manipulative kind.

She nodded, sauntering away with what I could have sworn was a little extra sway in her step. I supposed if you had it, flaunt it, right? Objectively, she was stunning, after all. With envious curves and rich, bronze hair. I bet she didn't have so many scars she forgot the origin of most. She probably didn't know the hollow clawing of starvation. Or the ache that lived in bones broken too many times.

I turned back to find Sin watching me. I felt his attention like a physical caress and shuddered at the intensity.

"What?" I asked.

His lips twitched. "Nothing, poison. You just amuse me, is all."

I pulled a sour face. "Dinner and a show, huh? Lucky you."

"I am lucky, actually," he drawled, ignoring my sarcasm. "Let me guess, you're ordering a carbonara?"

My eyes narrowed. "What is your weird obsession with my food habits? It's creepy, even for a denizen of hell."

He chuckled. "I make it my business to know everything about my prisoners. Can you say the same?"

If anything, I knew a little too much about him after yesterday.

"Other than food preferences, you know nothing about me."

Sure, he'd had a few lucky guesses about my hostile work environment last night outside the demon club, but he didn't know *me*.

Sin reached out, stroking a claw tip along the back of my hand, fisted on the tablecloth. I relaxed my clenched grip, annoyed I'd shown a visible reaction to his taunts.

"You'll pretend to sip your wine, but won't drink a thing, because you want to stay sharp in a pathetic attempt to escape me later, even though I already told you I'd be able to find you anywhere."

"That's pretty obvious," I scoffed. "I'm literally your captive, collared and all." I pointed to his ridiculously soft tail at my throat. "Who wouldn't be trying to escape? Also, that was practically food related." I poked my tongue out like the mature adult I was.

He rolled his starry eyes. "Fine. Then tell me something real about you."

"Like what? You're a demon, and I'm a human. We aren't exactly friendship material," I drawled.

"You know the feeling of my barb locking your sweet cunt onto my dick. We're way past anything as mundane as *friendship*, poison. We're forming a blood bond. I want to mate you. The thought of watching your belly swell with my offspring runs through my mind on loop until I think I'll go insane."

My cheeks flamed at the reminder of what we'd done, and I subtly glanced around, hoping nobody was close enough to hear all the crazy he was spewing.

I chose to ignore the mating and blood bond comments for my own sanity.

One of us had to get it together, and I was hoping whatever weird bond he kept bringing up would just fade with time and distance.

I'd cross the pregnancy bridge if it came to it. I might have been dreaming of starting a family of my own for years, but raising a half-demon baby on the run wasn't exactly what I'd had in mind.

He leaned closer, radiating threat. "But why don't you start by telling me the things I really want to know? Like which hunter prick liked to beat you. Why you were starved. Why you kept experimenting on demons when you didn't want to." Menace seemed to spark the air around him. "Why you were even a hunter in the first place."

Were.

Somewhere in the past few days, Sin had stopped thinking of me as one of *them*.

The realisation that I agreed with him rocked my foundations. I'd always been a hunter. Born and raised in their violent creed. Even if I didn't quite believe in the cause anymore, I still wanted to protect people.

Who was I now?

Just a broken woman trying hard not to think about all her past wrongs, desperate to start over.

"My father," I whispered.

His lips peeled back into a sneer. "The one hurting you?"

I shook my head. "He's dead." I swallowed thickly, eyeing my wrist on the table, sleeve pushed back enough to expose the spotted tiger-lily inked into my pale skin. "But he's the reason I am...*was*...a hunter."

Sin followed my gaze, voice gentle. "Your tattoo... What does it mean?"

I shifted in my seat, curiosity luring me in. "I'll tell you mine, if you tell me yours."

His horns canted aside, a crooked smile playing at his lips. "An unfair trade, given how many I have compared to you."

I smirked, the cruel expression he loved taking over my face.

He chuckled, shaking his head lightly. A break in the clouds had sunlight filtering through the bay window, turning the longer strands of Sin's hair pearlescent where they fell forward into his eyes.

He brushed the strays back between his curved horns, forcing my eyes to the flex of his bicep. "Fine, but toxins first."

I huffed, but my lips curved upward without my permission. The expression died as I thought of my only tattoo.

"When I was twelve, I watched a blood demon kill my father," I said.

Sin's expression shuttered, but he didn't interrupt.

My jaw worked as I took a moment to compose myself. "I loved him, but he was a bastard," I said simply. "He used to call me Tiger-lily, and when he died, I got this to remind me that even the strong get hurt, and family can mean many things."

Not that I'd needed the reminder.

My expression wiped clean. I'd already revealed too much to the observant demon.

Sin considered me for a long moment. "You fed a blood demon, even though one of my kind murdered your father?"

I shrugged. "What can I say, maybe not all blood demons are bad." Guilt squirmed through me on the heels of that thought. I jerked a chin towards his chest. "And yours?"

"The tribal art is the story of my heritage. It honours those who came before me, and the bonds of family."

The idea of celebrating family like that was foreign, but something I longed for in the quiet hours of the night when loneliness bit at me with sharp teeth. What would it be like to have such strong ties to be thankful for, not twisted ones that held you down?

My tongue darted out, moistening my lower lip. "And the others?"

He leaned back in his chair, crossing his arms over his broad chest until I worried for his T-shirt seams. "In hell, I lived in one of the smaller blood kingdoms, working as an enforcer for our laws. My subtype is fairly traditional, and historically closed off, but one day, the King and Queen let in a new group of blood demons. At first, they seemed to settle in well. Then they murdered my mother." His eyes hardened to shards of ice, voice dropping. "I slaughtered them all. Made it hurt. And I *enjoyed* it."

An ache built in my chest. I knew the pain of losing a parent. The horror of witnessing it.

Was this the shadow at his back from his tattooed script? Or was it the violence that followed? I knew all about the guilt that came from such bloodshed.

Some sense of understanding passed between us as I held his starlit gaze.

"She'd always look up at the sky with a smile on her face." His fingers reached up, grazing the pointed star tattoo that wrapped his neck. "And she'd have loved you." He chuckled, but the pale glow in his eyes wavered. "She'd have cheered you on for poisoning me after the way I hurt you with my venom, because she was bloodthirsty like that, and she'd have respected the fires out of you for your fierce nature as a huntress, even if you were going about things the wrong way. You're a protector with blood on your hands. Like me."

I thought back to the script on his chest. We both sought redemption.

I swallowed hard. "I avenged my father too."

He inclined his horns. "I'd have expected nothing less, poison."

The pop of a cork startled me from the intensity flaring between us.

The waitress grinned, holding the wine out like she was giving Sin a gift and fluttering her lashes seductively. "Would you like a taste, sir?"

Ugh. Was she trying to die horribly?

Sin's attention didn't shift from my face. A bright grin slashed through his dark features. "How could I resist?"

Chapter 35

Sin and I spent the whole day traipsing around my hometown, and I was embarrassed to admit it hadn't been the worst day of my life.

My feet had started to ache late in the afternoon, but I didn't complain. If blisters were the worst thing I had to face today, I'd take it gladly.

The demon had watched me touch far too many items in the various shops, all with an intensity that made me squirm. He'd bought me anything I'd even hinted at wanting.

Leo had always earned more than me for his hunter duties, not to mention his part-time job as a security consultant, but he hadn't paid for much in our relationship. Especially near the end. If I'd wanted to go out on a date, I had to pay. He'd always said if he'd suggested it, he'd pay.

Unsurprisingly, he'd never planned anything for us.

Not that I'd wanted him to support me, but it would have been nice for him to treat me sometimes. He knew how much I was struggling. Financially, amongst other things.

Most hunters had a day job as a cover story, and for the money, sometimes strategically in the emergency services or local government, but my uncle had forbidden me in order to keep his leash tight.

I took in the neat brick structure as we approached with a sigh. Dying rays of sunlight slid over the pub, almost setting the bricks aflame and reflecting off the windows until they were blinding to look at.

It was like walking towards the entrance to hell. Not that I'd ever seen one of the portals between our realms.

Sin's last suggestion for the day was the most likely to see success, but it wasn't like I could dissuade him. Didn't mean I hadn't thought about it.

The pub before me was one of many the hunters liked to drink at. There was a chance we'd run into any survivors inside, drowning their sorrows.

Sin walked beside me, his tail collaring me in a way that felt shamefully familiar. I'd almost forgotten it was around my neck, and I berated myself for getting so comfortable with my demonic captor.

"I'm tired. Can't we just call it a night?" I asked, feigning a casual shrug and a very real yawn.

Long days in the lab had made me soft if I found a day of shopping and eating proper meals this tiring.

A cruel smirk curved full, grey lips. "Very convincing. Now say it like you mean it."

I rolled my eyes.

Soft and a terrible liar, apparently.

The sounds of chatter and clinking glasses reached out as we neared the open doorway. Sin entered first, in what I might have called a protective gesture from anyone else. I trailed behind him, eyeing the back of his head like I could burrow through and read his thoughts.

A few groups of patrons already laughed and drank around sticky wooden tables, despite the early hour.

My eyes homed in on one in particular.

A sandy-blond head, cut through with three distinct slashes of scar tissue, bent towards a glamorous woman seated beside him. Leo peeked down her low-cut top before flashing his roguish smile, complete with a single dimple. His hand drifted up to caress her doll-like face, and she smiled coyly, peachy lips curving as she fluttered false lashes up at him.

Anger sparked embers in my chest. The bastard had been engaged to me last month. Our wedding would have been yesterday. He probably thought I'd *died* two days ago.

Yet here he was, hitting on a random woman.

Or maybe she wasn't random. Maybe she was just another person he'd been cheating on me with.

The thought sent me into a spiral of rage.

The urge to storm over and beat him bloody was so strong I could almost feel his high cheekbones shattering under my knuckles.

I gritted my teeth, trying to rein in the vicious thoughts. That was the problem with being raised in violence.

It was my default setting.

Taking a slow breath, I turned my attention to the rest of the table. A giggling woman sat beside Leo's latest conquest, and a stocky male flexed his impressive biceps at her, a too-wide grin on his squashed features as he gestured with his pint glass.

I recognised him immediately: another alpha squad hunter. I'd fought beside Arsen for years.

Yet the stocky hunter was just another traitor who'd left me for dead and then had the audacity to shun me when I'd miraculously survived and transferred into the science division instead.

He noticed us first, eyes bugging comically as he choked on a sip of his beer. He slammed the glass down and his mouth moved, but the sound was lost to the buzz of the other patrons.

Familiar navy eyes left perky cleavage and landed on the towering demon, half blocking me from view. Leo stood, his chair screeching against the floorboards loud enough to pierce the chatter.

The hard indifference on his face contrasted the slack fear on Arsen's.

I stepped out from behind broad, spiked shoulders, giving both men a sarcastic, tinkling wave.

I wasn't sure what reaction I'd expected from my ex-fiancé, but I'd thought seeing me alive and collared by a demon would invoke some kind of emotional response.

I'd been wrong.

His expression remained unchanged. Cold. Unfeeling. His stare leaped straight back to the demon, like my presence meant nothing.

Something in my chest crushed further. I didn't need more evidence that he was a piece of shit, but it would have been nice to be pleasantly surprised for once.

Obviously, my taste in men needed work. Something to think about when I was trolling the desolate forest of eastern Europe.

Arsen rose from his chair, eyeing Sin. He glanced around at the pub patrons nervously before saying something to Leo. The cold bastard jerked a thumb at the back exit, his meaning clear.

Most hunters wouldn't risk harming innocent civilians, and it was good to see that hadn't changed.

Though I wondered whether Sin would start brawling right here in front of all these witnesses.

The demon chuckled, grinning like a maniac. "I'm going to kill your friends."

Nausea rolled my stomach, but I clenched my jaw. No matter how hard I tried, violence followed me like a deranged stalker.

"I have no friends." The words escaped my lips so softly, the laughter in the pub drowned them out.

Sin shot me an unreadable look over his lethal spikes. "You don't need any. You have me."

I didn't know what that meant, but I'd have nothing when he found out the truth of what I'd done to Silvanus.

The demon trailed leisurely after the hunters as they made excuses to their confused dates and headed towards the unlit emergency exit in the back, easing past the cheery humans.

I remained rooted to the spot until Sin's tail tugged at my neck, forcing me into motion.

Dread built with every step.

Sin waltzed through the open fire door, and straight into a trap.

The pair of hunters stood with pistols raised, pointed straight at the demon's chest.

Leo grinned, a malicious baring of teeth. "I'm going to enjoy this."

I swallowed thickly. Tension suffocated the wide alleyway snaking behind the noisy pub we'd exited.

Sure, I could have warned Sin that the hunters would ambush him like this, but why should I?

A niggle of guilt wormed through me, and I stabbed it ruthlessly. I was his *captive*. If anything, I should be cheering at the turn of events.

Any self-respecting fighter would have seen this a mile off, anyway.

Arsen's hand shook slightly, and I took a moment to assess him. Bruises marred his throat, half-hidden by his shirt collar. Scabbed cuts and angry scratches lined his neck and hands.

Leo, on the other hand, looked perfectly unscathed, apart from the old scars slashing his temple. Somehow, he'd not been injured in the raid.

Demons were stronger and faster than us. There was no way they'd failed to land a single blow if he'd been in the melee.

"I took you for many things, Dozer, but never a traitor," Leo sneered, his glare stabbing me for a brief second.

My ex-fiancé had me all kinds of twisted up inside.

I scowled, stepping further from Sin so his thick tail pulled taut between us. "You think I'm here by choice? He's a fucking demon, Leo. What am I supposed to do, unarmed and alone?"

He shook his head, blond locks falling into his face artfully. "This is because of Tia, isn't it?"

My lips parted, rage burning me up from the inside. "You think I'm working with a demon because you *cheated* on me?" My voice rose in pitch, but I was too angry to care that I was practically screeching behind a crowded pub. "I'm. A. Fucking. Prisoner." I snarled. "Just like I've always been. Not that you cared back then, either."

He flinched at my venom, but lifted his chin, glaring right back at me as he kept the gun on Sin. "Grow up, Liliana. You could have left me at any time."

"Once again, it's not always about you." Little pinpricks of pain dug into my palms as my fists curled at my sides.

Sin watched the two of us, a cruel smirk playing on his lips like my emotional pain was so damn enjoyable.

Maybe the evil parasite was more than just a blood demon.

Sin released me and darted forwards, slamming Arsen's hand aside just as he popped off a shot. It went wide, pinging into the bricks somewhere to my left.

Before I could react, Sin buried his fangs in Arsen's neck, using the hunter's struggling body as a shield from Leo.

The monster drew back with bloodied fangs to grin at the other hunter.

His tail lashed out, wrapping my wrist and dragging me to his side.

"Sorry to interrupt the lovers' spat." The demon glanced between me and my ex with a sinful smirk. "Please, continue."

Arsen whimpered in Sin's grip, and his thrashing slowed before he slumped, limbs dangling uselessly.

I assumed he was still alive, given Sin needed people to question. The dead made for poor conversationalists.

Leo snarled, his gun aimed steadily at Sin through the unconscious hunter doubling as a shield. My ex couldn't take the shot without hitting Arsen, but I wouldn't put it past the maniac to try.

He'd always thought very highly of his skills. In all departments.

"Great, Dozer. Now you've killed Arsen too," Leo growled.

I raised a brow. How was this a me issue?

Other than a little anger, Leo didn't seem that upset. He ignored the demon like he wasn't even there, glaring daggers at me instead.

I cocked a hip. "Are you high? Or is your head just so far up your own arse you can't think past the bullshit?"

"Fuck you. You're the damn hunter princess of Riverside, pampered and pretty," he scoffed, full of bitterness. "Your uncle has done so much for you, and this is how you repay him? Repay us?" He shook his head, backing away through the alley, pistol raised.

Normally, a hunter would strike first and talk never, but Leo had been outmanoeuvred by a psychotic demon and his not-so-willing sidekick.

I batted my lashes, twirling a lock of my plain hair around a finger. "Aww, you think I'm pretty?" I drawled, putting on my best vapid expression.

Sin's dark chuckle filled the air. The bastard was probably seconds away from grabbing some popcorn to watch the train wreck that was my life.

Leo glared harder at me, if that were possible.

"You were once," he sneered. "Now you're just a skinny, used-up whore."

My own dark chuckle spilled out, layering over the growl spilling from Sin. "How am I the whore, when you were the one fucking around behind your fiancé's back?"

"Because you're the one spreading your legs for evil," the hunter snarled.

"You'd better shoot, human. Or I'll tear your spine out through your throat and flay you with it." Sin's voice had dropped to that silky octave that spelled danger.

I side-eyed the monster. Clearly, he was losing patience with this game.

Leo sneered. And pulled the trigger.

A distinct pop sounded, muffled by the silencer, but no pain followed.

Sin grunted, and cruel laughter spilled from him, louder than the gunshot. My heart squeezed. An exit wound marked his shoulder.

The bullet had missed both Arsen and me. Just barely.

Pistols weren't known for their accuracy, and Leo wasn't exactly at close range. He'd seen the odds of both a hunter and his ex-fiancé dying and had taken the shot anyway.

My hands curled into fists. "Leo, you fucking bastard." Anger strangled my vocal cords until the curse came out as more of a whisper.

A smug grin wrinkled his scars.

The demon's chuckle simmered low. "Sorry, I should have specified. Shoot *well*."

Leo's sneer dropped as Sin burst into motion. The demon released Arsen and me, racing towards my ex. Leo turned and ran, shooting back wildly over his shoulder.

I yelped as a ricochet pinged and sliced through my forearm, knocking me back a step. Pain sang through my flesh in the next breath.

Sin turned, eyes wide. He scanned me from head to toe instead of chasing his prey.

"I'm fine!" I called out, straightening with a wince.

Sin's eyes darkened to pure black, and he roared at Leo's retreating form disappearing around the edge of the building.

The demon stalked back towards me, kicking the unconscious hunter out of his path.

Rage contorted his features until he was almost unrecognisable. Purely demonic.

"You're. Hurt," he growled, reaching for my injured arm.

I chuckled, ignoring the line of pain burning across my forearm. I'd had much, much worse. "It's barely a scratch. Us humans aren't that weak. It'll be gone in a week or so."

He bared his fangs. "Unacceptable."

"Sorry if my body's natural abilities aren't quick enough for you," I drawled.

He nodded like he accepted my apology, and my mouth popped open in shock.

Before I could berate the idiotic demon, he brought my arm up to his lips. His forked tongue slid out, lapping the blood running slowly down my skin. A look of bliss stole the rage from his carved features.

I watched, stunned, as he gently cleaned the wound, a complete change to how he'd roared like a feral beast just seconds ago.

Dark blood seeped from the bullet wound in his shoulder. He'd gained another through his bicep, but as I watched, they both closed, until only ashen scars graced his charcoal skin.

Glowing eyes pinned me. "I'm going to show you a secret, and you're not going to share it with anyone. Do you understand me, poison?"

I bit my lip. Who was I going to tell? I was his captive—for now—and then I'd be living free, off-grid somewhere until all the hunters and demons forgot about me.

Ignoring the dumb pang in my chest, I nodded, succumbing to my curiosity instead. Sin raised his tail, spikes out. The longest one on the tip dug into his wrist. Blood welled, and he held it over my cut.

The heated drop seemed to fizz as it hit my wound. I bit down on my tongue at the odd sensation but didn't pull away.

I already knew this secret.

Chapter 37

My arm tingled as the edges of the cut pulled to together, zipping closed until nothing but a faint pink line remained. It probably wouldn't even scar.

Guilt strangled me until I was rendered mute.

When Silvanus had saved my life by forcing his blood down my throat and showering it over me, he'd passed out beside me right before I'd followed him into unconsciousness.

If anything, I'd tried to convince myself it wasn't that miraculous. I'd refused to think about the incident at all. The thing was too painful, because it meant that I'd probably murdered innocents in my quest to protect humans.

Even as a hunter scientist, I hadn't been doing much good until Sin came along.

This whole time, I shouldn't have been messing about with my blood though.

I should have been studying his.

Unlike with my saviour, Sin only seemed mildly drained. His tail drooped enough to brush the ground, and a tightness lurked around his hypnotic eyes. I was exhausted too, but nothing on last time.

Was it because Sin was stronger? Surely the amount of damage to heal had an effect too? How much demon blood was needed to heal what size of wound? Could all blood demons do this?

"You've got that mad scientist glint back in your eye, poison." Sin sneered, the mocking expression as familiar as it was infuriating. "Don't waste your time thinking about it. I'm not going back to playing your lab rat."

I huffed and pulled my arm from his warm grip. Maybe I was more scientist than hunter. Or probably just a cruel mixture of both.

"Thank you," I murmured, unable to meet his inhuman gaze.

"That coward was your ex?" Sin's voice was barely a whisper, yet still artic cold.

I nodded, studying the cracked paving slabs under my blood-splattered trainers.

"I thought you were meant to be smart? Why would you ever choose to be with a weak creature like that?"

I swallowed thickly, his question ricocheting around my skull like a gunshot.

"I guess I was just a little too desperate to be loved, flaws and all." Bitterness coated my tongue as I forced the words out past the lump in my throat.

Warm fingers tilted my chin upwards, and I scrounged up the courage to meet the twin stars lighting the darkness of his eyes.

Sin studied my face with a consuming intensity. "You don't have any flaws, poison. Every part of you is perfection to me."

Tears flooded my vision from one blink to the next. "You can't mean that."

"I've never lied to you, poison." His gaze held me captive.

A dark laugh left my lips, and I brushed aside the evidence of my weakness spilling down my cheeks. "So you really will snap my neck?"

He grinned, so at odds with the vicious topic of conversation. "Sure. When I get bored of toying with you. But I'll never be done with you, Liliana. You will always be mine."

I narrowed my eyes at the wicked demon. "You don't get to just say psycho shit like that."

He stepped in close, hand fisting in my hair. I couldn't look away from his starlit eyes, trapped in his hold.

"Then let me prove it."

His lips pressed to mine, sweet and sinfully slow.

There was a promise on his lips.

And it terrified me because I knew mine were answering right back.

Something warmed in my chest, like my heart was basking in sunlight.

An eternity passed as he kissed me like I was the answer to every question he had.

He growled deep in his throat, vibrating my lips. His hands tightened in my hair, pricking my scalp. He deepened the kiss as heat sparked through me. I craved him with a desperation that took my breath away.

"Liliana," he murmured against my lips, pulling back just enough for me to gasp a ragged breath. "I'm addicted to more than just your blood. Everything about you is intoxicating."

A loud bang had me shoving out of Sin's hold, preparing to attack.

A man stood in the pub doorway, a scowl etching his craggy features. "Hey! You two can't be out here fucking like horny teens."

Sin pursed his kiss-swollen lips, looking wholly unconcerned by the shouting human. "Come on, poison. Let's get your friend back to our home."

Our home. Those two words mocked me with a sense of longing that I shouldn't have.

"Sorry," I cringed, giving the man an awkward wave. At least he hadn't spotted Arsen's body sprawled by the brick wall. "We're just leaving."

"If you're not gone in five, I'll call the police on your canoodling arses." The old grouch slammed the door behind him.

Sin's low chuckle rumbled beside me, and I shot him a glare, but quickly looked away.

I didn't know what to make of him. Of us. Things were spiralling out of control so fast I was dizzy.

I'd hurt him, and he'd returned the favour. He took my breath away, but half the time threatened to do so for good. He claimed I was his with sweet words and collared me like his captive. He protected me. Cooked for me. Healed me.

We were sworn enemies, yet the sparks between us caught fire until I burned for him.

Nothing made sense.

And he'd still execute me when he found out what I was hiding, regardless of whatever demonic blood bond may or may not be forming.

I had to escape him before it was too late. Despite the insanity he made me feel.

My attention snagged on the hunter still passed out. I was no doctor, but being unconscious that long seemed unhealthy.

The demon followed my gaze to his other prey. "He'll be out for a while longer after the dose I gave him."

I blanched at his implication. "Are you saying you could have knocked me out with your bite at any time?"

He flashed me a fanged smirk. "You're not the only poisonous one here."

I swallowed thickly. I'd been in more danger feeding him than I'd realised.

Hard to push a lethal collar remote if you were unconscious. He could easily have torn open my arteries, bleeding me out.

My life had been in his claws for weeks without me knowing.

"I see you're finally noticing how nice I've been." He bared his teeth in a vicious smile. "You're welcome."

"Yeah, your sainthood is in the post, I'm sure," I drawled and made a sweeping gesture to the side of the building. "Beast before beauty."

The demon snorted, scooping Arsen under one arm like a rolled yoga mat. I shot him a pointed look, but it didn't seem like he was willing to retract his spines to throw him over a shoulder.

I followed Sin's spiked back down the dim alley, the opposite direction that Leo had fled. The fighting was over, for now, yet adrenaline sizzled through my veins as we circled the pub to where we'd parked the car further along the quiet street.

I kept my eyes peeled, but nobody was around to witness the crime I was an unwilling accessory to. Unlocking the vehicle, I slid into the driver's seat, watching in the rear-view mirror as Sin slung Arsen into the car boot and slammed it closed. He climbed in beside me, comically big for the space, despite it being a generous-sized SUV.

Stewing in tense silence, I drove towards the house Sin had claimed. Every second that passed was one less in Arsen's life, and guilt squirmed through me.

Maybe I should crash the car.

Would I be able to slam the passenger side into a lamp-post or tree hard enough to injure Sin without killing myself too? I could run out and grab Arsen, the pair of us fleeing, before the demon recovered enough to hunt us down.

"What are you scheming, poison?" Sin's voice was laced with mocking. His hand came to rest just above my knee, searing like a brand through my borrowed jeans. "Your pretty features betray you."

I pulled a sour face, still watching the road, even as a dumb, girly part of me instantly latched onto the word *pretty*. Did the demon find me attractive?

And why did I care?

This had to stop.

I needed to get away from him before things got any more complicated.

Drawing a deep breath, I let everything quiet inside me. I'd made my decision.

I yanked the wheel aside.

The car slammed into a lamp-post with a squeal of metal on metal and the crunch of shattered glass. The airbags exploded, bouncing off my head in a dizzying slam. Something slapped my chest, halting my momentum.

"Liliana!" Sin roared, oddly muffled over the ringing in my ears. "Poison, are you okay? What the fuck just happened?"

My chest heaved. Sin's tail had caught me before I could impale myself on his shoulder spines. I'd almost got more than a little headache.

Any fledgling hope was crushed like the passenger side door. Sin seemed wholly unhurt, cuts from the broken glass of his window already closing over before my eyes.

I'd failed.

And now Arsen and I were both going to die under Sin's claws.

"Whoops." I straightened, an unhinged laugh spilling out. My heart pounded in time with the dull throb in my thick skull. "There was a squirrel in the road. The red ones are super rare now."

The demon pursed his lips, eyes narrowing dangerously. "You're hurting my feelings, poison. Here I thought we were both just pretending to be captives for each other. Apparently I'll have to try harder for you to choose me too."

I looked away, heart pounding for a different reason now.

Had he *chosen* me? In what way?

I shoved aside the hope trying to creep in at the edges like a monster in the dark. It didn't matter what he thought of me. I escaped, or I died. Either way, we'd never see each other again.

To my dismay, the car worked perfectly fine as I restarted the engine, finishing the final few minutes' drive with an odd shrieking rattle coming from the SUV.

Not only had we made ourselves at home in a stranger's house, but now I'd wrecked their car too.

I screeched us onto the driveway, quickly escaping the confined space and slamming the car door hard enough to rock the already damaged vehicle.

Sin punched the warped passenger door clean off its hinges, his reinforced spiked knuckles apparently tougher than steel.

He climbed out opposite me, a knowing smirk playing on his pouty lips.

I huffed, waiting for him to fetch his other prisoner.

The demon yanked Arsen out by the arm, letting the man hit the gravel. I winced at the dull thud. The poor guy would feel that when he woke up. Along with whatever injuries I'd given him by recklessly crashing the car.

"Oops." Sin sniggered gleefully to himself and dragged the hunter along the ground.

I followed the monster into the house, stewing in my uselessness. He slung his prisoner into the downstairs bathroom and fetched a dining chair from the kitchen, propping it under the door handle and blocking half the corridor. It wouldn't trap the hunter but should slow him long enough for Sin to reach him with the commotion.

I eyed my demon captor. "How much longer will he be out?"

He smirked, brushing past me and catching my wrist with his now smooth-tipped tail. "Enough time for us to get dinner."

The demon tugged me into the kitchen, jerking his chin towards my usual chair at the dining table littered with his claw marks. I swallowed at the evidence of what we'd done together. The line I'd crossed with the enemy.

I sat quietly, and he headed straight for the fridge.

My stomach growled at him, matching my mood.

What kind of sick sociopath kissed her captor? Ate dinner with him at the table they'd fucked on?

Would we sit and pretend to have another civilised meal, all while waiting for his other prisoner to wake up, ready to be tortured for information?

Information that would get me killed.

Chapter 38

The last rich bite of pesto gnocchi slid down my throat as I savoured the final treat.

Another delicious meal prepared by the bizarrely skilled monster-slash-chef.

It had taken Sin mere minutes to throw together the meal, and we'd eaten in tense silence. My head still throbbed from my own stupidity.

Who decided a car crash was a good idea? And why did my escape attempts always involve writing off a vehicle?

Of course, Sin looked perfectly at ease, dwarfing the furniture and cutlery as usual.

I was on edge. Thoughts racing to figure a way out of this.

I eyed the back door, and the freedom promised by the darkened garden, but I'd never be able to outrun a blood demon at full strength.

A low groan rose from the bathroom.

The gnocchi turned to lead in my stomach.

"Sin... Don't do this," I said, desperation tightening my vocal cords.

I wasn't sure I could watch him torture someone, let alone a hunter I knew. Someone I'd trained with. Worked with for years.

"This bastard helped your ex shove me into that fight ring. He electrocuted me and others until we hurt each other for their amusement." His tone was level, despite the harrowing tale. He settled back in his chair, eyeing me over the wrecked dining table. "Do you think he deserves mercy after that?"

"I..." Words failed me.

The never-ending guilt drowned me, shoving me beneath dark waves. I'd let that happen to him. I'd let it happen to so many before him too.

He rose silently, not the faintest protest from the chair. I followed like a ghost. Spikes slid out from his spine, jutting through the tight fabric of his shirt, as he returned to what I thought of as his warrior mode. The white points gleamed under the warm lighting as he stalked into the corridor.

He kicked out the dining chair, sending it tumbling along the carpeted hallway to hit the front door with a thud. The monster yanked open the bathroom door and prowled inside, but I was rooted to the spot.

A scream sounded, and then Sin was striding back out, a struggling man clutched by the shirt. The demon threw his captive into the wall. Plaster cracked, loud as a gunshot.

Arsen panted in fear, pushing himself up shakily. His usually burnished skin was a sickly pale shade. Blood smeared his throat from the messy bite Sin had used to poison him. The demon backed the man into the cracked wall, leaving just enough space for false hope.

The hunter eyed the oak door only a few metres away, but it might as well be miles.

His glare swung to me next, a sneer on his lips. "Fucking Dozer, of course you're the first one to turn traitor to the cause. What? Because Leo dumped you, you're sucking demon dick to get back at him?"

My cheeks reddened like he'd psychically slapped me. Shame rushed in the wake of his words, stunning me. It wasn't anything to do with Leo, but I'd done a lot more than that with Sin.

A low growl filled the space, contrasting the cheery décor. Sin's attention locked onto Arsen, a predator sizing up his prey.

It wasn't aimed my way, yet the ferocity was like a bucket of ice water, breaking me from the heat of embarrassment.

"I don't usually enjoy causing pain...*much*." Sin's grin was viciously cruel. "But I'm going to take great pleasure in making you bleed for that."

Arsen whimpered, terror stealing his vitriol.

Violence filled the corridor, squeezing out any air.

Sin caressed the spikes of his tail along the man's arm. Arsen quaked at the casual threat, but there was nowhere to go. Sin had the hunter trapped against the magnolia wall, his sheer size mocking any hope of escape.

The front door lurked close, taunting us both.

"Just get it over with, vile beast," Arsen spat, jerking away from the demon's touch. "Whatever it is you want I ain't giving you," he scowled in my direction. "I'm not a traitorous whore."

This time, I was ready, my mask firmly in place. "I was kidnapped in the raid, you idiot. I'm not here by choice."

"You sure about that? There's not a single mark on you. Did you trade your body for your life?" he hissed, shoulders squaring as I became an outlet for his terror. "You're nothing but a hole. To our kind or theirs."

The words knifed through me, cutting away the barely healed wounds from Leo's betrayal.

Sin chuckled, a dark and bloody sound. "By all means, keep insulting her. She's the only reason your entrails aren't already wrapped around my claws. If she leaves because of your petty words, I'll get to play with you for even longer before I finally let you die screaming. I will make you beg for her forgiveness until the last name on your lips is hers."

My brows shot up. Rage carved Sin's cruel features as demonic as I'd ever seen him. His tail flicked side to side, the sharp weapon only inches from the cowering human.

"Feeling particularly violent today, parasite?" I asked.

I didn't know how to process this side of him. Nobody had ever defended me before him. It made zero sense, considering I'd been the one keeping him captive and actively trying to poison him.

His gaze snapped to mine. "How many times do I have to tell you, poison? You. Are. Mine. Nobody will hurt you without suffering tenfold for their stupidity."

I sighed, all the energy draining from me in a rush.

My emotions were a tangled mess.

One minute, the demon seemed to care for me. He kissed me so passionately I thought I might burn up. He fed me when I was starving. Protected me when I was attacked. Rescued me from my prison.

But was it all so he could keep feeding from me?

Arsen was wrong about me. I wasn't a hole. I was a fucking vein.

Yet I refused to stay that way. I would break free from all the toxic bullshit and start a new life. One where I lived for myself, and nobody else.

Even though something in me recoiled at the idea of leaving behind the one man who made me feel alive. Who understood the darkness tarnishing my soul and didn't balk at my violent side.

I watched on in silence, unable to voice any of my whirring thoughts.

Suspicion flashed through his narrowed gaze before his attention returned to his newest victim.

"All you have to do is answer one question, and the pain stops."

Sin whipped his tail out and slapped the hunter.

Arsen screamed, lifting his arms to block too late. Blood ran down his face from multiple punctures.

He touched a hand to his cheek. A sneer twisted his features, causing more blood to run. "Fuck you, beast. I ain't telling you shit."

Sin purred, the sound positively evil, "By all means, try to hold out as long as you can for me."

I shivered, reminded again why it had been so easy for me to assume all demons were malevolent beasts. Even the ones who seemed to not want us all dead were still bloodthirsty by nature.

Sin reached out, casually running a claw along the man's chest, slicing right through his shirt to open up a thin line of red. Nothing too deep or painful. Not yet.

Arsen sneered, holding strong, but his body betrayed him, trembling against the wall. It wasn't usually the physical torture that made someone crack.

I knew that better than most.

"In the last month, have you seen a male demon who looked like me? A few inches shorter, yellow eyes?"

I swallowed hard at the reminder of Sin's goal. And my insidious secret.

Sunshine eyes. Kind smile. Gentle hands. Blood.

Arsen laughed, a cruel sound to rival Sin's. "What, lost your daddy?"

Sin's hand snapped out, bony knuckles cracking Arsen's bloodied cheek. "My brother, actually."

My heart stuttered, terror filling me with enough dread to curdle my gut.

If Sin knew what had happened. What I'd done. He'd kill me.

No more stolen kisses and confusing declarations.

He'd finally snap my neck.

How could he not? His brother had saved my life, and I'd got him slaughtered for his mercy.

I hid my trembling hands in my pockets, watching the scene unfold. I needed to get out of here before Sin found out the truth.

Arsen had been there. He hadn't been the one to kill Sin's brother, but he'd watched as Leo slid his blade into the vulnerable demon's chest.

Malice sharpened the hunter's bloody smile as he aimed it my way. "He doesn't know. Does he?" Maniacal laughter followed. "Oh, this is just priceless."

Sin's attention flicked towards me. "Know what, poison?" His voice dropped to a deathly low octave, so soft and yet so deadly.

Arsen cackled like a damn witch, the unhinged sound seeming to echo through the bright corridor. "The bitch you're fucking got your brother killed."

Sin tensed, betrayal slicing through his expression before rage swallowed him whole. An animalistic roar shook the walls as he vented his anger.

He reached forward and grabbed Arsen's throat, ripping it out with his claws.

The hunter collapsed, blood gushing over the cream carpet in a bright torrent. Sin dropped the flesh in his grip. He turned to face me, eyes pitch black like the stars had been snuffed out.

I didn't recognise the demon before me.

But I knew death when it snarled in my face.

Chapter 39

Sin slammed me into the wall, right next to where he'd just murdered Arsen.

I braced to meet the same fate.

The demon snarled, but his claws hovered inches from my face. Blood dripped from their lengths, splattering the front of my shirt.

My chest heaved for air. Any breath could be my last.

The usual starlight in his eyes was gone, lost to a dark abyss.

Anguish tore apart his mask of rage. "Why?"

His fist clenched, dropping back to his side. His solid heat pressed me against the wall, trapping me in.

I opened my mouth. Unsure where to begin.

Technically, I hadn't killed his brother.

I'd just watched while my hunter team had come back and killed him where he lay beside me.

Whatever power he'd used to save me had knocked him out. If he hadn't spent all his energy healing me, he wouldn't have been there, vulnerable and defenceless.

He'd saved my life, and it had cost him his.

How was I not responsible for that?

"I'm sorry," I breathed, the broken sound like shards of glass in my mouth. "I didn't kill him, but...it was my fault."

Pain tightened his inhuman features. He stepped back, a new mask falling into place. Cold and unfeeling. "Go."

I blinked, shocked my heart was still beating. "What?"

"Leave." Stars flickered back to life in his eyes, bright enough to burn down to my blackened soul. "It's what you wanted all along, right? To escape. You never felt a thing for me. A hunter to the core."

"Sin... No. It's not like that, I..."

"You lied to me!" he snarled, cutting me off with a vicious sound that raised the hairs on my nape. "Just go, hunter, before I change my mind. I want to feel your tiny neck snap under my fingers, but I can't do it. You might be a heartless monster, but *this*"—he gestured a bloodied claw between us—"was real for me."

Moisture swam through my vision as I stumbled back a step. A nauseating mix between relief and devastation struck me. My lungs wouldn't expand.

"It's real for me too," I whispered, voice barely audible over Sin's low growl.

His eyes narrowed, accusation clear on his stony features.

I took in every detail I could, crystallising this one final moment in my mind. The last time I'd ever see him.

With a last look at the demon I'd begun to care for, I turned and fled.

The front door slammed shut behind me as I escaped into the cool night. Wind blew the angry tears tracking down my cheeks, and I swiped them away from under my glasses.

Some ridiculous part of me felt betrayed. Worse than when Leo had abandoned me to die on the battlefield.

I'd hurt Sin. What right did I have to be so upset about his reaction to it?

At least I was *alive*. But whatever bond had been growing between us was dead.

I'd killed it.

My hands shook, but whether it was the cold or the adrenaline, I didn't know. I started walking, leaving Sin behind, and all the confusing things he made me feel.

Hours passed as I trailed through the streets, reeling from the ache knifing my chest.

This was what I'd wanted. To finally be free of demons and hunters and violence.

So why did I feel like someone had carved open my chest and shredded my insides?

You knew your life was messed up when your enemy treated you better than your family. When a demon showed more kindness than the humans sworn to protect people.

But it was more than that. Every time Sin taunted me and I bit back, it revealed the backbone I thought I'd lost under the years of brutality my uncle dealt out.

The wicked demon made me feel alive. Like a real person worth more than my last name or the lives I could take.

Being around him had chipped away the loneliness and guilt smothering me, until hope seeped in through the cracks, despite the sins of my past.

Swallowing the bitter lump in my throat, I tried to scrape the tattered pieces of myself together. Now was my chance to flee. To start a new life.

A small voice screamed inside my head, *What life?*

I couldn't get the image of Sin's face out of my head. That flash of betrayal in his eyes sliced through me. More silent tears overflowed, chilled by the harsh night.

My hands curled into fists, nails biting into my palms. The pain helped focus me, even as it paled compared to the ache in my chest.

I altered course, heading for the trio of high-rise buildings lit up in the distance. My cramped flat had the cash I'd been saving up for an opportunity just like this. I needed to break in, pack my meagre belongings, and leave Riverside behind. Along with all the hunters and demons. The violence and heartache.

Time blurred as I jogged through the dark streets in the early hours. The suburban houses were silent apart from the occasional barking dog. More sounds filtered in as I passed into the rougher neighbourhoods: parties spilling bass-heavy music, yelled arguments, revving engines.

Finally, I slipped into my building, quickly heading up the stairs towards my floor, avoiding the broken glass littering the worn carpet like confetti.

I didn't have my apartment keys, but the peeling door was flimsy enough.

I kicked it in with a loud bang, enjoying the satisfaction that came with destroying a part of the place that had trapped me for so long.

None of my neighbours even popped their heads out to investigate the noise.

I huffed under my breath, storming inside. Everything looked exactly as I'd left it when I'd hurried off to work three days ago.

The only thing different was me.

I snagged my emergency go bag, packing a couple more essentials, and grabbed my pouch of cash, stored in one of the many fist-shaped holes in the plasterboard. A fun decoration from a previous tenant.

Slinging my pack onto my shoulder, I took one last look around my apartment.

Everything was dingy. Worn. Tired. Broken.

If that wasn't a depressing metaphor for my life, I didn't know what was.

My chest ached. The past few days playing house with Sin had really put my depressing life into perspective.

Somewhere out there, a family was living my dream life. They had smiling pictures of their loved ones on the walls. Meaningful trinkets from adventures worth remembering. A cosy, safe space to rest. Enough food to eat. Money to waste on trivial things like scented candles and hair conditioner.

I bet they didn't have scars covering their bodies. A constant patchwork of cuts and bruises adding to the collection. I bet you couldn't see their ribs poking through. I bet they weren't a quick turn away from passing out.

I bet their hands weren't drenched in blood.

I bet they dreamed at night, not woke up sobbing with a cry on their lips.

My mind tried to fracture under the weight of everything.

Through sheer stubborn will, I held myself together.

I just needed to get far away from here, and then everything would be all right. I could find a safe place to have that breakdown that had been looming for years.

Maybe then the nightmares would stop. Not that I deserved the peace.

Starlit eyes filled with betrayal pierced my mind. My heart ached, but I ignored it, accepting the hurt until it numbed me.

I turned my back on my old life, walking out of the broken door.

"Ah, Liliana. I've been looking for you."

The familiar gruff voice froze me.

My uncle waited in the corridor, grizzled features sharp.

Behind him, Leo grinned.

Chapter 40

Oh goodie, my family was here to make sure I was okay.

If only.

Seeing my uncle only ever caused pain.

The two hunters looked a little worn at the edges, with bruised smudges under their eyes. Leo even had a fresh cut on his tanned cheek, and harsher lines seemed to bracket my uncle's thin mouth. They'd dressed identically in black cargos and suspiciously large coats, clearly armed beneath.

My first instinct was to attack. Yet I couldn't fight my way past both men.

Leo I could probably take in a fight. I'd used to let him win sometimes, much to my shame, but now I wouldn't be holding back to protect his fragile ego.

My uncle was a different story. He might be greying at the temples, but he'd been hardened in the forge of violence long before I was born. I wouldn't delude myself into thinking his age hindered his capacity to put me firmly in the grave.

I swallowed thickly. The freedom that had glimmered so close was ripped from my cold, bony grasp once more.

Any hope I'd had left was crushed, along with my already battered heart.

I scraped some logic from the ruin. It hurt, slipping back on the mask of the devoted hunter, suffocating and pinching like it no longer fit.

But choice was a luxury I'd never been able to afford.

A tight smile stretched my brittle lips. "Uncle. I'm so glad you're okay."

He nodded, like he accepted my concern but didn't particularly care either way. "Let's go."

My last living relative turned his back to me. Leo smirked as he let my uncle pass, starting down the stairs with glass crunching under his boots.

I clamped down on the urge to scream.

For a second, I wondered what would happen if I just refused to go with them.

Then I remembered the last time I'd tried to escape. Leo had driven me off the road, again almost killing me, and physically dragged me back here.

I took a step towards them. Then another. My feet kept moving, but my dreams were left behind.

Leo grinned as I approached, gesturing for me to follow my uncle first. Having him at my back set my teeth on edge.

"We've been busy since the attack," my uncle said, oblivious to my discomfort. "Luckily, Leo and I were with the North London chapter, discussing alliances and reinforcements."

I nodded mutely, as if I'd been paying close attention to all hunter-related matters and was somehow fully aware of his movements without being informed.

We marched out of the building, and he continued, "I'll get you up to speed once we arrive."

More nodding.

I followed my uncle to a subtly armoured SUV, parked right out front across two accessible parking spaces.

Leo opened the door for me like a gentleman and invaded my personal space like a creep.

"Where's your beast now, slut?" he whispered so only I could hear.

I stiffened but refused to bite, sliding into the back seat of the car. My ex-fiancé slammed the door shut, sealing me inside. Considering the last I'd seen of him was the back of his sandy-blond head as he left Arsen and me to a demon's clutches, he was being awfully superior.

My uncle twisted in the front passenger seat, colourless eyes boring into me. The silence thickened with unspoken accusation, but I refused to buckle under the strain.

Leo hopped into the driver's seat, breaking the stare-off, and peeled away from my building with a revved engine and the squeal of tyres.

My thoughts blanked as he sped through the streets, empty at this time of night.

Minutes ticked by, agonisingly slow and yet somehow too fast. We pulled off the main roads, winding through the countryside in the darkness. The headlights illuminated fields of wheat and rapeseed as we left the city behind.

After twenty minutes of tense silence, we arrived outside a familiar cabin. My father had bought this section of woodland before I was born. He'd built a quaint cabin on the land, and my uncle had been expanding it ever since.

He'd brought me here countless times, testing my survival skills and using the privacy it offered to teach me strength and discipline. I'd learned how to hunt, how to use weapons, and how to suffer.

My stomach churned at the sight of the wooden monstrosity.

Leo parked next to a suite of other vehicles in the mud. We exited, walking towards the raised entryway in silence.

Leo stepped into the cabin, spilling warm lighting and the sounds of muted chatter.

My uncle stopped me outside with a raised palm.

Flinty eyes tried to stab through my mask, but I waited him out. We lurked on the front porch, staring each other down.

Finally, he nodded, seeming to decide something. "We can address your failures later, Liliana. For now, we have work to do."

With that ominous statement, he strode inside the building that featured in too many of my nightmares.

I steeled my spine and plunged into hell after him.

Four alpha team hunters lounged in the main living area, a sprawling open-plan space complete with a fireplace and a set of horns on the wall, as if this really were the luxury hunting lodge the outside promised.

I didn't look too closely at the branching antlers mounted on the wall. They weren't from deer.

Jayce caught sight of me and spat out a mouthful of his drink. "*Dozer* survived?!" He slammed his tumbler onto the side table as every hunter turned to give me a once-over.

I huffed at his dramatics. "I was alpha squad long before I chose omega. Long before *you*."

My uncle glanced at me as he strode past, disapproval furrowing his brows at the emotion-driven outburst, but said nothing, jerking his chin towards the back.

"Pfft, barely," Jayce muttered under his breath.

I ignored him and trailed behind the man still holding my leash after all these years.

A pained groan rumbled from somewhere along the sparse corridor, and I stomped down the urge to see what was behind door number two. Instead, I followed my uncle into his study, once my father's favourite room in the cabin. I wondered what he would have thought of the bloodstains that painted it now, little flecks of my pain left behind on the floorboards.

To my annoyance, Leo hovered inside the spacious office, leaning casually against the bookshelf. He took the seat beside me as we faced my uncle across a polished desk.

The monster cleared his throat, devouring my attention. "Leo reported a demon kidnapped you." There was zero inflection in his tone. Anyone else might have been concerned about the abduction of their niece, but not the mighty hunter prime. "Not everyone was so lucky. Your omega colleagues didn't make it out. Congratulations, Liliana. You're now head of our research division."

My nape prickled at his declaration. Sin had snapped Martin's neck right in front of me, but I hadn't realised Cara and the others were also dead. I had mixed emotions on the subject.

"We're not exactly in a position to continue our work…" I trailed off.

I swallowed as my uncle's inscrutable features twitched at the hint of dissent.

"You're mistaken. I've secured assistance from our London allies, and the team recovered several fridges from the labs while you were off gallivanting. It's now more important than ever that we purge the evil haunting our city." He slammed a clenched fist down in a rare display of emotion that had the sheathed knife on his desk jumping.

Good to know killing demons ranked as more important than whether I'd died.

I nodded, as if the idea of experimenting on demons didn't cause bile to rise in my throat.

Leo slung an arm across the back of my chair, and I stiffened at the contact.

He twisted in his seat, invading my personal space like he had a right to it. "Despite our...issues, I believe in you, Liliana. You were always smart. If you just worked harder, I know you'd find something to help us win this war."

Wow.

The audacity of this boy knew no bounds. Literally none.

For some reason, my mind latched onto that word: *smart*.

My lips twitched as I remembered all the times Sin had questioned my supposed intelligence. The mirth died before it could fully form. I'd ruined whatever strange connection had grown between us.

You know, by getting his brother killed.

"Yes, I'll try super hard." Even to my own ears, the sarcasm leeched through. I cleared my throat, ignoring the tightness as I buried my true feelings. "For the good of humanity."

But I'd never again be responsible for torturing another soul. Not that I could tell my uncle or ex.

"I knew we could count on you." My uncle's bland tone really added to his dedicated serial killer vibe. "Leo will show you to your new lab to set up." He turned to the hunter in question. "Let her have her pick of the beasts and don't touch any she chooses. We can't risk hindering her progress."

Oh god. They already had captives.

I choked back the manic laughter that bubbled up. A naive part of me had hoped the screams from down the corridor had been an injured hunter getting first aid.

Leo stood, the abrupt screech of his chair on the hardwood grating on my frayed nerves.

This couldn't be happening.

On autopilot, my body copied my traitorous ex. I nodded as if the unhinged movements would cause both psychos to think I was in complete agreement rather than descending into my own madness.

Leo shared a final pointed look with his leader before striding out of the office.

I couldn't look back. Instead, I followed my ex down the stark corridor. Agonised groans echoed louder with each step.

I braced as he unlocked one of the unmarked doors, and promptly threw up on his shoes.

Chapter 41

A battered cage dominated one wall. Inside, three demons huddled together. The tallest one's horns almost brushed the top bars, and she half hid the other two behind her bulk.

A fourth demon writhed in metal restraints on a dining table in the middle of the room, giving the others a prime view of the broken male. Navy blood dripped off the wooden surface to pool onto the tarp lining the floor beneath.

"The fuck is wrong with you?" Leo snarled, glaring down at the wet chunks on his combat boots.

I wiped a shaky hand across my mouth. "Must have eaten something dodgy," I croaked.

"Bathroom is at the end of the hall." He jerked his thumb, as if I hadn't been here countless times, disgust curling his upper lip. "I'll get you something to clean this up." He strode off before I could respond, disappearing back into the main reception area.

I ignored his directive, stepping over my vomit and deeper into the nightmare.

The demons remained silent, except for the one strapped to the table, whimpering with every exhale. Deep slashes decorated his body like someone had sharpened their knife with his flesh and bone.

My mind swapped his gaunt face for Sin's.

More bile rushed up my throat. I lurched for the metal sink in the corner, losing whatever acid still clung to my stomach. I dry-heaved, groping for the tap and letting the water wash the evidence down the drain, before rinsing my mouth out and sucking in a ragged breath.

I turned back to face the demons, ignoring the dizziness threatening to make me stumble.

The bruised demon in the cell pulled a young female, barely older than ten by human standards, further behind her and bared her fangs at me in threat. A slim teenage male pressed closer to her other side, tears tracking down his cheeks.

They all had the same blueberry complexion and bright-yellow eyes. Both younger demons had curly emerald hair and ram-like horns, matching the male bleeding out on the table.

A family.

The hunters had kidnapped *children*.

It was an unspoken rule, a line even the most brainwashed cultists wouldn't cross. On the rare occasion any were even found, hunters ended them quickly.

Thankfully, I'd never found myself in that kind of situation. Even raised in blood as I was, I wouldn't have been able to do it. There was a world of difference between putting down a man-eating wolf and murdering an innocent pup.

"Oh god," I whispered, meeting the mother's enraged glare. "I'm sorry. I will end this. One way or another."

My uncle had taken it too far.

The demon snarled, her fists throttling the bars as she blocked her kids from view. "We don't want any part of your twisted mind games."

I shook my head, thoughts rattling around in my skull.

How could I have let this go on for so long before? These were *people*.

People like Sin.

Demons that protected others. That cared about their families. Enough to get themselves captured by the enemy and tortured just to find out what happened.

My heart gave another pitiful squeeze as memories of Sin flickered through my mind.

I wrenched myself from the pity spiral before I could become any more useless.

Sin had finished the change in me that his brother had started, and determination hardened my resolve.

Nobody else would suffer while I stood idly by like a selfish coward. No matter what it cost me.

"Stay here," I said and instantly cringed at how dumb that sounded. They were literally prisoners in a cell. "I'll be right back."

"Oh, whoop-de-do, a hunter is coming back for us," the female hissed.

I gave her an awkward double thumbs-up and walked out, avoiding the puddle of bile on the floor.

There was an armoury in the basement. The thought of picking up a weapon again, coating my palms in even more blood, made my hands tremble.

But if I wasn't armed, that family died here.

First, I had to get the keys though.

I strode towards the main living area at the front of the monstrous cabin, braced for more heckling.

"Leo," I barked, purpose giving my voice a snap that reminded me of my father's. "I need the keys to the armoury and cages."

Once more, every head turned towards me.

My ex wiped the last traces of my sickness from his boots, ditching the rag in the bin with a scowl.

I should have aimed for his face.

The twisted bastard had captured children. And tortured their parents in front of them.

"Glad to see you've made a full recovery, *princess*, but you can't get everything you want with a snap of your bony fingers," he sneered. "Besides, how are you planning to take a beast out for testing without the others ripping you apart?"

My eyes narrowed. Leo shifted, pushing his blond hair back from his forehead.

"Then make yourself useful for once." I cocked a hip, planting my fist against it in an outward show of confidence even as my thoughts churned. If I had to put him down, then so be it. "I have important work to do, remember?"

He glared back but grunted in begrudging agreement as he gestured for me to lead the way, pulling a ring of keys from his pocket.

I turned on my heel and stalked back out, my ex-fiancé stomping behind me.

Adrenaline flooded my system. I was about to betray another person.

Though, my ex had betrayed me in so many ways, I was losing count. A little violent payback was more than overdue.

"You armed?" I gave him a cursory once-over as I assessed my target.

He snorted. "Only a moron would be unarmed at a time like this."

The brute had me rolling my eyes. "Right, well, I'm a moron, so let's start with the armoury." I waved him towards the unassuming wood door that led to the most secure room in the house.

Back in the base's lab, we had tranquilliser darts, but my uncle rarely kept any here. This was a place of training and suffering, of the human variety.

Leo barked out a laugh. "Well, you *did* leave me, so clearly, you're not the most intelligent being."

I flashed him a sarcastic smile. "Yup, that's me, the idiot who dumped a cheating sack of shit." I pressed a hand to my chest in mock devastation. "How will I ever move on?"

He chuckled, as if we weren't bitter enemies. "I don't remember you having such a sharp tongue. You must have knocked a little personality loose when you crashed your car."

My fake smile stiffened, but I refused the dangling bait.

I hadn't "crashed." He'd forced me off the road when I'd tried to escape my violent life as a hunter.

Leo slid the panel beside the reinforced door aside, revealing a keypad and keyhole. He punched in a code, then grabbed a shiny key ring from his pocket and unlocked the door.

It swung open on well-oiled hinges, and I followed him inside. Cold sweat broke out across my lower back as I took in the sight of so much weaponry. It was brutal evidence of the war that my uncle had been waging for longer than I'd been alive.

I hadn't picked up an actual weapon since the incident with Sin's brother. I wiped my clammy palms on my trousers and stepped up to the case of knives. Quickly arming myself, I grabbed a few blades and their holsters, securing two to each of my thighs before moving on to the pistols. They filled a drawer in the metal cabinet, each placed into its own foam cutout. I chose two of my favourite handguns, letting their cold weight fill my hands before I holstered them in a utility belt.

"And here I'd thought you'd gone too soft for weapons," Leo huffed.

I ignored him, eyeing the assault rifles on the wall with a sense of dread and longing. If I was going to take down my uncle and an entire house of psychotic hunters, I'd need more than a few pistols and knives, but my uncle had cameras in here.

I needed to play it smart.

I flashed Leo a syrupy smile. "Almost dying tends to have an impact on people with feelings. As a sociopath, I'm not sure you'd get it."

Leo chuckled. "Come on, Dozer. The remnants of beta squad will be back soon with more monsters for you to play with. If you want one of the current ones, it'll be easier to grab it while the cage isn't as full."

My middle twisted into knots. Thankfully, I'd already lost the contents of my stomach.

With more hunters on the way, I'd have to take down over a dozen highly trained killers if I wanted to free those demons.

The odds weren't in my favour.

Jaw clenched, I nodded, waving for him to lead the way back out. "Let's do this."

His eyes narrowed. Leo never liked it when I told him what to do, but he was right when he called me a princess. I was as close to hunter royalty as you could get.

We made our way back to the holding room, and a sense of calm washed over me. I'd struggled under the weight of so much guilt, hoping I could one day outrun it, but now the kilos shed with every step.

Redemption was worth fighting for.

"Find me the least damaged one, would you?" I asked, pretending to look inside the humming mini fridges dumped in the far corner.

Leo hesitated in my peripherals but finally stepped as close as he dared to the tarnished bars, sneering at the cowering family. "They all look the same. Beasts waiting for slaughter."

The demon shackled to the table had passed out, chest rising and falling as I swept around him on silent feet.

Holding my breath, I crept up behind the hunter. He turned as I whipped my pistol up and clocked him across his scarred temple.

My ex-fiancé crumpled to my feet.

Chapter 42

Blood trickled from the gash I'd left on Leo's head, dripping onto the plastic sheet covering the wooden floorboards.

With him sprawled on his back, his features had slackened in unconsciousness. It made him look younger than his cold eyes and scarring implied.

Silence echoed throughout the room.

"Holy fires. The crazy lady might have been telling the truth," the teenage male whispered.

I flashed them a wide grin. A sense of righteousness filled me as I swiped the keys from Leo's belt. "We need to move fast. Don't bother with revenge. Get out with your lives, okay?"

I hurried to undo the locked bolts welded to the cell door, keys jingling in my grip as I shook from the adrenaline.

Unlocking the last one, I swung the cage open. "There's a back exit through—"

A bang cut me off.

"What the fuck!?" a male barked at my back.

I spun, gun outstretched, to face the hunter gaping in the doorway.

"Back off, Jayce," I warned. "They're not all the monsters you think. They're just people. Please, let us go."

The hunter frowned before shaking his head. "Demons murdered my entire family, Liliana. I won't let these bastards take any more lives."

"They're a family too," I hissed. "Humans murder each other all the time, Jayce. Think about it. They're just like us. Good and bad."

His head cocked aside, as if he were really considering it. "Maybe you're right... I can admit they're intelligent beings."

Hope soared in my chest. I'd been trying to speak to hunters and scientists about this possibility for days after my incident, but nobody would hear it. That Jayce, of all people, would be receptive was baffling.

"Yes," I breathed. "Just step aside. You can blame the whole thing on me when we're out."

He drew back with a pitying expression. "If you really believe what you're saying, then talk to your uncle. But you know I can't just let you go. Sorry, Dozer."

He yanked up his pistol.

I popped off a shot first.

It slammed into his leg, knocking him to the ground with a pained yelp.

"Stay down, Jayce. I mean it. They're children, for fuck's sake. *Innocents*. I will not stand by while they're hurt." I aimed steadily at his head, despite the adrenaline coursing through me. "Not again."

I didn't want to kill him, but I would if I had to.

He hissed through gritted teeth, pressing one hand to the ragged hole above his knee, the other raised in surrender.

I kept my gun on his prone form, stepping close enough to snatch his weapon and pocket it. I gestured for the demons to move.

They slipped past, the mother and teenager clawing through the wooden table to free the metal restraints on the bloodied male and hauling him up, supporting him between them as the young girl held on to her mother's tail, following closely.

The one good thing about the cabin was that gunshots and pained screams were the norm. Nobody would come to investigate. Not yet, anyway.

The mother peeked out through the door. "It's empty."

I edged around Jayce, leading the way into the corridor and quickly locking the door, leaving Leo and Jayce trapped inside.

"We don't have long." I urged the family behind me as I raced down the corridor, turning at the end to speed through the mud room littered with hanging coats and dusty boxes and out the back door.

"Go!" I hissed, pushing them out into the waiting forest. I grabbed the adult female by the wrist, halting her.

She turned, a snarl on her lips.

I ignored her rage, meeting her feral eyes. "Run straight for about a mile and you'll hit a stream, wade through it to the far side and then head right until you hit a road. If you can get into a vehicle from there, you'll be safe."

"Thanks, human. I can—" Her eyes widened, catching on something over my shoulder.

I spun.

A boom sounded, and the demon staggered aside, but I was already surging forward. Cries blared out behind me as I slammed my palm into the side of Leo's gun, knocking it askew as it spat another bullet. This one finding a home in the wall rather than flesh.

I risked a glance over my shoulder. "Run!"

The mother staggered, blood pouring from her arm, but managed to drag the rest of her family along as they stumbled towards the tree-line.

"You dumb bitch," Leo roared. "I'm going to take them apart in front of you, then help your uncle beat some damn sense into you."

His gun swung back towards me, but I was ready. I ducked under and surged up, knocking the weapon from his hands.

I slid a knife from my holster, fisted his shirt, and yanked him forwards onto the waiting blade.

Navy eyes met mine, widening in shock. "Liliana," he gasped, clutching my hands and the knife I'd buried in his stomach. "How could you?"

The betrayal in his expression sliced into me, and I released the handle, pulling from his touch like it burned. He groaned in pain, hurt creasing his familiar features.

Everything we'd been through hit me at once.

We'd fought side-by-side for years. Joking with each other after battle. Pushing each other during training.

Him kissing me. Holding me at night. Asking me to marry him. Planning a future together. A home. A family.

He'd been my lifeline in an endless sea of violence. Even if it turned out he'd been betraying me all along. I'd thought I loved him.

Victory suffused his features in a malicious grin. "Pathetic."

His fist slammed into my temple before I could move.

Everything went black.

Chapter 43

A loud slap rang in my ear.

Stinging bloomed through my cheek, joining the throb in my skull.

The world filtered in through painful increments.

My head lolled forwards as I struggled to drag myself from the depths. I blinked slowly, staring at the plastic dust sheets beneath my trainers, and realised I was sitting on a chair.

"Ah, the traitor awakens." A gruff voice sliced through the confusion.

I lifted my head, taking in my worst nightmare looming over me and meeting his arctic gaze.

"Uncle," I spat.

Disdain curled his upper lip. "A traitor like you is no family of mine. Your father would be ashamed."

A bitter chuckle spilled out. "Probably."

I'm sure he thought it would cut, but his words held no more power over me. Neither did the memory of my father. A naive part of me had loved him, despite what he was capable of. He wasn't too different from his brother, and I knew neither of them would stop killing demons even with proof they weren't all preying on our kind.

Life was just a cycle of violence.

My uncle cocked his fist back and threw a punch, purposefully slow enough that I had time to brace, but couldn't do anything to avoid the blow.

Knuckles hit my cheek, whipping my head aside.

Pain burst through my face. Bile rose in my throat as the pounding turned sharp, but I swallowed thickly. Facing the monster, I kept my expression clean despite the pit of rage welling up inside me.

I hated this man.

Every fibre of my being screamed for his death. Yet I'd done nothing. I'd only really tried to escape after Sin's brother had opened my eyes to what was happening right in front of me.

I'd let him hurt me for years before that, vaguely hoping to find my freedom in retiring to have a family of my own with Leo. I'd been a coward.

But I wouldn't submit meekly without a fight. Not now, not ever again.

"You've gone soft, Uncle," I said, imitating Sin's cutting sneer. "No wonder your chapter is in pieces."

His jaw clenched, but he didn't hit me again. Yet.

"So this is the real you, huh? The real Liliana that's been hiding behind the blank stares and meek acceptance." He shook his head. "Pathetic."

I grinned through the pain as he echoed what Leo had said before he'd knocked me out. I'd never realised how alike they were until now.

Yet neither of them had any idea who I was, and until a certain vicious demon had entered my life, I hadn't either. Sin had seen me at my worst, and still thought I was worth saving.

If he could spare me after how I'd wronged him, surely there was hope for me yet.

Even if he never wanted to see me again. I knew I cared about him. More than I'd ever thought possible.

I should have told him how I felt before it was too late. Now, I'd missed my chance for something real, but at least I could go out knowing my last act had been good.

I'd rescued that family. Those children could grow up with parents who loved and protected them.

The insignia ring glinted on my uncle's finger a second before his fist impacted my other cheek, knocking my glasses off. I grunted, bindings stopping me from falling out of the chair he'd strapped me to.

The cosy wooden walls fuzzed slightly, but the small room meant everything was relatively sharp.

Both sides of my face throbbed, but I forced my split lips into another cruel smile. "That all you got, uncle? You're shaming our family with your weakness." I chuckled, throwing back at him one of his favourite lines from our bloody "training" sessions.

He pounded his fist into my stomach, and I wheezed, curling forwards as far as the bonds would allow. My lungs refused to inflate for a second and I struggled not to flop and gasp in panic.

"What were you planning with the demons?" he asked, false calm settling over him like a wet blanket. "What have you told them about our organisation?"

I wheezed out a grating laugh. "You think I'm working with demons like a mole? To what...? Take down your chapter? It's already gone, old man."

Now I wish I had been. I should have been working with demons and educating the hunters. We still needed fighters willing to protect innocents. They just had to learn that some of those innocents had horns too.

"You know this is about to get a lot worse for you, Liliana. I'm giving you the courtesy of starting gentle because of your service history. Mark my words, you will tell me what I want to know."

My service history? Like I was an elevator?

I fought not to cackle at my own dumb thoughts. Clearly, he'd knocked a few brain cells loose.

I nodded, despite the pain in my skull.

He was right, and he didn't even need to beat it out of me.

"I'm not working with the demons, but I discovered a very important fact we've all been overlooking. Demons are just people. They're not mindless, evil beasts. They're good and bad, like us."

He rolled his colourless eyes, a long-suffering sigh filling the space between us. "Nice try, Liliana. Even you're not that stupid."

Why was everyone obsessed with my perceived intelligence? It was exhausting.

I arched a brow, but I'd already known I was fighting a losing battle, repeating the same thing over and over to different hunters. "It's stupid to think other sentient beings might have more than one personality? One singular goal or focus? Not all dogs are feral and yet some of the most docile pets still bite."

He rolled his eyes. "We already lost the damn hell-mutts."

I narrowed mine right back. "I wasn't talking about those poor creatures."

"Stop wasting time." His features hardened. "Tell me what you've done."

I notched my chin, waiting for the next blow to fall. "I told you the truth. It's not my fault you refuse to hear it."

"What about the truth of your corruption, hmm?" he asked, a deadly stillness overcoming his grizzled features as he tried a new angle.

My heart raced.

"Your fiancé—who is still stitching himself up after you stabbed him—told me all about your *indiscretions* with one of those beasts," he spat.

My own ferocity rose to meet his. "Ex-fiancé," I hissed. "And so what? Sin treats me better than any human."

Memories slammed through my thoughts until the ache in my heart rivalled the one in my head.

His panic when I'd collapsed in front of him. His rage when I'd turned up bruised from my uncle's fists. Feeding me after I'd been starved. Protecting me from his own kind. Drugging kisses. Intoxicating pleasure. Whispered words.

I should have told him the truth when I had the chance, and trusted what I'd felt growing between us. Even after I'd betrayed him, he still hadn't hurt me.

He'd set me free.

My uncle's expression clouded, thunder rolling in. "So it's true? You're the devil's whore."

A distinct scrape sounded as he unsheathed a knife from the small of his back.

My uncle had always enjoyed getting up close and personal with his kills. Guns made the experience too removed. A "necessary evil," he'd concede in most circumstances.

But not executing a prisoner.

The reaper lurked in his flinty eyes. "No blood of mine will disgrace our family like this."

I yanked on my bonds, but the zip ties along my wrists and ankles wouldn't give.

"We were never family." I notched my chin, bracing for my fate.

A booming roar sounded outside the room. Snarls layered with the sharp retort of gunfire and screams.

I drew my final breath.

The blade halted inches from my chest.

"Fuck!" my uncle snarled, running for the door instead.

It burst apart as he reached it.

Wood shattered, and with a deafening roar, Sin crashed through.

Chapter 44

Starlit eyes raked over me, eclipsing with dark rage as they leaped to my uncle.

The old hunter was already moving. His blade sliced through Sin's chest as the demon reared back just in time to avoid the strike turning lethal.

"Sin!" I screamed, yanking on my restraints, but it was no use. Too many plastic ties held me. The tight angles making all force impossible.

I didn't have time to feel the shock at Sin's arrival. Panic consumed my world as he traded blows with the monster who'd dominated my life.

Rage consumed the demon as he snarled, raking claws along my uncle's arm. "You're the spineless maggot that's been beating and starving her."

"Training her," my uncle sneered. "She'd be dead if it weren't for me."

"You're more evil than any demon." I thrashed harder in my restraints, but nothing budged.

"Well, you should have trained the others better. I killed every human here." A cruel smirk etched his features as he darted his tail forward to stab the old hunter in the leg.

A distinct boom sounded.

Sin jerked back before his blow could land, blood spraying from his shoulder.

I gasped, helpless to do anything but watch as he staggered upright with a snarl, tail twitching as he watched both the door and my uncle like a cornered predator.

"Not all," a familiar voice drawled.

Leo shuffled into the room, pistol shaking in his raised hand. Bloodstained gauze wrapped around his middle, the bare skin of his chest too-pale.

A violent smirk curved my lips. "Not looking so hot, Leo. What's the matter? Can't handle a little prick all of a sudden?"

"You again." Sin snorted, unfazed by the fresh wound seeping blood down his chest.

"I could say the same." Leo grunted. His eyes flicked to me for a millisecond. "I hope some demon dick was worth dying for."

The icy façade of my uncle cracked. "So you're the monster corrupting my niece?" The hunter prime snarled, switching the grip on his blade, holding it along his forearm and slashing out.

Sin evaded him, spiked tail lashing side to side in threat.

A cruel twist held his lips in a familiar gesture that made my heart ache. "*Corrupting*, huh? We're a little past that, old man. I love her."

I sucked in a gasp, eyes flying up to Sin's. They met mine, honest and vulnerable, for a single moment.

My uncle jolted as if struck. Sin took advantage, darting forwards to finish him with a swipe of claws aimed for his throat.

But the hunter dived aside.

And right into me.

I jerked in the chair, my uncle's body slamming me hard enough to snap the ties on my wrists painfully. My lungs couldn't inflate under the weight crushing me.

Gunfire thundered, flashing in my periphery as Leo fired everything he had at Sin.

My uncle's grizzled face loomed above me. "No family of mine."

Wetness drenched my front, and I looked down in slow motion.

The hilt of a blade jutted from my chest.

I was going to die.

But he'd never hurt anyone else again.

"Liliana!" Panic suffused Sin's voice before gunfire swallowed it.

I drew the blade out.

And sliced my tormentor's throat.

Blood rained in a torrent of heat. Colourless eyes widened. His mouth worked, but only a gurgling sound escaped. He slid off me, slumping to the floor on his back.

The weight lifted, and I could breathe at last.

Pain caved my chest as I finally felt the lethal wound. My breath stuttered, a low rattle that reminded me of the last time I'd plummeted towards death. But I couldn't look away.

Within seconds, the cold light dimmed from my uncle's eyes, leaving a blank stare of shock.

"Sin," I whispered, fighting to stay conscious through the agony carving out my heart. My gaze found him across the room.

My demon roared, ducking and charging into Leo as the gun clicked to empty. His shoulder spikes pierced my ex's chest, sending him flying into the wall and thudding to the ground in a broken heap.

Sin ripped a knife from his thigh, stumbling towards me as a mess of gunshots and blood.

"S-Sin...," I tried again. My voice came out in a raspy exhale as I tried to process his declaration. And my end.

His eyes met mine, stars gleaming around hollow pupils.

At least he'd be the last thing I saw.

He closed the gap, dropping to his knees before me. "Liliana... What have they done to you?"

The low whine of a wounded animal reverberated the air between us as he took in the damage to my chest.

His fingers dug into a deep slice through his chest. Blood pooled in his hand before he pressed it to the hole in my sternum. Pain flared white-hot, and I hissed out a breath as stars eclipsed my world.

It simmered to a steady ache, winding hope through my veins, but dark blood still gushed around his fingers as my vision cleared.

Panic struck his rugged features as he came to the same conclusion I did. He savaged his wrist, fangs tearing messily, and shoved his new wound hard against mine.

"What are you doing here?" I gasped, struggling to unlock the tightness squeezing my vocal cords, my chest pulsing and hollowing out even as his blood fizzed hotly where it met mine.

Was I hallucinating? Had my uncle hit me so hard that I'd keeled over in this chair, brain conjuring a tragic fantasy of Sin coming back for me?

Blood painted him. Too many gunshot wounds gaped across his bare chest and arms. Precise cuts, like those from a blade, littered his body.

I'd never dream of him this badly hurt.

His other hand gripped my cheek, starlight tunnelling down to my soul. "They tell you that you're not worth fighting for, but I'd go through eternity in a cage for you. No matter what you've done. I know who you *are*, poison. I know you're worth any suffering they could inflict on me. How could I not come for you? I should have never let you go in the first place."

Nobody had ever saved me. Not my mother. My father. My uncle. My fiancé. Not anyone I'd called family or friend.

I'd learned to survive on my own.

But in such a short time, Sin had shown me what it was to truly feel alive. And I was as addicted to it as I was to him.

My chest ached, the feeling of his blood mixing with mine too warm as it attacked the ragged edges of damaged flesh, but it couldn't cover the fact that I was losing too much.

"They could have tortured and executed you. I-I'm not worth getting you killed too..." I choked off.

His breath sharpened at my unspoken meaning.

Like his brother.

"I should have listened to you instead of letting my emotions spiral out of control. I'm sorry, poison. You didn't kill Silvanus, you said it yourself." His thumb brushed my cheek, catching a stray tear I hadn't realised was falling.

"He healed me," I whispered. "I've seen your party trick before."

A small smile played at his lips, gentler than anything I'd seen. "Of course he took the time to revive a pretty hunter during a fight."

"He showed me not all demons were evil, and you showed me there's more to them than I could have ever imagined." My voice sounded thin, and exhaustion tried to drag me under.

"My sweet poison." His attention dipped to where his wounded arm met my chest and his features tightened. "It's not enough." Desperation laced his tone. "I can't lose you, Liliana."

He lifted his bleeding wrist to my lips.

Starlit eyes, filled with pain and hope, tried to hold me to this world. "Given all we've shared, if you drink from me now, you'll live, but it will cement our blood bond. You'll never be able to escape me, poison. Mine for eternity."

Everything we'd been through flickered hazily through my mind. But unlike with Leo, I knew what I felt for Sin was real. It was gritty and vicious and all-consuming, and I wouldn't have it any other way.

"I already am." I leaned into his offered wrist and sealed my lips to his skin.

Warm blood spilled across my tongue. It was like a shot of ambrosia. The most divine flavour with a citrus edge.

Joy like I'd never known filled me despite the pain, and it mirrored the expression suffusing his stunning features.

My chest grew hot, burning hard enough that I pulled back with a hiss. Rich blood sat thickly on my tongue. The caving sensation in my torso lessened with each passing beat, replaced by something full and tangible. A sense of *more*, somehow.

Soothing warmth glowed beside my heart, centring me around the feeling I knew was him.

A wicked grin curved my demon's lips. His eyes brightened like a supernova.

"My bonded." His fingertips brushed my face in reverence, tracing the parts I knew were bloodied and bruised, but even the pain there was fading.

I was still alive. And I was finally free.

Because of him.

Chapter 45

Sin's fingertips left my cheek, and I mourned their loss.

Heat pulsed through my chest, as if to reassure me that our bond was there.

That *he* was there.

The coldest parts of me infused with power. My limbs felt lighter, my blood fizzing with energy, despite my brush with death.

The pearly strands of Sin's hair glowed under the artificial light. It caught on the sharp tips of his horns and shoulder spikes, highlighting the dangerous creature even as it cast his cruel features into shadow. Blood splattered his charcoal skin, smearing brightly over the white tattoos hugging his broad chest and thickly corded arms. Power brimmed through every muscular inch of my demon, overflowing from starlit eyes. Even on his knees, wounds healing across his bare chest, Sin was a formidable sight. A warrior to his core.

And he was mine.

"Shouldn't you be rolling over for a nap right about now?" I asked, my voice embarrassingly husky after the way he'd stolen my breath.

He ran the spiked heart tip of his sinuous tail along the last zip ties around my ankles, freeing me completely. The sharp tips trailed up my calf, sending shivers racing through me.

"Healing is draining, but our bond is powerful. Its energy flows to strengthen us both." He pressed a clawed hand to the centre of his chest. "I can feel you here, where you were always meant to be."

I nodded, understanding the warmth that radiated from a single point beneath my ribs. A sensation I now realised had stirred more than once over the past few weeks, that odd heat that seemed to nestle against my heart.

Stars glowed through the blackness of my demon's eyes. "Poison... My beautiful bonded... Unless you want me to fuck you on the bodies of your enemies, you'd better run."

Sparks ignited low in my body, and I bit my lower lip to stifle a gasp.

"Your demon is showing again." I tutted, struggling to unstick my vocal cords.

He grinned, flashing pointy fangs glistening with venom. "You haven't seen anything yet, Liliana. I'm going to hunt you down, and when I catch you, you'll scream yourself hoarse."

I smirked back. "*If*, not when."

Shoving him aside, I surged from the chair, leaping over the monsters of my past as I raced out of the room that I'd almost died in, heading straight for the cabin's back door.

Mocking laughter followed me, drenched in violent promise. My lips spread wide, even as adrenaline flooded my system at the demonic sound.

I burst out the backdoor, racing into the starlit night.

Blood coated my arms, highlighted under the cabin's rear lighting. It should have turned my stomach, but the warmth in my chest seemed to soothe away the panic before it could steal this moment from me.

I grinned, darting between slender birch trees, plunging into the dark forest.

Footsteps echoed behind me.

My nape prickled. I was being chased by a monster.

Excitement hastened my steps.

I swept around tall trunks, flowing over roots and fallen branches. I'd trained in this forest for years as a teen, and I knew exactly where I was going. A bird cawed in the distance, piercing the quiet.

"Run faster, poison!" A raspy masculine voice taunted behind me. "Or someone might think you want to be caught."

I drew a deep breath, racing quicker until my heart pounded. I reached the stream I knew would be there and turned right, heading for the road.

Shadows moved in my periphery, and I put on a burst of speed right as claws raked out from the darkness, slicing into my sleeve. Only years of training had me swallowing the scream lodged in my throat.

Sin snarled at my back. A low growl flooded the woods as his footsteps pounded the earth. I swore I could feel his breath fanning my neck as I fled along the riverbank, trainers sinking in the soft mud.

Moonlight pierced the forest up ahead, and I burst through the tree-line, suddenly exposed to the midnight sky. A dark vehicle sat abandoned on the side of the quiet country road.

Victory surged through me at the sight.

I raced towards it, but something slammed into my side, knocking the world out from under me. The air burst from my lungs as I fell, tumbling and rolling on top of something hot and hard.

Sin chuckled, pinning me to the tarmac as I gasped for breath, blinking the world back into focus.

Stars swam behind him, paling in comparison to the silvery glow trapped in his eyes. The moon haloed him, outlining his curved horns and casting his dark features deeper into the shadows.

He dipped close, and his nostrils flared as he inhaled my scent, before speaking directly against my parted lips. "You're the sweetest fucking prey. My hunter turned hunted."

His claws fisted in my hair and dragged me aside.

I hissed at the sharp tug, scrambling onto my hands and knees to lessen the pull.

Sin sat back on his heels, spreading his knees wide, and tore the fly of his trousers open.

My demon snarled, yanking on my hair to tilt my face to meet his burning gaze. "Take your cock out, bonded, and suck it like a good girl."

I bit my lip to hold back a moan at the heady dominance and shot him a dark glare, as if the very idea of tasting him again didn't have me soaked. "Or you can do something useful with that forked tongue for once, like a good demon."

He chuckled, fangs gleaming in the moonlight. The smooth head of his tail slid under the ripped waistband of his trousers and freed his steely length.

Pearly liquid already glistened from the pointed, heart-shaped tip, and I literally gulped at the sight of his diamond-studded shaft, tail wrapped around the thick base.

He gave me a single moment to take it all in, then yanked me forward.

My lips parted as his wet tip bumped them, and he slid into my mouth, hitting the back of my throat.

I choked on his hard length, struggling the pull off as he chuckled darkly, claws tightening in my hair as he finally pulled me back enough for me to breathe.

"Such a naughty hunter," he purred, running a thumb across the corner of my mouth as I panted around the pulsing head of him, "sucking a demon's cock out here in the open like the greedy little thing you are."

"—uck yuu—" I tried to snarl, gagged by the heart-shaped tip between my lips.

His hips rocked forward as he held me still, slowly fucking my mouth, demonstrating his absolute control. I groaned around him, tongue playing with the textured bumps of his gem-studded shaft as I let him use my mouth.

Someone could drive past at any moment, and the thought of being caught like this sent an extra thrill running through me.

Just as his hardness began to throb in my mouth, he slid free with a lewd pop.

I strained for another taste, and he loosened his cruel hold just enough for my tongue to trail along the velvety smooth skin of his balls. Their heavy mass had my core fluttering in appreciation.

"Fuck, Liliana, the way you drive me wild…," he hissed. "But tonight all this cum is for that greedy pussy of mine."

His tail wrapped my throat in my favourite necklace and yanked me back, laying me across the tarmac as he prowled over me, huge hands pinning my wrists on either side of my head. His hard length rested heavily at the apex of my thighs, hot enough that I felt it through my clothes.

"Ah, sweet poison." His forked tongue flickered out to wet his full lips. "This is where you belong, trapped beneath me, at my mercy."

I bared my teeth, struggling in his iron hold even though I revelled in every second of his feral dominance. "Fuck you, Sin. You should be under me. After all, you were my prisoner first."

A raspy chuckle rumbled from the thick column of his throat. "Oh, poison, my silly little hunter. You were always going to be mine. From the moment I laid eyes on your stunning face, your pouty lips parting just enough to beg me to widen them fully, I knew I'd have you. I just didn't realise I'd need to keep you. Forever."

My heart squeezed, and that soothing heat from our bond pulsed in my chest.

He slammed his lips against mine, stealing my words and my breath right along with them.

The kiss deepened until his forked tongue lashed against mine in a sensual dance. He retreated after a dizzying second, letting his fangs drag deliciously over my lower lip before he released me with a growl.

Before I could stop him, his claws shredded my clothes down the middle. Even my underwear succumbed to the sharpness. He ripped the tatters aside, leaving me vulnerable to the cool breeze. I tried to sit up, but his tail tightened around my throat, restraining me against the tarmac.

His eyes shone, running over my exposed skin, trailing heat in his wake. "Beautiful."

I gasped, but somehow the monster ready to devour me made me feel safe in a way nobody ever had. He was a protector to the core.

"And all mine to play with." He grinned.

He lunged, fangs slicing into the mound of my breast. Heat shot through the instant sting, radiating through my chest until my nipple hardened into a burning peak of sensation. I moaned, and he repeated the venomous bite on the other side. My chest throbbed with delicious heat.

Claws skated up my arms, along my ribs, viciously teasing me before he gripped my hips, kissing and nipping his way down my stomach. The lingering taste of his citrusy pre-cum on my tongue only heightened my desperate need.

A small moan left my lips as I realised where he was headed.

He didn't waste any time spearing his forked tongue straight into my pussy. I bucked on the tarmac, letting my legs fall wider as he fucked me with his thick tongue, lashing my clit before thrusting back inside.

He growled against my lower lips, and the feel of his fangs grazing me ever so slightly pushed me right to the edge. Threat and pleasure combining in a devastating mix.

He pulled back before I could tumble into bliss, kneeling between my thighs and looming over me like a brutal demon come to claim my soul.

A cruel chuckle flooded the night as he watched me moan and writhe on the road beneath him.

I snarled, fighting to sit up and grab his horns to bring him back down to where I needed him. A wicked laugh rumbled his chest as he evaded me, the sound low and deep and oh so sinful. He slammed me back to earth with his tail at my throat.

I choked for a second, coughing as he grinned down at me, malice written across his heart-stopping features.

"Oh, poison, you should know better by now," he drawled, licking the evidence of my arousal from his lips as he leered at me. "You're *my* captive. Mine to do with as I please. Mine to pleasure and devour."

"You teasing bastard," I hissed back, feral against his mocking composure.

He smirked at the insult and slapped his palm over my nose and mouth, cutting off my oxygen. My eyes widened as I realised I couldn't breathe, my hands instinctually reaching up to yank at his wrist, nails scrabbling for purchase in his blood-slicked flesh.

The demon shifted lower between my spread thighs.

"Open wide," he sneered.

In one thrust, he forced himself deep into my pussy. I screamed against his hand smothering me. It felt like he was splitting me open but in the best way.

The bond in my chest brightened, like the connection between us sang with a sense of rightness.

Spots danced across my vision as the lack of oxygen caught up to me. Euphoria swam through my veins, stealing the harsh edge to the burn in my core. I floated on a cloud of pleasure, my inner walls fluttering around the monster lodged deep inside me.

Sin released his cruel grip, and I choked in a ragged breath, my lungs on fire.

"You fucking psycho," I spluttered, my core clenching the thick intrusion practically splitting me in half. "You really are trying to kill me, aren't you?"

A dark smirk curved his lips. He pulled back and thrust in to the hilt. His wide hips forced my thighs further apart, and I panted raggedly, my own hips bucking at the textured glide, silky enough that it felt like he was coated in lube.

"At least you'd die doing what you loved, my bonded." He chuckled, wicked as sin.

"You're more likely to bore me to death," I sneered, trying and failing to keep my breathing even as high-pitched moans threatened to spill from my lips instead, even with him holding still.

An unhinged grin sliced through his dark visage. Venom dripped from his fangs, splashing warm drops onto my throat.

He unleashed his demonic fury with a feral snarl.

The monster pounded me into the tarmac. His hips pistoned, until only his tail at my throat kept me in place.

I moaned, instantly overwhelmed, as he fucked me into submission.

A growing rumble joined his growl. Sin paused, brows furrowing, and I cried out in protest, trying to claw at the back of his neck.

Before I knew what was happening, he wrapped his arms around me and rolled us aside. The world spun once more. The sound grew, punctuated by the scrape of Sin's bony spikes against the road as he took us straight off the edge into a grassy verge, leaving me dizzy. My core clenched around him as he pinned me beneath his muscular body.

I sucked in a breath. "What the f—"

Headlights pierced the night, cutting me off.

A van hurtled past, running right over the spot where Sin had been fucking me.

My lips parted, and Sin's cruel chuckle took over from the dimming rumble of the vehicle speeding away.

The heat his body threw off countered the chill trying to seep in from the damp grass at my back. His shoulder spikes loomed enormous, backlit by the full moon and sparkling stars as he stared down at me, a look of dark hunger etched into his stunning features.

"Now that I've saved your life again, bonded, where were we?" His forked tongue traced his lower lip. Clear venom splashed little drops of fire onto my bare chest as his fangs peeked out.

I feigned a yawn. "I believe you were trying to lull me to sleep," I said, but my words came out too husky to be convincing.

His low rumble shook his cock inside me, and I had to stifle a whimper, fighting to hold on to a bored mask even as my lips twitched.

"Well, if it's sleep you want, poison, I'll happily fuck you unconscious," he sneered, vicious and cruel, and so damn sexy it made my inner walls flutter around his steely length.

He pulled out to the pointed tip and slammed home.

I couldn't stop screaming as he took me. Stretched my tight channel, forcing his enormous studded length into me. Over and over. Harder and harder.

He unhooked his tail from my neck, and his lips peeled back in a feral snarl. He struck, fangs sinking into my throat as he fucked me into oblivion. Heat flooded my arteries, racing through my body until it felt like he'd set me aflame.

Sin reared back, my blood coating his pouty lips. Starlit eyes flashed bright silver. "Break for me, poison."

My body obeyed.

Pleasure smashed me apart on the rocks, waves breaking over me as I drowned in bliss.

Something pressed into my inner wall, swelling and pushing until a keening left my lips. Sensation overloaded my body as Sin's barb locked his throbbing cock into me.

I lost all sense of self, unable to do anything but scream and *feel*.

My demon roared, claws curling into my shoulders as he thrust deep and stilled. His cock kicked inside me. Heat flooded my channel, searing in the best way as I writhed through the onslaught of pleasure.

The venom from his bite had invaded every part of my body, driving me to my peak and shattering me all over again.

Twin stars glowed in my vision, the last thing I saw as the world faded, drowning me in harsh pleasure and searing heat.

Something warm tickled my cheek, feathering a light touch along my jaw. It soothed down my throat and across my shoulder, reaching lower to circle the side of my breast. A satisfied mumble was pulled from my lips. Heat sang through my body in a blissful symphony, lifting me high as I drifted up from the depths of sleep.

"Mmm," I hummed, shifting on a hot, firm surface beneath me.

My core clenched around something girthy and impossibly deep. An extra thickness poked at my inner walls.

I inhaled sharply, eyes flying open.

The world swam into focus through my glasses, and I frowned at dark-grey skin graced with curling white script, kissed by soft light.

"Ah, my bonded finally wakes," a raspy voice drawled.

A hand reached up to join the tail tip that had been stroking me. Sin curved a pearly claw under my chin, tipping my face up to his with a sharp prod.

I was lying on his muscled chest, sprawled out across him in a familiar king-size bed, the sage-green duvet thrown over us. My knees were spread either side of his toned abs, leaving me curled up yet open wide for him.

I frowned, realising where we were. "How...?" I trailed off on a moan, feeling Sin's cock pulse inside me, flooding me with more liquid heat.

Bliss stole across Sin's carved features, softening the harsh angles for a single moment. He blinked his eyes open, long white lashes fluttering as the stars beneath refocused on me.

He ran his clawed thumb across my lower lip, his own twitching in wry amusement. "When you were so bored that you fell asleep stretched around my dick, I carried you to the car and drove us home."

My core tightened at the thought, and I bit back a needy moan at the pleasure seeping through my body. "But your barb..."

He flashed me a cruel grin. "Yes, poison? Are you wondering if your greedy pussy has been milking my cock this whole time?"

My lips parted, and he pushed his claw inside, eyes devouring me as I tasted the faint salty flavour on his skin.

"The answer is yes." He smirked, full of masculine satisfaction. "My barb locked us together, and I drove home with you in my lap, pumping you full of cum even while you were unconscious. I've been inside you ever since, waiting for you to wake up. I want you to scream while I breed you, poison."

I moaned at the heady thought. That he wanted me that desperately. That his primal instinct had been driving him to take me.

Something was clearly wrong with me because the idea of him filling me up while I was passed out from the intense pleasure, no doubt combined with his wicked venom, was undeniably hot.

"Sin," I whined around his thumb in my mouth, unable to stop the roll of my hips.

I ached, so full I thought I might burst, but I couldn't stop pulsing and fluttering around his thick length. The liquid trapped inside me swished in a sensation unlike anything I'd felt before.

He groaned, and claws raked lightly down my back as he held me to his chest. "I'm going to knot you with my barb over and over, poison. Until your belly swells with my offspring."

The thought shouldn't have turned me on as much as it did.

He reached down, grabbing my hips and forcing me down harder on his length. I gasped, eyes flying wide as his tail pushed my chest, sitting me upright on him. He rocked me back and forth on his cock, lodged so tightly inside me I could barely move. My hands spasmed high on his pecs, blunt nails sinking into the firm muscle.

Every movement sent shock waves of pleasure through my lower body, fizzing through me with a tingly heat.

"Oh god, Sin," I cried out, feeling the pressure build and build.

"Yes, poison. I'll be your god," he snarled, claws digging into my flesh. "I'll be anything you want."

His smooth tail slapped my arse, the sting ceding to a delicious heat that only propelled me higher. His hips drove up hard, bouncing me on top of him.

Pleasure sparked deep in my core. Stars burst through me as everything seemed to swell. Sin's feral snarl rumbled through us, and he tensed beneath me with a loud roar. I screamed as blinding light surged through me, orgasm shattering me apart as I followed Sin into ecstasy.

I slumped forward onto his chest, his tail catching me and lowering me gently as I panted hard, completely spent. His arms wrapped around me, and the bond in my chest seemed to pulse, making me feel whole.

Everything had a dreamlike quality, and I hummed in contented pleasure. My connection to Sin swelled like a warm hug around my heart, trying to fill the jagged cracks from so many years of hurt.

Sin kissed the top of my head and whispered against my hair, "I love you, Liliana."

Tears filled my eyes, spilling over to run down his chest, and he held me tighter against him. Warm and safe, at home in his arms.

"I love you too, Sin."

Epilogue

"Keep your eyes closed, poison. No peeking," Sin said, chuckling with what could only be described as evil glee.

I huffed but couldn't help a small smile as I took tiny steps forward on what felt like grass, given the tickle against my ankles where my trainers ended. I couldn't peek, because he'd wrapped his tail around my eyes in a warm blindfold.

"Let me guess, it's a glass cell and you're kidnapping me all over again," I said, tone wry with amusement.

Sin had held me all night as we'd passed out in our borrowed bed, locked together in the most intimate way, recovering from everything that had happened, both good and bad.

We'd won, but it had still cost us both.

A part of me mourned the loss of my family and the only life I'd known. My uncle had abused me for years, but the image of his gaping throat and the feel of his blood rushing down my front would haunt me, along with the sight of Leo's crumpled body.

"Ah, my silly bonded mate," Sin drawled, tugging on my waist to draw me back against his broad chest. "You're already my captive."

I snorted but felt the pulse of something warm in my chest where the bond between us seemed to live, as if reminding me of the unbreakable connection we shared.

"Well, what's this surprise, then?" I tugged at his tail blindfolding me. "I was planning to go back to the cabin and burn it to the ground later, with all the bodies inside before the police can find them. Maybe I'll build a new base on top of the ashes to spite my uncle and create an anti-hunter team to stop the cultist infection spreading back to Riverside."

The idea had occurred to me a few hours ago, when I'd woken up in Sin's arms, wondering what the future held for me. For us. It had been swirling through my thoughts ever since.

What did I really want when I wasn't just fighting to be free?

"You're not alone anymore, poison. If you want to start a war against the hunters, I'll be at your side, revelling in your viciousness and cutting down anyone who threatens you. Or if you don't want to fight anymore, I'll do it for you, gladly."

My throat felt too tight for words, and I was glad his tail was covering my eyes so I could avoid his gaze without feeling like a coward. "I don't want to stand by while innocent people are hurt again. No matter their species."

How could I have ever tried to poison the man holding me? I'd always regret the wrongs of my past, but I wanted to do good things with my future. I'd been raised to save people. I just hadn't known I was killing as many innocents as I'd saved.

An approving rumble shook my demon's chest. "Then we fight together. I already knew you were a protector, poison. It's in your nature as much as mine." His lips brushed my cheek as he curled himself tighter around my back, sheltering me before stepping back and letting the cool air rush between us. "You can open your eyes now."

His tail inched down to my neck in a collar I shouldn't like but found too soothing to care.

I blinked, the late morning sunlight obscuring my vision for a second before it cleared.

The cosy suburban house we'd just left fifteen minutes ago sat before me.

I twisted to face Sin with a quirked brow, but the expression slid from my face.

The hulking demon waited on one knee, a tiny velvet box in his raised hands.

"Poison...you had me intoxicated from the moment I saw you. This little waif of a human, hiding the soul of a fighter. You looked so sweet and innocent. All I wanted was to corrupt you, to break you. Yet it was me who fell. I love you, Liliana. I will love you until the blood in my veins turns to ash, and then I will find you in the afterlife and love you there.

"You are my family. My home. My entire damn world."

He drew a deep breath, tattooed chest widening, and I realised I was holding a hand to my mouth, shaking so hard my wrist rubbed against the velvety softness of his long tail.

He opened the box, and a stunning gold ring, topped with a raw orange gemstone struck through with flecks of black, stared back at me.

It reminded me of a tiger-lily.

"Liliana, will you marry me?"

I swallowed thickly, feeling a million different emotions streak through me.

He waited on one knee, starlit eyes outshining the sun.

I sucked in a deep breath before I could lose my nerve. "I've never met anyone who's felt like home. Until you. The first time I can remember feeling safe was when you wrapped this damn tail around my neck and promised to watch over me while I slept. It doesn't make any sense, but...somewhere along the way, I realised you're what I've been searching for all along." My lips peeled back into a grin so wide my face ached. "Yes, Sin. I'll marry you."

His grin rivalled mine, and he slid the ring onto my finger and swept me up into his arms before I could even get a good look at it.

Laughter bubbled up my throat until it overflowed. He spun me around with a low chuckle before setting me back down.

His lips found mine, swallowing my mirth and stealing my breath. He kissed me until I was dizzy, lighting a fire in me that only he could tame.

He pulled back with a huge grin, tugging me towards the commandeered house.

I chuckled, following him up the patio driveway. "Wait, why on earth did you drive me around in circles, blindfolded, just to bring me right back?"

He glanced over his spiked shoulder with a wicked grin. "I brought you home, Liliana."

I frowned. "What are you talking about?"

"This is yours." He rubbed the back of his neck, toned arm flexing. "I bought it for you. For us."

My lips parted as he knocked me on my arse for the second time in minutes. "You bought the house we've been illegally squatting in?"

"When you told me you'd never had a home, and you looked around this house with longing in your beautiful brown eyes, I knew I'd do anything to change that." He shrugged, an almost sheepish expression on his stunningly sharp features. "I made a cash offer after that first day. The estate agent said the owners were on holiday, but this morning, they accepted. Sure, there's some legal hoops still to jump through, and we'll have to pretend we've not been staying here, plus they'll need to move out officially when they're back, but...it's yours. If you want it. If not, pick a different one. I don't care where we live, as long as I'm with you."

Tears filled my eyes, spilling down my cheeks. "It's perfect."

I'd never had a real home. Somewhere I felt safe and loved.

I'd always thought my future would be dictated by my uncle, filled with violence even if I did manage to settle down with another hunter, or that I'd live a hard life on the run.

But Sin had changed everything.

My captive had set me free.

Afterword

I'd just like to take a moment to thank you for reading this saucy tale!

If you want more spicy paranormal romance, then sign up to my newsletter at sakurablackbooks.com/subscribe for exclusive bonus content, character art and release updates.

As an indie author, it would mean so much to me if you could please leave a review.

This helps other readers to find my wild stories and take a chance on me so I can keep on writing and working towards my dream of becoming an author full-time (help – my day job is way too sensible for me!).

The next instalment of the Playing with Demons series will feature Eve – the demon-witch hybrid – and Killian – the demon enforcer who longs to protect her. Hellish Witch is an irresistible forbidden romance between a broken healer and her brother's best friend.

Acknowledgements

This is just a quickie to say a huge thank you to my awesome beta readers – Mandy, Emmy, Cheri, Chauncey, Anne, Amber and Taylar. Your feedback made all the difference, and I can't thank you enough for taking the time to help me out and encourage me. That last spice scene is for you cuties!

I also want to give my editor, Lyss, a big shout out for whipping this book into shape.

My ARC team has been simply amazing too. Thank you for your support in getting this book in front of more great readers like yourself!

Also By Sakura Black

Fae Mate Hunt Series *(complete)***:** A spicy reverse harem monster romance novella series

0.5 – The Nymph's Dark Pleasure

1 – Selected for the Shifters

2 – Hunted by the Minotaur

3 – Burning for the Fire Nymphs

4 – Fleeing the Feline King

5 – Their Concubine Queen

1-5 – Fae Mate Hunt: Complete Series Collection

.

Monster Mate Hunt Series *(complete):* A spicy reverse harem monster romance novella series

1 – Rattled

2 – Get Foxed

3 – The Stones for It

4 – Reeled In

5 – Their Crown Jewels

Playing with Demons Series: A spicy demon romance connected standalone series
1 – Take Me to Hell
2 – Capturing Sin
3 – Hellish Witch

For all the latest book release information, subscribe to Sakura's newsletter at sakurablackbooks.com and for a limited time, get a FREE bonus short story – The Nymph's Dark Pleasure – the prequel to Selected for the Shifters, all about Newbury's hot night with a dark stranger. Warning: it's a steamy one!

About the Author

Sakura Black is a writer of steamy fantasy and paranormal romance, often dreaming up wild stories about frightfully sweet monsters and the women they're lucky enough to fall horns over tail for.

For more saucy action head to Sakura's website: sakurablackbooks.com

You can also find Sakura's Author Page on Amazon or reach out on Instagram / Facebook / TikTok @sakurablackbooks - she loves hearing from readers (but is crap at social media so the best place to find her is her Newsletter)